MW01181568

# The Judge's Demon

## K.M. Pfeifer

To my family, but especially my husband,
who supported and motivated me the entire journey

# Preface

25 November 1798


She ran as fast as she could into the trees. There was only a short distance before the wall; she just needed to get past it. She ran so quickly that she didn't see how deep the snow was getting. Charles was catching up; his hands nearly touching her. He was after her and her alone while James and his guards were chaotically rounding up the others. She could feel the cold air filling her lungs in her panicked pace, but she pushed herself all the harder to make it out of the city. She could see the wall. It wasn't much further, and she was determined to make it there.

She was focused on it so intently that she missed the small drop. She lost her footing and tumbled down the side of a hill, rolling through the snow. She looked up as he was standing near the top trying to figure a way down. She was so close and knew she could make it. Charles was fat and wouldn't get over the wall anyhow. She picked herself up and brushed the snow from her dress. That's when she saw him; James had come to find her as well. She continued on, finally reaching the wall but soon realized she wasn't tall enough to climb it. She searched for a crack, an opening, anything, but when she finally found one, it was too late. Charles shoved his hands into her back, throwing them both to the ground. She struggled to get away, but he pinned her down.

"My, my sweet girl," he snarled as he ran his finger down her chest. "It's just like the first time we met," his voice whispered in her ear. She kicked his stomach and almost escaped, but didn't make it very far. James had gotten there as well and caught her. He wrapped his arms around her tightly, and his hand pulled the hair behind her ear to ensure she heard his next words clearly.

"You should stop fighting this, it's over. You will watch as they all die."

# Chapter One

03 October 1778

It was a very dark day, and the air smelled of rain to come in Paris. Rosa, the house maid, helped Claude into his black coat. He stared into the mirror as she brushed back his hair. It was long and sleek but had a neat trim. It slicked back over his head in dark, thick layers. He stood tall as he tightened the lace of his waistcoat. The rigid draw of his binds was a strict impression of his overall personality. He held a strict posture as he inhaled and pulled at the strings, hoping the tension would ease the grip of despair in his chest

"The service is starting," he heard a woman whisper through the door as he buttoned his sleeves; the final touch.

He didn't want to go. He couldn't bear to see the man he once revered in the highest regard lying in a box lifelessly. It wasn't right, but it was expected of him to be there. He took a solid breath, but stood erect, frozen in his pose as his gaze pierced into his tired reflection. The room was ill-lit and accentuated the bags of sleepless nights under his eyes. He was just over nineteen but with the appearance of a much more mature man. His face was long and had a fullness in shape that was very becoming on him, and his jaw was cut to accentuate the potential for a cunning smile that could be quite charming. Such details aided him in his authoritative career, but nonetheless made him feel less appealing to his peers.

His father was the only man that had ever truly cared for him. He was more than a role model to him. He considered his father a friend, and he was now gone. He walked into the annex of the cathedral without greeting a soul. He didn't have the patience for thoughtless sympathies or meaningless condolences. His poise was strong, but he could feel himself shaking with anger and hurt inside as he pushed himself to the front. He knew these people may respect his father, but they were no friend of his. They simply feared him. Even Claude feared him. He threw himself down and slumped on the pew. In that moment he was no longer concerned of how he appeared to others. His breaths were heavy as he attempted to distract his thoughts.

"On this day, the third of October 1778, we gather to mourn the loss of the great Judge Claude Augustus Fontaine II," he could hear the speaker say, but he couldn't focus on the service at all.

Claude's mind wandered to a night just three months before; one that would always haunt him. He was on a night patrol, because he could pick up on sounds in the dark hours better than most people. He recalled a small carriage that had driven to just outside the woods, barely able to be seen in the moonlight. It abruptly stopped, and three figures crept out to unload some bags. When the last case touched the ground, the carriage disappeared back to the woods as fast as it had appeared. Claude and Charles had charged the group and were quick to surround them. It was more of the illegal gypsy criminals. Claude remembered the feeling of disgust as he uncovered the men bringing a variety of rifles and cages with small, rabid creatures into the city. He could recall the voices of the smugglers pleading, but there were strict laws regarding weapons and exotic animals. As they gathered the gypsies to the hold, a man on a horse raced towards him.

Claude tuned back in to the funeral, and felt even more hurt. He watched as his friend Joseph made way to the front to pay his respects and then sit next to him. It reminded him again of that night. The rider was similar in appearance and build to Claude, but with an even more slender face and higher cheek bones. He was hurried and nervous. Charles raised his sword in preparation for an attack, but as the man got closer, they recognized him. He was disheveled but kept a straight posture as he approached them. His long brown hair was usually properly set back, a style common for most prominent men, but in that moment, it was untamed as he rode through the night. It was Joseph, but in that state, he was unrecognizable.

Joseph had come that night to inform Claude of his father's critical condition. Claude thought back to the feeling in his chest as he jumped on his horse and quickly followed him. His Father was being kept at Joseph's family's private hospital. Few people were permitted to go there. The Beauchene family was a legacy of physicians and surgeons. They built a hospital for family, close friends and anyone of wealth or prominence. Just thinking about running through the halls behind Joseph seemed to tighten his chest and shorten his breath. He tried to distract himself, but his heart sank again as he remembered kneeling at his dying father's bedside.

Claude sat on the cold hard bench, broken inside. The more he listened to the other guests speak, the more frustrated he became. The events after that night had forever changed Claude's life, and he found it hard to hold back his emotions. His face was burning with rage and sadness. He let his anger well up inside of him as the people spoke of his father in the church. He tried to pay attention as the Bishop made his speech. His father was a well-known man amongst the clergy and other people of the church. Many made their appearances at the funeral, all expressing their deepest sympathies for his father's passing.

Hearing a man refer to his father's death was his breaking point, and he felt a deep rage overcome him. He stood to speak. He held a deep secret to his father's death, unknown to anyone, that tore through his heart like a knife. As he opened his mouth to begin his passionate rant of their ignorance, he felt a hand on his shoulder. It was his dear friend Charles. He placed his hand over his friend's and let out a deep sigh. Charles was just a few years older than him, but he had the demeanor of a boy... a rather unappealing boy. He was larger than most which suited him in his addition to the king's guard, but many compared his features to that of a rat. He did not have many friends except for Claude. They had been close since they were very young, but even he was unaware of the secret Claude held deep inside.

Afraid of releasing any more emotion, Claude quickly pushed the hand off and shoved his way from the church. He couldn't stay for the burial. There was a deep pain in his chest, and without any more thought, he went straight to the king. He knew what needed to be done. It was for his father's honor. His stride was heavy and quick. He insisted on walking to get his words straight in his mind before he spoke. Still, all he could think about was that night he learned of what had happened to his father. The hard truths he learned as he kneeled at the man's bedside, and the realizations he had come to. He began to see it all so clearly now. He remembered a conversation he had just months ago as he lumbered his way through the palace and demanded to speak with the king. The guards attempted to subdue him, but he was strong for his build and would not be settled easily.

He was relentless in his attack of the palace's best men when the king himself finally appeared. Claude looked up to him, and he knew this man, the highest authority in France and his father's dear friend, could sense his desperation. The king left to wait in his meeting room for a guard to help them all to their feet and escort Claude to him. He invited him to a private chamber and sat Claude down for a drink. He could sense the king's sincerity and finally took a breath of relief. He'd been holding onto so much and knew he could trust him. The king was near the far window pacing with concern. A long table separated them, stretching almost the entire length of the room with thirteen chairs on each side and one at each end. When he noticed Claude, he stopped and sat down at the table.

"Please, have a seat. There is nothing to be afraid of."

Claude nodded and took a deep breath before he found a place about halfway down the right side of the table. He didn't want to be rude and sit too far away, but he also didn't want to be presumptuous and sit too close either. He knew his entrance had caused enough trouble.

"Your Highness, I came here to accept your offer of taking this city under my wing. I will do anything for it. The gypsies are as you and my father spoke. He always told me they're like an ant pile. At first you don't notice them under the ground except when you step in the area and one or two bite you. I didn't truly believe him, but I should have," he admitted.

"The ants have been constructing a home under the earth. Building and scheming. They are soon to have their filthy pile built up over our beautiful city. Your father shared this analogy with me when he was alive. I'm devastated over his passing," the king said as he bowed his head in remembrance of his old friend.

"It is they who have murdered him with their evil doings." Claude felt a deep and painful lump in his throat as he pushed himself to speak. His chest felt tight, but he tried his hardest to continue, choking on every word and forcing back every emotion he felt.

"We will cleanse our home of such filthiness before they build and destroy us all," the king replied.

"They worship false gods, fornicate with whomever they please, destroying the great in our parish. These people are infinitely less intelligent, and most are just beggars with no trade. They surely aren't productive citizens, but do you really think the gypsies are such a problem as to start colonizing and taking over?" Claude questioned.

"They know we are superior to them and they can't stand it. I believe the gypsies are up to something. We have to stop them before they destroy our society and bring down everything we have worked for."

"I understand. How may I best serve my country?"

"I don't want to put too much on you. You're already in line as the next sheriff, and an acting lawyer. Should the people elect you as judge, you will have quite the career on hand. It can be a lonely life to hold that sort of title."

"I'm nearly twenty, Your Majesty. I was the best in my class for this very reason. I was destined to do this for you."

"We desperately need more patrol at night. That's when the dirty vermin do their business. They must be squashed!" the king demanded. He felt it was necessary to target all gypsies out at night and anyone else who may be helping them. He insisted Claude do whatever he needed to. He ordered public chastise for small offenses, floggings, hangings… The king was willing to do whatever it took to regain order and create fear in the people.

Claude had doubts that this would be a Godly way to deal with the problem. He expressed that would be almost considered gypsy genocide and warned him the people may try to over throw him for such a thing. Claude considered himself a sensible man despite the rage he felt deep inside and knew that not everyone felt the same of these gypsies as they did. He was hesitant, but the king was reassuring. He wanted his late dear friend's son to feel just in the request. After everything he had been through and dealt with, he believed Claude deserved to be a hero in Paris.

"The people respect you, criminals fear you. I believe you will do great things under my command. Your father would certainly be proud."

"Thank you, Sir." Claude bowed his head in gratitude for the king's kind words.

"Your father was a brilliant Judge. I know you will do well in his stead." The king was comforting in this difficult time for Claude. He felt lost and wanted to do anything he could in the name of his father.

"We would never go after innocent, law-abiding citizens. We only want the ones who step out of line, the ones who don't follow order. You're doing this to protect them. Relate to the families, the middle and higher class, the hard workers of Paris… They need to be saved from this epidemic! Highlight all the crimes and hardships on the rebels. Make them hate the crooked gypsies. Make them understand they are dangerous to their wives and children. Show the people that you are their savior. The good people of Paris will hand them to you on a platter. I will make sure of it. Your father was my oldest friend. I am doing this for his honor."

"As you wish your Highness. I will not fail you." Claude felt a twist in his gut, it felt wrong, but it was also his duty to protect others.

"I know you won't. You are only doing what is right and just for our people. They need-" As the king spoke, a small child burst into the room. "Elaina! What is she doing in here?" he shouted.

"I'm sorry, Sir, she's been so active today. She has been wanting to come see you. I tried to stop her," the woman cried.

The girl ran up to Claude, she had a big smile on her face. She was small with long blonde curls, but her dialect was not French. She danced and pranced about the room as her nurse tried desperately to catch her. The child couldn't have been more than seven. She grinned as Claude took her hand and greeted the young mademoiselle and inquired to who she was.

"I'm Annalise!" She sang. Her voice was proud and confident for her age.

Claude was confused by her. The king's first queen had died of illness, and it was known she had not carried any children. He tried not to impose too many questions, but the king gladly explained the girl was a gift from America. He continued on that when she was of age she would be the queen alongside him.

"America? Why would they do such a thing?" Claude inquired.

"They are planning a war against Great Britain, but I am not convinced we're ready to help when so much is going on here. We have three surrounding countries at war that have caused this disgusting rise in migrants here. This is their way of buttering me up to join their forces," the king told him.

"I see. And what is your plan?"

"Don't worry yourself with the matters of the world. Elaina, get her out of here!"

"Of course, Sir." She picked up the girl and quickly brought her out of the room.

Claude watched the young girl being carried out. She was so happy, full of life and completely unaware of what life would have in store for her. He pitied her. He thought of his own maid, Rosa, who he also considered a dear friend. She too had been taken by a man as a very young girl. That was no life for a child. A child bride; the thought made him cringe. How some families could have a daughter and willingly push her to a man two or three times her own age just for status and money was beyond his comprehension. It troubled him deeply, but he had to push it out of his mind; there were matters far more pressing to be dealt with. Claude nodded and left. He felt that he would avenge his father and make the gypsies pay for their ways.

When Claude was gone from sight, the king shouted for a guard to retrieve Charles immediately. The guard left and swiftly returned with him, who seemed quite disgruntled.

"Your guard said it was urgent. What was so important that I had to miss tarts?" Charles complained.

"Settle down Charles. I will have a whole tray of tarts made for you."

"Ah, very well, my King."

"Now to why I called you here. Claude and I have a plan to destroy these insects we call gypsies and I need your help. I need you to rattle the town's people, make them feel unsafe at even the thought of gypsies." The King checked to make sure no one was around to hear of their plot. His tone lowered as he shared his ideas with one of France's most ruthless soldiers. He knew Charles would do even the most vile of things he commanded him. He handed him ragged clothing that was similar to the Romani culture. He instructed Charles to terrorize the wives of the French men, making them afraid to leave their families alone. He encouraged him to scare the children and even commit crimes in public, robbing houses in the night. The king wanted to instill fear in the people of Paris of the gypsies.

"Do whatever you can, but don't let anyone, even Claude, know of your deeds. He must gain the people's trust. He must be the hero of our great Parisian culture. I trust you, Charles."

A twisted smile grew on Charles face. He took the clothes and went immediately to work. The king had given him complete freedom to do anything he wanted to anyone he pleased, and he was sure to induce horror amongst the people. Charles committed to doing everything his twisted mind could imagine to terrorize its citizens and make them desperate for a hero.

# Chapter Two

26 September 1787

     The king's plan was working after just a few short weeks, but it continued on through the years. Claude handled the gypsies that were arrested and was able to manipulate the juries and the justice system against them. Charles's actions began to isolate the gypsies, and soon the people of Paris were becoming more cautious of the migrants. They watched them more carefully and were quick to report any wrong-doings they witnessed. Some of the gypsies were able to fit in and live peacefully in the city; others were marked as trouble makers or rebels and left exposed and vulnerable. Things were going accordingly and the king's power was magnified. There was a blanket of fear that hovered over Paris. The town's people elected Claude as the Judge, keeping his current position as Sheriff, along with taking on the responsibilities in the city. There was an overall sense of peace knowing Claude was there to protect them. He now had been granted the power by the people to do whatever that may take.

     The years following that day brought about a silent chaos in France. The king was keeping a tight rein, especially on his beloved Paris, but at the expense of his best men. His experiment proved tiring amongst the people, yet all seemed to be exactly as the king demanded. Claude had been given a ruling power over Paris, but tried most often to remain fair. He was cunning to the people, and was loved by many. He was tough, but the people believed he was what brought on peace amongst those who had been living in fear. He was seen as a hero, even amongst those who weren't in favor of the monarchy. He'd won the people by numbers, and his power seemed to only gain momentum.

While there was currently an illusion of safety and peace, Claude knew it was just a veil over a much deeper-rooted issue. Still, he tried to live his personal life as normally as he could. Just inside his front door and to the right was a rather large fireplace. It did well to keep the entire level warm during the colder months, and Claude favored this spot more than any other. He'd been gifted an exorbitant chaise that he often looked forward to resting in at the end of each day. Rosa, who had cared for Claude's home since they were both young, sat with him. They were around the same age, yet she had the face of a much wiser woman. Her hair was long and curled down her back. She kneeled on the floor with a young boy and read to him.

It was in their routine every night. She ruffled his hair as he attempted to learn new words. His name was Julien. Claude had taken him in when he was a small baby at the request of the Monsignor. The boy was half gypsy, and Claude thought of him as less than valuable, but he tried to treat him well and educate him because of his partial French heritage. Julien tried to concentrate, but he knew tonight he had to take a chance he hadn't before. It may be the last opportunity had had for a while, and he shut the book with a thud loud enough to capture the attention of the room. While he had always thought of Claude as a father, and Rosa was certainly a mother to him his entire life, he knew they were not the ones that had brought him onto this earth, and he wanted to know more.

"Are you finished with your studies, Julien?'

"Almost, but I was really hoping that you could tell me of my parents. Please, Master?"

Claude insisted the boy was not old enough to hear such stories. It was a complicated matter that a child may not fully understand. He rolled his eyes at Julien's persistence and was annoyed to be robbed of his own simple peace due to nonsense inquiries of the past.

"Please! I beg you to tell me. Rosa will not tell me."

"As she shouldn't." He looked to Rosa who remained quiet. He knew that she had a better understanding of her place in his home and would remain silent. She nudged to Julien to quit, but the boy would not give up. Lost of all patience, Claude finally gave in.

"Fine, you're eight years old now. You want to know the truth?" His tone grew deeper in his frustration. He wasn't sure if it was a good idea, but Julien would keep wanting to know.

"Yes." Julien smiled.

"Your father was a prominent French man. He was married to a beautiful French girl for years until she died of illness. In his grief, he was bewitched by a gypsy, your mother. She plagued him with disease and was going to kill you as a sacrifice to their god, but the monsignor saved you. I have taken you in since."

"Why would you take me in? You hate gypsies."

"Not all. There are a few who behave properly and conduct themselves in a civilized way in a community. It is wrong in the eyes of my God to kill the innocent, especially as a sacrifice to a false god. Most gypsies are dark worshippers and evil doers, but children have innocent hearts. They can be trained to live the right way under Him. The good gypsies, like Rosa, are the ones who live like the good French people and learn the ways of God. I told you what you wanted to know, now get back to your reading."

"Yes, Master." Julien wanted to please him. All He wanted was a family. He knew Rosa loved him and that Claude at least cared for him, but he wanted a real family, like how Mary and Joseph were family to Jesus.

Claude spent much of his free time teaching him to read larger books and scripture, but Julien remained distracted. He did not have the normal life of a child, and was not allowed outside. Claude could see he longed to play with other children and make friends, but he did not want the people of his neighborhood to see the boy and gossip with false assumptions of who he was. Claude was a prominent man in the kingdom, he had a reputation to uphold and would not let even the child he took in out of good faith taint his name.

"Why must I learn all this?" Julien complained. He was tired, but Claude felt studying would keep him distracted enough to keep him quiet.

"There may come a time when education is beneficial to you. If I am to visit with you, you will be of some sorts, intelligent. Reading will also help you pass time in the church when you are not serving."

"Is that where I am going tonight?"

"Yes," Claude looked to Rosa. "pack all of his things. It's time for him to get ready to go. The Monsignor is expecting us."

Rosa loved the boy as her own. She quickly organized his clothes and a few other toys and small items to remind him of home. Whether or not she created Julien in her womb, he was her boy, and she adored him. She insisted on riding with Claude to deliver him to the church. When they arrived, the Monsignor quietly led them inside and down to the servants' quarters where they found a small, empty bed.

"This is where he will sleep," the man pointed.

Rosa put Julien, but he immediately reached up to her. His breathing became panicked which made her heart feel torn. She closed her eyes and took a deep breath as she prayed for strength to comfort him and let him go.

"Are you leaving me? I'll be good! Don't leave me here!" he cried. He was scared. Rosa knelt down to his level and looked him in the eyes as she spoke. She pushed the hair from his eyes. Her voice was gentle and soothing to the frightened child. She assured him this is where he would belong and that he was a very good boy for being so brave. Julien wiped tears from his eyes and hugged her tightly.

"My sweetheart... you must serve here for God. This is a good thing, I need for you to go and do this. I promise this will not be the last we see of each other."

"I can do that for you, Rosa," the boy whispered.
Rosa kissed his cheek and picked herself up. She felt heartbroken to have to leave him there and immediately went to Claude.

"Can he please come back soon? Just to visit every now and again? He can travel in the night so he won't be seen. I will even continue his studies on my own."

Claude was reluctant, but he saw the sadness in Rosa's eyes. He knew she had been through so much in her life and had never once asked him for anything and decided to show compassion for them.

"I suppose I could do that for you. But only if he keeps up with his lessons and is obedient in the church. He must never leave here otherwise. He is a servant now, and he will abide by my rules."

Rosa knelt down to hug Julien. "I know you will," she whispered.

"Say your goodbyes, I have patrol tonight." Claude interrupted.

"Goodbye Rosa!" He reached up and kissed her cheek.

"I love you child." She wiped her face and then brushed her fingers through his hair as she held him in her arms and prepared herself to leave.

"I love you Rosa." He looked up to Claude. "Goodbye Master."

Claude reached out his hand to shake Julien's. "God's blessings to you.

He brought Rosa home and then immediately left to meet Charles and the king at the palace to prepare the nights plan before patrols. They enjoyed a drink together as they discussed their success in keeping order and what the future may hold. As the meeting went on, screams echoed from outside the room. It was high-pitched and shrill. Someone, a girl, was clearly upset. They then heard the crashing sound of glass breaking on the floor.

"What in God's name is going on out there?" Charles asked.

"Annalise... she has been especially temperamental these last few weeks."

"What is the matter with her?" Claude inquired.

"Sir!" Elaina burst into the room. "Sir, this is the worst yet. She's ripped the dress and already ruined one cake. We're trying to calm her, but she can't be reasoned with," the woman cried.

"Do what you can. Lock her in her room until everything is ready. Fix the dress and tell her that if she tears it again, she will be forced to wear it torn in front of everyone in the kingdom to see."

"Yes, your Majesty." Elaina left the room in hopes she could settle the girl.

"Now don't come back! I'm busy!" The king scowled.

"Dress? It can't be that time already, can it? Didn't we just celebrate her thirteenth year?" Claude inquired as he could hear the girl's screams outside the door, she must have been terrified.

"Yes, but she's bled! She's ready whether she thinks she is or not. She can continue with her tantrums, but it changes nothing."

"That's understandable, but don't you find thirteen to be a bit young?"

"Nonsense! Her body is fit to bear children now. She has a few months before the wedding, but I will wait no longer than that. Now you two must go, you have more important things to worry about." The king was stern and would discuss the issue no more. Claude felt uncomfortable, but he had to push the thought from his mind... This wasn't an uncommon practice, in fact, many young girls were married off at such an age, but it bothered him nonetheless.

He washed up his face in a hurry and then followed Charles to the courthouse just after dark.

"Anthony tells me they have found some gypsies he believes to be smugglers. He and Benjamin are laying low until we get to them." Charles informed him.

"Is everything ready to go?"

"Yes, the horses and wagons are out back." He assured him as they left to meet up with the two soldiers who were waiting. They observed as five gypsies carried goods out of a small cart.

"When I give the signal, we will surround them." Claude prepared the others. They each took their positions, awaiting his cue. Charles noticed one woman in the group. She was young and very lovely with a small frame, yet curved in sensual places. Her corset was especially tight and left little to the imagination. Charles never took his eyes off of her as they stalked the group, and when Claude gave the signal, he grabbed his cuff and locked her to the side of the wagon. He then helped gather the others. It was a tough fight at first, but extra soldiers had been waiting on guard and quickly arrived to relieve the situation. When all the gypsies were restrained, Charles unlocked the girl's cuff, and tied her hands behind her. As he walked her to the wagon, he kissed her neck and whispered something in her ear. The girl began to fight him and hit him. He pushed her down, and she kicked him in the leg. He jumped back in pain as the girl got away.

"Why did you let her go?" Claude shouted.

"Oh no! We've got a runner!" Benjamin and Anthony chimed, laughing.

"I love the ones that run; they think they have a chance." Charles shouted back as he ran to her with a malicious grin.

The prisoners grew in an uproar in the cage as Claude turned away to lock them up. "I'll never understand that. They're known to carry disease."

"He wants what he wants I suppose." Anthony brushed it off. He had worked many patrols with Charles and had seen it happen many times. "I guess there is something mysterious and exotic about them."

"Well he better hurry, it's freezing out here," Claude complained.

"The winter months are approaching fast this year," Benjamin added.

Charles chased after her into to a dark alley. He threw her into the wall, and she fell. As she laid there, Charles unbuttoned his pants. She tried to get up and leave, but he threw her down and forced himself on top of her. She kept screaming, but no one came out to her rescue. No one ever did. Rue de Baker was a notorious neighborhood for such crimes, and the people were known to keep to themselves, some out of fear, others out of apathy, but few ever helped another in need.

"I love when you scream. Such a beautiful sound," he scoffed. When he was finally finished with her, he laughed as he drug the distraught girl back to lock her away with the others and joined his mates.

"I don't know how you do it. What makes it worth the risk?" Claude was disgusted but his curiosity won.

"Well let's talk about it over a pint. I need to change up and so do you."

"I'll meet you after I bring the prisoners to the jail and get ready."

Claude locked the prisoners away and changed into a clean shirt. He didn't particularly want to go out, but he had nothing better planned. He slowly made his way to the nearby tavern and sat next to Charles at the bar.

"I'm glad you could make it," Charles greeted.

"What else would I do? My life revolves around work and this place."

"You need a lady, Claude; it would be good for you. I can tell you what I will be doing when I leave here," he chuckled.

"Is it true you visit the prison at night?"

"It's easier. French women expect you to spend months or even years courting them and buying them fancy things. And even then, they may never truly satisfy you. Prison gypsies love the attention you give them and expect nothing in return. They are all sexual savages; it's all they want so I can save my money."

"How have you not been diseased yet? The gypsies are filthy." Claude was still disgusted.

"It's a science really, I can just look at a girl and tell if she is or isn't."

"Excuse me?"

"Must be a rare gift, I can't explain it," Charles smirked.

"Are there any virgins left, or is virtue and morality lost at a young age?" Claude sighed. He could picture his life with that perfect woman, the one he knew had to be out there, but Paris was riddled with women caught in the midst of gambling and prostitution. Many girls did start young or were married off by their parents, but Claude didn't have such luxuries. His parents had both perished when he was young and had never pushed any prospects upon him. But even when he did court, none were truly promising.

"I think the children are all doing it nowadays. You're quite late in your quest, wouldn't you say?" Charles laughed.

"I just haven't' found a woman I can trust. After what happened to my father, I just think it's important to be as careful as possible."

"What about Lady Eleanor? I've never seen a lady so smitten with anyone."

"She's been married twice."

"But I have it by the highest authority that she's never been with other men than her husbands. She loved you back in the day, before them. If you had married her then, she most likely would have been yours forever."

"Or I would be her first dead husband." Claude joked. He did care about Eleanor, but that had faded in the years. He didn't want a woman touched by another man; he wanted his own love. He longed for someone he trusted to only be touched by him. Charles laughed, "indeed, but you know what I mean."

"Yes, well I was an apprentice building a career and a life. I didn't have the time to slow down with her. All she wanted was to settle with a family, but I had goals and a destiny to fulfill," he explained.

"And that's all you have to show for it. Women love you, they want you."

"And none of them interest me, most can't even speak properly. And all the women that can seem to abuse it and have few morals or virtue. They use their beauty for sex and money. It's a disgrace."

The thought of his best friend being attracted to girls who were simply well spoken was almost boring to Charles, but he attempted to remain encouraging as he nodded to a pretty young woman on the other side of the tavern. He signaled for another drink for them both and continued listening.

"What about Rosa? She's lived with you our entire lives. You've never been interested? She speaks very well," he suggested.

"After...? Are you mad?" Claude thought of Rosa as family to him.

"I would."

"Well who wouldn't you lay with? I will find someone one day. God will lead me to the right one, I know it."

"Well I hope you do, you don't know what you're missing." Charles told him.

# Chapter Three

25 February 1796

     With every radical plan for an illusion of peace comes its own set of sacrifices to freedom of the people it aims to protect. Strict laws had been approved that put the city under intense pressure. Rebels fought to destroy the monarchy, and often the country of France would divide, but the opposing militia was weak. The king's men remained victorious for over ten years before the Directorate was formed just the year prior. This committee consisted of men picked by the king to serve as acting order.

     These powers served him and his agenda and only strengthened Claude in his crusade. He had put aside any hopes for love and a family-oriented future, and in his spare moments he began to focus on continuing Julien's education. It became routine, and Claude took it very seriously. To the world, Claude was a charismatic and charming mystery. He was highly respected, and many even found him to be a caring official who led for the people, but Julien knew a deeper and sometimes even darker side to the man. When Julien did well in his lessons, he was allowed to return home with him to visit Rosa for a night or two every week, but when he didn't do well or disobeyed, Claude was harsh and many times beat him with his cane. He felt Julien needed more guidance than most boys his age. He could sense his disorderly nature and believed a strict routine and discipline would best train him to be a productive member in society.

Still, Julien felt the physical punishment was nothing compared to the pain of when he was not allowed to visit Rosa. He tried to be as good as possible, but it never seemed to be enough. In an attempt to keep his mind occupied and positive, Julien found an old pottery wheel and taught himself to use it with materials Rosa would send for him. He was talented with it and made many pots, vases and dishes.

One day, after a particularly harsh punishment, Julien began to carve out a piece of wood he had found in the courtyard. At first it was merely angry and hurt cuts and gashes, but then a funny thing happened. The outline of a face began to appear in the grains of the block. It immediately calmed him, and he slowed his pace. The impression of a small face gradually peeked its way through the layers. He took his time and finished the sculpture in the wood. That's when the idea came to him, and he covered it in clay to create a mold. He began to make masks and faces, but it wasn't enough. He wanted to make a beautiful doll. He began carving a full figure into wood, using them as molds to make their bodies. He laid the sculptures in the sun to dry and harden.

Rosa began to bring him paint and horse hair to give the dolls true appearance and even identities. They would be his friends. Julien longed to see people, to talk to them, enjoy a day with them, but he knew that would never be allowed. To distract his desires, he made more dolls to occupy time. He could name them, give them lives, and teach them. It was up to his imagination what they could be. He learned to sew them clothes and designed elaborate dresses with dramatic accessories and hats. Each had a name. Each had a persona, a relationship with the others, and an identity. They were becoming real to him. It wasn't long before the other servants and the clergymen of the church noticed his work over filling the rooms. They unanimously agreed to help Julien in his venture and set him up a workshop in the tower of Notre Dame. It was the perfect place to overlook the city and inspire his art.

Claude came for a visit one afternoon after his court hearings. Julien had never shown him the full extent of his work, but his hobby had become his life work, and he wanted to share that with the ones he loved. He opened the glass case he kept them in to expose all of his beautiful creations.

"This is very good Julien. You have a gift for clay work."

"Thank you, Sir, I have spent many years perfecting them, making them what they are now." Julien sat straighter, proud of himself.

"True dedication to your craft. You indeed have talent." Julien reached to the top of his case. He pulled down a small doll from the back with long black hair and an elaborate green frock and bonnet.

"Here Master! It's my best work yet. I made this one for Rosa! The dress is made from an old shirt she had made me a long time ago that no longer fits." He was excited to show his creation. The doll had a beautifully painted face to resemble the woman who had cared for and loved him like a mother.

"Well she is beautifully done." Claude was impressed. "Speaking of, I have brought you something. It's from Rosa for your birthday." He handed Julien a basket who opened it excitedly. He rarely received gifts.

"Some wine and a slice of cake!" Julien shrieked. Claude opened the bottle while he set the table. "You're eighteen now, and Rosa feels you are responsible enough to handle it, but only one glass at a time. We can't have a drunken doll maker in the church." Claude poured them each a glass and then put the bottle away in a locked cabinet.

"How old are you now?" Julien asked him boldly.

"I was eighteen when you were born. You are eighteen now. How old does that make me?"
Julien grabbed a piece of paper and wrote down the numbers.

"This is addition, right?"

"Yes."

"So, I put '18' at the top for your age, and I'm eighteen now, so, I add '18' under that. Am I right so far?"

"So far. Now, what is '18+18', Julien?"
Julien thought for a while. He had only learned addition of large numbers a few weeks ago and had not yet mastered it.

"Twenty-six?"

"How did you come to that?"

"Well one plus one is two and eight plus eight is sixteen. And when the numbers have a '1' in front of it, you drop the '1'?"

"You tried to solve the problem backwards. Just because the first numbers are easier to add, doesn't mean you are allowed to start there. You have to start with the last numbers. So, if eight and eight equal sixteen, you carry the '1' to the next sequence. Now you add the '1' to the '1+1' and what do you get?"

"Three."

"Very good. So, how old am I?"

"Three- no… thirty-six?"

"That is correct."

"You are a very good teacher. I wish you didn't have patrol tonight, Master. I would very much love to spend time with you and Rosa again."

"Next week for sure. Now enjoy your treat. I must be going," he said as he packed his things for the evening.

Julien waved to him as he left for patrol. Claude and Charles quickly loaded their wagons with supplies and immediately got to work, but they hadn't even settled at their posts that evening when they noticed Anthony was quickly riding to find them. Anthony only ever left his post if he had big news or information so Claude knew to be prepared. It had been years since their patrols had ever uncovered any major dealings, and seeing Anthony made him nervous of what may be to come.

# Chapter Four

26 February 1796

Anthony rode as quickly as he could to meet Claude. He was a much shorter man than average, but he had a confidence in himself that made up for his height. His hair was kept short, and the brown almost appeared to have shades of red in the subtly light. The features of his hair perfectly complimented his light and freckled face. He was neither graceful or the smartest, but he was loyal to Claude and shared in his mission.

"Judge Fontaine! One of the private detectives has witnessed an underground shed to harbor gypsies! I'm told they are hiding at least twenty," he informed the two. Together they worked to devise a plan of action and retrieve the appropriate back-up in case there was any trouble.

Anthony led them to where he had last met with the other officers on the case, but as they traveled closer Claude began to recognize the property. It was a vegetable farmer's land. The other guards had already began rounding up all of the gypsies from the shelter.

Claude found the guard arresting the land owner. He knew the man and was sure to express his disappointment and then led the siege on the property to find what else may be hiding besides the illegal gypsies. Claude waited with the landowner and watched as the officers cleared out the underground storage, and what they found confirmed the king's fears. Something big was happening in Paris, and it hadn't come about overnight. This was years of planning and preparing and it had occurred under Claude's watch.

Stock piles of food and water covered multiple crates weapons, armor and gunpowder. He felt a deep anger with himself. Yet again, he had failed to listen to what his father and the king had told him for years. He was lenient and gave chance after chance, and this is where it got him. Claude feared for what could have become of the city had his men not found the farm.

"Arrest this man and his wife for treason!" He commanded.

"No please! My wife had nothing to do with this. It was all me. I beg of you, Sheriff, we have children! They have no one else."

"You should have thought about that before William. We've allowed your half gypsy family to live on this land and even prosper well under the king. You will pay heavily for your betrayal. Now, Anthony, find the children appropriate accommodations until after their incredibly stupid parent's trials." Claude directed two guards to keep watch for any that may have eluded capture, and the rest of the officers transported the prisoners. Anthony brought the children to Madame DuPont. She had become widowed early in her life and had never found any other love than that of her children. When problems arose suddenly, she always took in and cared for orphans or other children in need of a home. Claude and Charles returned to their post after everyone was on their way to where they'd been instructed. Anthony managed to return quickly. He enjoyed any help he could give Claude and was eager to follow in his footsteps. He checked that Charles's prison wagon and Claude's carriage was secured. He and a fellow officer made sure the horses were fed and ready should anything else happen, because their shift had barely begun for the night.

The evening's events created a buzz amongst the guards. They were ridden with excitement. It was the largest case that had happened before them, and the guards all stood by at their stations when Claude noticed something in a nearby area just after midnight. He woke Charles who had dozed off in their wait and whispered to him. "Look, across the alley way. They've gathered a few, four maybe five of them. The women are most likely selling themselves."

Charles became excited. He knew they could catch them. It seemed to be an easy arrest, and they hadn't taken down this type of crime in a while. He eagerly charged on his horse and quickly jumped off in front of the group. He raised his sword to the largest man's throat so none of the others would run.

"Don't move! You are under arrest!" He shouted with a smile. The man trembled. He feared Claude and his men and insisted they were not doing anything wrong, but their pleas for mercy were ignored. Claude kicked the man to the ground and threw Charles a couple of bundles of rope to bind the prisoners.

"Whatever you claim to have been doing is irrelevant. You're out past dark with these women. Prostitution is punishable for both the whore and her mate." Claude snarled.

The older of the women became enraged.

"We're not prostitutes! You only come after us because you think your kind is better than us! We've done nothing wrong, you cowardice pig!"

"I am an official of the law! I go after only the sinful and unrighteous insects of the city. Don't blame me because you got caught! You know the curfew laws," he scorned. He could feel his anger taking over. He stepped down from his horse and towered over the woman as Charles continued to bind the others who had left the younger of the girls for last, and when he finished putting the men away, he made his way back to her. She was small and timid. She held her breath as he stood behind her and pulled her hair back. Charles removed his glove to feel the soft skin of her cheek. His fingers caressed her as he reached around to kiss her neck. She began to cry as his hand reached around her neck and moved down her chest. "What a pretty little thing you are," he whispered into her ear.

"Don't touch her!" The woman jumped on Charles's back and wrapped her bound hands around his throat. She attempted to choke him and screamed for the girl to run. In the commotion, the man Claude was binding was able to elbow him in the face while he was distracted and knocked him to the ground. The girl was terrified by the chaos, almost frozen as she witnessed the struggle. When she noticed Charles gaining the upper-hand, she snapped back to her senses and ran as fast as she could towards the woods nearby.

Claude quickly regained his mind enough to grab his knife while the trouble persisted and stabbed the largest of them, cutting his Achille's tendon. The man let out an ungodly shriek and fell which forced the others to abruptly settle down in fear. Even Claude could feel the pain he'd caused like a phantom in his own leg, but he stood to enforce order amongst them.

"Enough!" He pulled woman off of Charles and threw her into the ground. "Charles, go get the girl! Anthony, lock them up in the wagon. Now!"

Anthony threw the men in the horse-drawn prison wagon while Claude grabbed the woman.

"Your daughter, I presume? You've just made a stupid mistake." He threw her in with the other prisoners and locked cage. He mounted his horse, but caught the woman's eyes as he attempted to let Charles have his way with the girl. Claude couldn't explain the thoughts running through his own mind. Maybe it was stress or exhaustion, but something in his mind told him to go after Charles and the girl.

Charles had chased the girl to a corner of the city where there was little light. There was a short wall separating the city from the woods. Another alley way led behind a stretch of flats. The girl knew if she could only reach the wall she would have a chance. She ran as fast as she possibly could, but it wasn't enough. Charles lunged into her and threw her to the ground. He picked her up and twisted her arm behind her, shoving her into the wall.

"No! Please!" she cried, terrified of what would happen to her. He started to reach under her dress. "The judge usually turns his head to what I like to do with the whores and runners. And you surely are the prettiest."

Before he could touch her, Claude caught up to him. Charles leaned into her and whispered into her ear how disappointed he was to have not been able to enjoy her and threw her down into the snow like common garbage.

"I caught her, now what shall we do with her?" Charles grew twisted with anticipation. He wasn't picky when it involved torturing others.

"You know that we usually kill the runners." Claude began.

"But I haven't done anything! Please!" The girl cried.

Claude sprung from his horse to catch the girl himself. He wanted to look her in the eyes as he taught her the proper way to speak to someone in authority. He grabbed her arm and jerked her to her feet.

"Stupid Girl! You know it's a crime to be out past dark! Only whores are out this late!"
She looked up at him. He was intimidatingly taller than she was, but she was persistent in her claim to innocence. She swore in the name of God, but Claude rolled his eyes.

"You stand in the alley like a common street walker in the night, yet you expect me to believe you? Charles, hold her," he commanded as he drew his sword.

"It's a shame to waste such a pretty face on a common gypsy whore..."

"No! Please you have to believe me! I'm not a... I've never even been touched by a man! I swear it!"

"Is that so?" There was something about her that made him slow to judge, but Charles grabbed her tighter as she struggled.

"She's lying," he insisted, but the girl continued to plead.

Claude pushed the hair from her face and lifted her chin. He looked into her eyes. They were dark, and her tears were genuine. She was so young and beautiful, if this girl truly was innocent than he must spare her. His posture straightened as he nodded for Charles to hold her tightly. He pulled the gloves from his hands and stuffed them into his pocket. Charles's arms wrapped around her and squeezed as hard as he could to prevent her from moving.

"I can tell if you're lying," Claude admitted to her, but she didn't understand.

She attempted to plead for mercy when Claude covered her mouth with one of his hands. She became afraid and tried to wriggle free, but he leaned into her to keep her from moving. With his free hand, he reached under her skirt. His hands were like ice, and she struggled more, trying to scream. He slowly slid his hand up her thigh. She kicked her legs, but it did her no good. She began to feel sick as his fingers seemed to crawl closer until she felt something like a sharp stab deep in her. She tried again desperately to scream as he felt around inside of her. He looked into her eyes and smiled at her devilishly.

"There we go." He mumbled. It was as if he were taking everything she had from her with just a touch. He did it with such ease. The smile in his eyes as he stared into hers assured her that he was taking his time, as if to make her feel less like a person with every moment. He eventually uncovered her mouth to allow her to catch her breath.

"Ow! Stop! That hurts," she cried. She didn't understand what he was doing or why he was doing it to her, but he wasn't letting up. He insisted he was almost done, but did not act quickly to be done. She was no longer even sure of what he was hoping to find when he finally pulled his hand from under her dress.

"Blood," Charles exhaled, seemingly disappointed. He dropped the girl, and she began to sob.

"It seems as though she's telling the truth," Claude reported as he wiped his hand and commanded his comrade to go wait by the wagon. Charles looked down at the girl and smirked as he walked away.

"It only gets better from here child," he sang as he left her there.

Claude crouched down next to the girl once Charles was out of sight. He touched her face with the back of his hand and pushed her hair from her eyes to behind her ear. He stared down at her chest, her corset was tight it made her breasts rise with every heavy breath she could breathe. His hand trailed down her neck. He grabbed her hands and pulled her to her feet.

"How old are you dear?"

"Fourteen, sir," she meekly responded.

Her words made Claude feel sick. He thought on the king's child bride. This girl was innocent. There was no reason to keep here there. He could let her go, and life could return to the way it had always been. He considered the thought when their eyes finally met. They were lovely, and her lashes were the longest he'd ever seen on anyone before. They pulled him into her, and he felt lost in her trance. He knew that she couldn't have just fallen into his life by accident. There was a reason she was there, and Claude wanted to know her.

"I'm so very sorry dear girl. You are so beautiful, and there's something about you." He pulled her closer to him as he whispered soft words of her seductive innocence.

"I don't know to what you are referring, Sir." She spoke softly, and her face burned as tears welled up in her eyes.

"Your voice is poetic. It draws me to you." His fingertips lightly touched the skin under her neck leading down her chest. Her breathing became heavier, she was too afraid to speak.

His hand grasped her jaw as his thumb brushed over her bottom lip. So soft... untouched... The way she looked up at him, when she spoke, everything about her was alluring. She was all Claude had ever hoped for in a girl. He wanted to feel her again. He needed to. He backed her into the dark alley and pinned her up against the wall. It was colder there, and she was shaking. He touched her lips, they were a beautiful color, a dark pink, and so soft. He wanted her in any way he could have her. He tried to kiss her, but she pushed back and begged hm to stop. He placed his fingers over her lips to command her silence. He continued and leaned into her with his whole weight, one hand over her face, the other on her hip working its way down. His knee shoved its way in between her legs as he lifted her skirt over her knees. He whispered in her ear. She was simply irresistible but the feel of her was just unbearable. Thinking of everything he wanted to do to her made him stiff and powerless to stop. He pressed his lips upon hers and tore the stockings under her dress. He quickly unbuttoned his pants and forced himself inside her. The girl was afraid. She clenched the wall, her voice muffled under his hand. She tried to scream but could barely breathe.

"You must be quiet!" He covered her mouth again with more force and thrust hard into her, his movements rapid. She closed her eyes as it became even more difficult to take a single breath. Everything became a blur, and she fell into the snow. She must have held her breath for too long as she realized that more moments must have passed. She looked up at him as he cleaned himself up. She tried to get up and walk but was bruised and in pain.

Claude pulled her up and brought her out of the alley way. She stood there in a confused daze, but she couldn't bring herself to even move. He paced in front of her, almost in a panic until they met eyes once more. His gaze turned from that of worry to anger. He grabbed her arms and began to shake her violently.

"What have you made me do? What powers of seduction have you used on me, gypsy witch?!" He threw her into the snow and continued to traipse back and forth. Her dizziness was worsened by his movements, it was almost as if he were skipping around her in circles. She tried to focus on a small twig in the snow as she listened to him accuse her of witchcraft. To be branded a whore was one thing, but to be named a witch was to burn. Her eyes widened at the thought and she forced herself up from the ground to defend the truth.

"I swear I have no power! I'm a stupid ordinary girl," she wept.

"A stupid child indeed, committing crimes in the night, I should put you and your whore mother to death right now!"

"We did nothing wrong! You have," she argued. Her chest pushed up against him, and she contrived the most daring glare she could fake into his eyes. She felt used, and her body was cold and weak. She was the most terrified she had ever been in her life, but she refused to just give up on herself.

"You are the only man who touched me! You can't do this! No!" She wanted to scream and fight, but the man stood cold in his emotion. In her mind, he didn't even seem to flinch as she became hysterical and kicked snow at him.

Almost shocked by her boldness, Claude stepped back to pull his knife from his waistcoat. He pointed the blade to her throat and lifted her chin with it to look up at him. His brows rose, and his eyes almost seemed to darken in that moment.

"Can you prove that? Stupid girl. Even so, who will hear the words of a dead gypsy? Your virginity is no longer yours to claim. So, it seems as though my dear, you...are...stuck..."

She began to cry more. She couldn't understand why he was doing this. Why her? She wasn't sure of her true sins or of what she could do to redeem herself, but she begged for mercy nonetheless.

Claude paused in thought for a moment. Whether or not she had bewitched him, he gave in to her. He took her innocence, her blood was on his hands, but he wanted more of her. He felt the weight of his sins on his chest, and it guilted him.

"There's only one way this can be made right in the eyes of God for what has happened here. You can fix this; for the sake of our souls and your family."

She looked up to the prison wagon where her mother was being held. She had no fear for her soul and especially not his, but for the sake of her family, she would do what she had to, even die for them.

"What must I do?"

"You must pay your mother's penance so she can care for your family. You owe her debt now, and only you can make everything right."

Her anxiety intensified, and her eyes began to burn. There was a knot in her. She couldn't pin exactly where it was, because it began to pain her body in random varying places. She could feel it in her stomach, her throat, and behind her eyes. The pain in her body was subduing her, but she tried to hold on to every last bit of strength she could as she assured him she had nothing left to give.

Claude paced behind her as he contemplated his actions but was halted by an intoxicating aura. He couldn't quite explain the scent, but it brought about a pleasant feeling that he didn't seem to have the words to describe. He followed it back to the girl and grabbed a handful of her hair. He clenched it tightly in his fist. It was sweet and a vague image of a flower hanging in the spring breeze came to mind, but he still couldn't quite put his finger on exactly what it was.

"Your innocence," he finally mumbled in his dreamlike haze.

"I don't understand, you just said..." Her voice was staggered as she tried to speak.

The cold was creeping in and began to burn her. She felt what seemed like her lungs collapsing inside of her and threw her hands into her chest as if to catch them.

Claude stood behind her, reached around her and placed his hand on her chest. He pulled her hair back behind her ear. The scent was strong, and he kissed her shoulder. He longed for more.

"Your innocence already belongs to me. Choose to come with me. Leave your family behind and be mine."

"I... I don't know..."

"It's what must be done to make this right by God. Your family as well as your soul will be safe if you stay in my home," he whispered in her ear.

She didn't know about God or what he would actually expect from a girl like her, but she looked to her mother in the distance and knew she would do anything to keep her and her sisters safe. The world fell silent as she closed her eyes and grabbed the necklace from around her neck. She began to mutter words that Claude could not understand... He became more impatient and pushed his knife, making a small cut into her chest near her heart.

"Choose now! I'm losing my patience!" He snapped.

"I'll do it!" Tears ran down the girl's face as she finally agreed.

"Very well." Claude tied her up, gagged, and blindfolded her. She was devastated and cried as he whispered threats in her ear of what he would do to her family should she dare move or run before he returned. She nodded, and he left her alone in the snow where no one could see her.

"Justice has been served to the gypsy whore! She ran into the woods and resisted arrest, which is a crime that is punishable by death," she could hear Claude in the distance shout to the others. She would be presumed dead to the world. It was the perfect plan to ensure no one ever searched for her. She could hear her mother scream.

"No! My baby!" the woman screamed again and again as she shook the cage bars in rage.

Claude ignored her and pulled Charles aside. He shared the deal he had just made with the girl and instructed Charles on exactly how to handle the prisoners and the girl's mother. For his secrecy, Claude agreed to turn his head once again to any indiscretions he may have with the woman once Claude was out of sight with the girl. Charles eagerly thanked him as they walked to the carriage to carry out their plan.

"Have the others gone back?" Claude questioned as he noticed they were alone with the prisoners.

"I told Anthony they could go home for the night. The prisoners are bound tightly and won't go anywhere. You and I can handle them on our own."

Charles grabbed the woman and brought her out from the cage. She tried to fight with them, but Claude overpowered and hit her. She was tough and tried to get up, but he hit her again.

"Hold her down! I need to get my carriage. When I give you the signal, let her go. Don't do anything with her until I am gone."

"What have you done with my daughter?"
Claude grabbed the woman's hair and pulled her head up as Charles spoke.

"She is alive and will spend the rest of her days hidden where no one will ever find her. The deeply blessed judge will enjoy her for the whore she has now become," he snarked as he shoved her face in the snow. The woman shook and cried in her devastation.

"So, when I'm done with her, you want me to just bring the rest of them to the prison?" Charles was skeptical of the plan working out the way he assumed.

"Yes, why wouldn't you?"

"Well... They could all be potential witnesses." Charles made a fair point. They had all seen the young girl, they may have even known her. They may be afraid now of the man that she was last seen with, but fear rarely kept rats from squealing. Claude realized he was right. He couldn't trust any of them. They would expose him in a heartbeat; he knew he was a mere complication in their vile lives. They would love nothing more than to taint his reputation and ruin everything he had worked for over twenty years accomplishing.

"Kill them all," he commanded.

"Of course. You should go Claude; the sun will be up in just a few hours."

Claude attached his horse back to his carriage and drove it to the girl. He threw her in and locked the door. As he drove away, Charles let the woman go, and she ran to throw a rock towards the carriage at Claude, and the girl could see her mother.

"Wait! I'm not ready! Mother! Wait, please," but they were too far away. She cried as the horse sped them away and stared weakly out the window of the carriage. She watched as her mother ran towards the woods and cried. How hard would her mother look? Would she know her daughter wasn't really dead? Where would her family search for her? She looked to her leg and noticed the blood running down. The sight made her head spin, and she laid back on to the seat to keep from getting sick. She stared at the window, watching the shadows of the night whirl by.

# Chapter Five

27 February 1796

      It wasn't a long ride before the carriage came to a quick halt in the darkness. She could no longer see out the window, and her body began to shake as she felt the wagon shift from Claude jumping down from his seat. With blurry vision, the girl watched as he appeared to unlock his gate. He immediately pulled her from the carriage, and she followed quietly behind him through the metal gate guarding his home.

      She was dazed and could barely speak. She wanted to shut her eyes to the world but found herself observing the home as they made their way across the courtyard. She could see his and the surrounding homes in the distance. His was only slightly larger than the rest, but it was also darker. This suited him well. The overall theme of the outer appearance was dreary and looked a bit neglected. She got the impression this place was even less welcoming of a home beyond the way she already felt about the man.

      As he pulled her along, she noticed his courtyard. The dreary confines of what she observed inside of that oversized iron gate confirmed her belief that this was a very lonely place. Most homes in this neighborhood had manicured courts and gardens, yet this home was very different. The property she realized she had been sentenced to endure did not contain such luxuries, at least not anymore. What looked to be a once beautiful garden was now dead. The lawn had been covered in dirt and brick with a narrow cobblestone path to the home.

This was not the kind of place that hosted guests often, or even a staff. The appearance of this particular home was designed to not require regular maintenance as the others did. She'd heard rumor that the great judge was a very private man and the life he must have lived to be so cruel, but she never imagined she would be the one to find out the truth for herself. She looked up to the man as he rushed to unlock the home. He was significantly taller than she was and far more intimidating as he pulled her closer to him.

"You will come inside with me without a fuss," Claude grumbled. He gripped her arm tightly as they walked inside. She found his voice to be plummy and began to resent him even speaking to her, but nonetheless, she nodded with a tremulous expression. She was dazed and couldn't even force herself to respond properly.

"Sit here, and I will get Rosa to come take care of you," he commanded. He pulled a chair from under the table for her. He intended to walk away when she finally spoke.

"Who?" she asked as she desperately attempted to collect her thoughts.

"Rosa. She keeps my house," he responded quietly.

The girl was still trying to understand everything that was happening, and Claude sat down next to her as if he were trying to help.

"Is she like me?"

"Like you, how?"

"You know... have you..." she whispered as she looked down at blood on her skirt.

Claude sat down in the chair next to her and held her hands in his. He began to speak, but all she could hear was the subtle creaks and cracks of the home around her.

"Dear girl." He reached for her hair, but she flinched, "I don't want you to be afraid. This is your new home... I want you to know, I have never touched anyone before in such a way. You are a beautiful, special girl. You made me feel something that I had never felt before. I'm sorry if I scared you."

She simply stared around the room with tears running down her face. The inside of his home was very different from its outward characteristics. The walls were light, and the mahogany cabinetry and furniture accented them well. The woods varied in texture and shades yet complimented the overall pattern. She contemplated if it was worth speaking as she studied her new home and didn't know what would even be appropriate to say. Claude stood and reached his hand out to her. She looked up at him and placed her hand in his as he led her around the house to a room.

"This is Rosa," he introduced. "She will get you cleaned up while I prepare you a room."

"Oh... and who is this?" Rosa seemed to be caught by surprise.

"This is our new house guest. Would you be so kind as to clean her up?"

"Of course, Sir." She was puzzled, yet knew not to ask too many questions.

"And be sure she stays quiet," the girl heard him whisper.

"I see... Come with me dear." Rosa led the girl to a washtub in a back room, "let me help you get this off." She helped her undress and get into the tub.

"I apologize the water is not very hot. I would have warmed it more if I had been given the proper time..."

"It's alright. I'm fine," the girl mumbled; staring off blankly.

"Tell me dear, what's your name?" Rosa wanted the girl to feel safe around her to talk to if she needed. She could imagine what the girl had probably been through in the previous hours.

"Marie."

"Marie? That's more of an English name than I would have expected. Aren't you- "

"It is, and I am. My father wanted my family to fit in here, but obviously it didn't work," she sighed heavily.

She could feel her hurt deep inside her and didn't want to talk about it anymore. She knew she may as well forget what her father tried to do. It didn't help her family, and it didn't save her from ending up where she was at that moment. She questioned Rosa of her job in the home and for any clue as to what her own future may hold with them.

Rosa sighed, trying to avoid answer her questions incorrectly. She was unsure of what the girl even knew or what Claude had planned. She didn't want to scare the girl, the child, more.

"I can clean well enough, but my sister always cooks better than me," Marie explained.

Rosa took a deep breath to hold back tears. "All clean dear, let's go." She brought Marie to a room. In it there was a just a bed with a seemingly large wardrobe in the corner. Rosa sat Marie on the bed and went to her room to grab a dress from her own wardrobe.

"You can wear one of my gowns for tonight. It's comfortable, but the corset gives a nice shape." She helped her dress.

Marie still didn't understand everything. "Will I be a keeper, like you?"

Rosa looked away. "I can't say... Just sit here, and I will see of the Master's plan," she whispered.

Marie looked around.

"Does anyone else live here?"

"No," Rosa told her as she tied the corset snugly on the girl.

Marie realized if this room didn't belong to Rosa, it could only be one other's room. She began to panic, and her breathing became heavy.

"He will be back any minute, I don't know what he wants you to do here, but getting in a panic will not help anything."

"I don't understand!" Marie looked around, her head rushing, she felt dizzy. "Please don't let him do those things to me again. I beg of you!"

Rosa tried to sit Marie back on the bed, but she got up and pushed Rosa aside.

"No! I can't do this!" She began to panic and ran from the room, making her way back to the door she arrived through.

"No! Marie! Wait!" Her voice was strong in its whisper. Rosa wanted to catch her before Claude could hear and become angry, but she couldn't get to her before she ran from the house. When Marie made it outside to the gate, she attempted desperately to open it and escape.

"No, no, no! It's locked!" She pulled at the latch and prayed it would open. "Help! Somebody! Please get me-" she tried to scream, but it was too late. Claude came behind her, covered her mouth and wrapped his other arm around her waist.

"What in God's name do you think you're doing damned girl?!" he scorned as he forced her back inside.

"No! Please!" Marie begged with all the energy she had left.

He carried her to the end of the hallway to a door leading to the cellar, dragged her down the stairs and threw her to the floor.

"Foolish, stupid girl! How dare you!" He grabbed his cane and struck her across her back as hard as he could. Her cries were vociferous, but it didn't serve her well.

"Scream as loud as you can! No one can hear you down here! You will learn how to obey me and behave yourself here," he shouted as he continued to strike her with the cane. Rosa grew even more worried. The girl was so young and frail. She knew the breadth her master's wrath could extend and quickly ran down the stairs to help her.

"Sir, you must stop! She's bleeding!"

"Leave! Get out Rosa! Shut the door!" Claude commanded, but he soon stopped and stared at the girl as she curled up on the floor.

"But, Sir!"

"I said NOW, Rosa!"

Rosa jumped back and left the room. She wanted to help, but didn't want to make him angrier for the sake of Marie. Claude dropped his cane and knelt beside her.

"I had to make you understand. I don't want to hurt you. We had a deal. Now you know how serious it is that you keep your end. I had hoped you'd obey and I could keep you upstairs with me, but now you will stay down here," he told her in a deep, low tone.

She nodded and shook as she kept her position on the floor. She couldn't force herself to say a single word as he left her down there. The room grew even darker the door slammed behind him. She wanted to scream out, but it wasn't until Marie heard the lock that she ran up the stairs and slapped the door with her palm.

"Please don't leave me down here! It's so dark! I'm sorry!" she pleaded.

Claude stood quietly on the other side and put his hand to the door. He could feel her energy flow through the wood, and he moved his hand to where he felt hers was. He could feel the pain and regret through the barrier that separated him. He felt guilty for hurting her, he wanted to let her out and make her feel comfortable but chose to walk away instead.

Marie couldn't bring herself to leave the door. She stared down the steps, unable to see yet fully aware of the darkness below. She'd always been terrified of cellars, and what had begun as a terrible dream turned into her most frightening of nightmares. Weakly, she tried to plead for someone to come back and open the door. Her cries were shaken and weary. When she finally realized no one was around, she went back down the stairs and felt around. The walls were cold, and the ground was like ice under her bare feet. There was nothing in the room but a small bed that she jumped into. It wasn't warm, but it would do. The tears streamed down her face as she prayed for guidance, but she wasn't quick to believe that anyone, even a god, could hear her down in that room. She didn't even know what to pray for. All she could do in that moment was stare to the dark ceiling above her. Her body felt warm, but she was shivering. She felt ashamed and ill at herself. She hid under its covers and desperately prayed for an angel of darkness to take her from the world and the pain it caused her.

The hours passed slowly, and Rosa couldn't manage to shut her eyes. As the morning sun began to peak, she got dressed and prepared breakfast. She was glad to be out of bed. Keeping busy would certainly keep her mind from thinking on the previous night. She had kept this house her entire life. While she maintained a relationship for so long with the late Master Augustus, she thought of Claude as a brother and close friend. She had admired that he spent so many years trying to not repeat the sins of his father, but today she felt that admiration crash down like a glass ornament. She worked hard on the meal; drawing out every step so as to take her time and collect the proper thoughts before she went to wake Claude for the day.

When he finally finished dressing, he came to the table and abruptly sat down. She was careful in her movements and words as she set his plate before him. She fixed her plate and sat in the chair across from him.

"If you don't mind my asking, what is your plan with the girl, Master?"

"As payment for a debt she has agreed to stay here. You will help care for her," he instructed as he ate his food quickly.

"I must be going. I expect you to stay out from down there for today, a lesson must be learned."

"I haven't heard a sound from her. We don't even know what condition the poor child is in. She could have very well bled in the night and lay cold in that cellar right now."

"She was hurt, but hardly in such a state when I left her. She will be fine. Now, do not test your bounds, Rosa. I told you we would check on her this evening, and I expect you to obey my order. Now get back to your duties, and do not question my authority again. Do you understand?" he scowled.

"I understand." Rosa felt guilty. She knew it was wrong but began to truly grasp the fact that nothing could be done except to help the girl adjust to her new home as the Master's slave.

He twisted the key to the door onto a small section of rope and tied it securely around his neck before leaving for his duties in the courtroom for the day.

# Chapter Six

27 February 1796


His horse trotted along the road to the courthouse. It wasn't a long distance, but Claude slowed the pace to draw out his time alone. He took the time to observe every neighbor and home as he retraced his route from the night before. He studied each face and demeanor as the people nodded him on his way. He had spent the last night unsure of what may have been witnessed or heard, and it troubled him. As he nudged his horse to speed up its gait, he realized the reactions were the same as every other day. Everyone was pleasant and greeted him as they always did, and he knew the people around him were oblivious to his new secret.

He tied his horse and immediately shoved through the doors of the back of the courthouse. He met up with Charles to begin their day, but there was no time to speak.

"The honorable Judge Fontaine," a bailiff announced.

Claude approached the bench. "Members of the jury, you have found these prisoners guilty according to the evidence shown in court. We appear in this courtroom today to assign rightful and just sentences. Am I to believe you have sentenced these persons who appear here today accordingly?"

The room grew silent as the first juror stood to read the list in his hands.

"We have your Honor. For the crimes deserving of a public chastise which can include, but is not limited to, a flogging in the public square, the mark of a criminal branded on their chest and their name listed in the public post of dangerous persons, goes as follows: Isadora Morariu for the crime of theft, and Marcolas Lazar for the crime of rioting in the streets. For the crimes deserving of time served in the prison for the rest of the criminal's natural life goes as follows: Ravena Hagi for the crime of attacking an officer of the law when caught with smuggled goods, Anthony Forwood for the crime of forging a bank teller's signature to gain a considerable amount of gold from the bank, and William Macek for the crime of harboring illegal gypsies in his home. And for the crimes deserving of a public hanging in the square goes as follows: Trevor Maddeaux, Anders Williamson and Ronald LeFleur, all for the crime of unitedly smuggling goods and illegal gypsies into the city and resisting arrest when caught causing injury to multiple officers of the law."

A second juror stood next to the first to continue, "Your Honor, we the jury have taken a considerable amount of time to discuss and think upon these sentences. These are our official decisions."

Claude was eager to finish early. The realization of everything that had happened the night before was creeping into his mind. He was finding it hard to focus, and didn't want to seem incapable because of his distractions.

"And so, it is decided and marked official. Bailiffs, take the prisoners to their destined sentences. How many hearings do we have in order for today?"

Charles checked his list, "it seems only three for today, Sir."

"Very well then, let's begin. Bailiff please bring in the defendants."

Barely paying attention Claude heard a voice.

"Case number 62643, the hearing of Felicia, no known last name, has been accused..."

Claude could barely pay any mind to the lawyers speaking. His mind was overwhelmed with the girl he was hiding. He wasn't just hiding a girl, he had stolen a child. Claude began to question his own sanity. He couldn't imagine why he would do what he had done. He wondered if he should just let her go. He thought of the innocence he had taken from her, he could never give that back. His guilt was building up like a fire in his stomach moving up his throat. He felt sick. He took a deep breath and briefly closed his eyes. Honeysuckle. That was it. That was the scent in her hair. It was sweet.

The image of her long dark hair flowing down her back infused in the smell of honeysuckle. She had to stay. He couldn't undo what had been done. Her innocence, her blood, was on his hands. She had agreed to stay with him, and that was final. He had to see her and feel her again. He refused to let her go. Her voice was soft and delicate, she had everything he wanted. He had waited years for this; God had finally sent his gift for waiting. He was aging; almost halfway through his thirties. He was running out of time, this was it; this is what he had always wanted, and he had to push the guilt away.

"Now you have heard the facts, and so we rest our case. Your Honor." The lawyer broke Claude's train of thought. His attention snapped back to the court hearing, although it seemed as though he had missed the entire thing. Nonetheless, the jury would decide in his favor so he had no worries of it.

"Yes. Thank you. Jurors, we will postpone the other hearings and recess for the evening. Please, take this time to discuss and deliberate all you've seen and heard today. Take your time and we will adjourn back here in the morning to continue. Oh, and one more order of business... The new laws regarding all the towns' people will be posted on the doors of Notre Dame before the next Mass." Claude turned to the bailiff and spoke. "All prisoners found guilty at any trials this week shall be moved tonight to be sentenced in the morning." He then turned back to the jury. "Thank you, jurors, your service is greatly appreciated. This court session is hereby adjourned."

Charles hurriedly caught up to him as the courtroom cleared. He checked his surroundings, but was eager to speak of what had happened.

"Sir, I made sure everything has been taken care of," he confided in Claude.

"Of what do you refer?"

"You know... the woman and the others from last night."

"I hardly think this is the place to discuss this, although, I appreciate that. May I ask you post the list of hangings for tomorrow for me? There are some errands I must attend to. Is it possible for you to meet at my home after dusk?"

"Of course," he nodded, and they each hurried on their own ways. Claude carried with him a list and discreetly obtained a few things he could guess he would be needing in his home now.

As predicted, it was nearly dark when he returned. Claude directed Charles to the items in his carriage and then went inside. He threw the key to Rosa and demanded she bring the girl upstairs and clean her up while Charles helped him move some things into the home. Rosa ran down the stairs and shone her candle light around the room. She silently prayed as she called out to the girl, who was curled in a corner of the room.

"I thought no one would ever come back down for me. I was so scared." Marie fell to Rosa

"It's alright. I'm here now, but we must hurry and get you fixed up again."

"I'm sorry, you had me clean, and now I have blood everywhere."

"Don't fret about it." She helped Marie up. "Let's get you cleaned up again, alright?" They went upstairs to the washtub, being sure to stay out of Claude and Charles's way. Rosa helped Marie into the tub.

"I was able to warm the water a bit, but with wounds like these, I don't want it to hurt you more than it will."
Marie flinched as Rosa poured the water on her.

"Ow, it burns..."

"You've got to be smarter than this child. He's a powerful man. Trying to escape will only bring pain to you." Rosa could feel herself choke on her words. She hated herself for speaking such ugliness to a girl who didn't deserve it.

"But I really don't think I can do this!" She started to cry. Rosa put her arm around Marie's head and pulled her close, trying to comfort her.

"I know it's hard and scary, especially at first... but I promise it gets easier and less painful after a while. Just relax and take deep breaths," she assured the girl.

"How do you know that?" Marie asked as she noticed Rosa wiping a tear from her eye.

"Never mind that child, let's get you dressed," she whispered. She led Marie to her room to find another dress. Claude came in behind her and grabbed her hand. He locked a metal cuff around her wrist. Marie felt a twist is her stomach.

Every new thing made it all more real to her. Her face began to burn behind her eyes. The tears were welling up. Her new life was in front of her, and it was terrifying.

"What is this?" she inquired meekly.

Claude had a serious tone as he explained it attached to a chain: one in his room and one in hers. She would be required to wear it whenever he was asleep or not home.

"Sometimes you will be in my room, but only under my own supervision. Now I have something to show you in your room." He grabbed her hand and pulled her back to the door of the cellar. Marie became very afraid and jerked back in a panic.

"Please don't make me go back in the dark," she begged.

"Hush now! You will come with me, or I promise things will only get worse for you."

"I'm very sorry." Marie almost gagged on her words as she spoke; trying her hardest to not cry.
Claude quickly led her back down the stairs. The room had changed. It was much lighter than Marie could have guessed in the darkness. Without windows, the room was a cold black without the aid of even a single candle. The new addition of light almost made the room a bearable sight.

"I put some things in here for you while Rosa cleaned you up. You now have a light, more blankets on the bed, a wardrobe with your own dresses and a table for you. Do you like it? You will be in here whenever I am gone."

Marie couldn't take her eyes off of the chain coming from the wall. The candles were intended to accentuate the light-colored furniture that had been added, but the reflection from the chain that extended the length of the room was all she could truly see in that moment. She anxiously forced a smile and complimented his efforts.

Claude held Marie's hands. He couldn't take his eyes off of her. He had thought of her all day. He wanted to express that somehow. He pardoned Charles and Rosa for the night to be alone with his new guest.

Marie grew more nervous as they left the room. She didn't know what to say or do, but her heart, and her hurting body, told her she needed to keep his mood pleasant.

"Sir, I'm very sorry," she began meekly, but Claude puts his finger to her lips.

"Let's start with a clean slate, shall we? You made a mistake that I know you will not make again." He laid Marie back on the bed and climbed on top of her, but his weight put pressure on the wounds. She tried her best to not cry out in pain, but it was a small battle lost. She quickly covered her mouth in hopes of preventing Claude from becoming upset.

"I'm sorry I didn't want to hurt you." He climbed down and pulled her up to the edge of the bed. He stood in between her legs as he lifted the gown over her thighs and grabbed her hips. He unbuttoned his pants and pulled her body onto himself, attempting to be gentle. She knew he was going to have her either way, so she tried not to make another sound. She put her face into his chest to cover her mouth. She felt very sore and hurt. She wanted to cry, but she couldn't stand him getting angry again. She closed her eyes and just prayed to make it through. He grabbed her back, touching her wounds. She allowed a tear to silently fall down her face while he continued. He rapidly pulled her into him and then finally let go. She fell off the edge of the bed onto the floor and tried not to let him see her crying. She was still unsure of what would anger him. He grabbed her arm and attached her cuff to the chain. Without saying another word, Claude left the room.

He could hear her cries as he left her alone to the darkness once again, but he couldn't let that stop him from what needed to be done. He quickly traveled back to the courthouse when the night was at it darkest and snuck inside. Claude knew he couldn't allow his personal life to divert his attention from his work. The king would be expecting results after recent events, and Claude held the secret to finding the answers he desperately needed. He knew nothing could ever be able to stand in the way of his mission as he shoved a bookshelf aside and made his way down the hidden stairwell that led below his office.

# Chapter Seven

03 March 1796

      In the courthouse, toward the back of Claude's chambers, and behind a rather large bookshelf, there hid a stairwell. The structure hidden underneath appeared to have been there for many years before the courthouse had even been constructed. There was no record of what it may have once been, but he found excellent use for it in the recent years. The layers of brick surrounding it kept it cool and barred any sound from escaping its enclosure. He and his men began to use this room for private interrogations that were unknown to anyone. It was the perfect place to extract any information needed, for practical rules of interrogation did not apply in this dreary cellar. The room was filled with many devices and equipment as means of torture.

      It provided the freedom to do anything that was necessary to extract the answer to any question, and Claude made sure to fully utilize it often. As he made his way down the steps that night, William, his latest arrest, was already there with Charles. He was tied in a chair and beaten. There were cuts and welts on his face and arms. His left eye a dark purple color, his right eye was bleeding and swollen shut. Claude believed William knew more about the growing gypsy rebellion. He had to get any information he could. He knew this was a family man. They could beat him all night, but that would only waste time.

"In exchange for your cooperation, William, I will consider reducing your sentence to prison time served and your wife will be released with chastisement as an associate of your crimes," he bargained.

"Why me?" William cried out.

"Because we've allowed your half-breed family to live in peace, and this is how we are repaid! It is shameful and a disgrace to your children who depend on you."

"Ok I'll tell you the little I know, just please let my wife go. The children need her."

"Tell me how a lowly vegetable farmer, who can't even afford the proper equipment, get the money to build the underground shed for hiding gypsies? There was enough food, water, and weapons to supply half the town!"

"It's all brought to me."

"By who?"

"A supplier. I don't know who he is or where it comes from. It just appears by my house in the mornings. That's all I know."

"How would someone know to anonymously bring these supplies to your home?"

"Word of mouth. I express my interest, and it eventually gets around to the right people, I suppose."

"And how do the gypsies get into the shelter, where did they come from? This all sounds utterly ridiculous; do you realize that?"

"I received a note to pick them up at the edge of the city and bring them to my home. I hide them in the vegetable crates during travel."

"Charles, have undercover patrols at every corner at nights until dawn, we will catch these suppliers." Claude turned back to William to continue, "why do you oppose the king? How could even think to rebel against his kindness towards you?"

"I don't! I was only told that these were the kin of gypsies in the city who had nowhere else to go. I was hoping to have a cold storage for my vegetables come the warmer season, so that is why it is underground. I would never oppose my king, I swear!"

"Kill him Charles."

"With pleasure."

"Wait, you said you'd reduce my sentence!" The man began to fight but was tied too tightly.

"I can't have you free to open your mouth and tell everyone what you told me."

He tried to scream as Charles cut his throat. Claude struggled to not feel guilty. He hated killing, but he knew this was no innocent man. He directly violated the king's laws. It was his job, his livelihood to protect the city from any and all wrong doers.

"I wish there was a better way to ensure these squalors stayed quiet without the mess of killing them," he complained.

"I've heard Joseph has a few interesting techniques. I've seen him work wonders when I was aiding investigations in the palace," Charles informed him.

"Then be sure we call upon him next time. This is merely the beginning. Something big is about to become of Paris; I can feel it. When you are done here, I want you to go to Anthony and have him help you collect as much gypsy clothing as you need to dress the night shifts. I want all soldiers disguised to catch these suppliers. We must move forward and end this madness as soon as possible."

Charles nodded and got to work immediately to dispose of the body and begin his mission. Claude, however, had different plans.

Claude could feel his inner power slowly returning to him after the events of that evening. He'd stayed dormant in the shadows of his career for so long, but life was changing. He could feel himself transforming with it. He made his way down the stairs of his own home that morning and saw her. This girl had reignited a force within him that assured him he was once again at his greatest in life.

She was sitting at her table in the middle of the room. It was a much more pleasant sight than he'd ever seen it before. What once was a cold and musky cellar, was now a tidy chamber. In the days the girl had been there, she'd brought a bright and clean look into a part of the house that had always been so dark. She sat elegantly at her table as she greeted him without looking up. She seemed entranced by her art, but upon closer view, Claude realized these were more than simple drawings.

"Hello dear," he nodded as he pulled out the extra chair and sat next to her. "I see you've really taken to the notebook I brought you."

"Just some poetry and prayers I can remember so I never forget them."

Claude was confused. He took the notebook from her. He only knew of gypsies to be illiterate and completely uneducated.

"You can write? I didn't know it was custom for your people."

"My people?" Marie was offended by his constant assumptions about who she was. She took a deep breath and looked up at him boldly. "I'm only half gypsy by blood, but my father was an Englishmen. My sisters and I attended the school for girls in London before we moved to Paris."

"I didn't realize... that's why you speak with such elegance."

"No, I can understand why you'd think... I never meant disrespect to you, it's an honest mistake. My mother is Romani, so I understand." She began to regret her decision to correct him. She closed her eyes, preparing for him to become angry and hurt her.

"I see... well I have a guest that comes here one night every week, and every now and then, he stays overnight," he explained.

Marie opened her eyes. She was blessed this time, but she knew she had to be cautious when she spoke in the future.

"So, I will not be staying in your bed this night?"

"No, you must stay hidden. I'm simply telling you as a warning for you to keep quiet. The consequences will be severe should anyone learn you are down here."

"Yes, of course." She felt the sting of her clothes on her back and closed her mouth.

"Perhaps we could spend a moment together before I leave for patrols. It's been a few days since I've seen you."

"Certainly." She closed her notebook and walked towards her bed. He laid her down and climbed on top her. She felt the pain but tried not to let it show. Claude was distracted, he hardly noticed her this time. His movements were off, he seemed to struggle to get into any sort of rhythm like usual so he began to show his frustration. He moved fast and fortunately for her, it didn't last much longer. He immediately stood to get himself clean and dressed in her room.

"Were you comfortable, child?"

Marie looked down shyly. "It gets easier each time, sir."

"Rosa will come to check on you. I must be going," he told her as he walked towards the stairs.

"Marie..."

Claude was instantly halted but didn't turn back to her. "What did you say?"

"My name is Marie. I've been here over a week, and you never said it... I wasn't sure if you knew."

"That's a lovely name... Marie." He smiled as he walked out.

He hesitated to take another step; something felt very wrong in his actions, but he had to keep going. He rode slowly and quietly to the church to continue in his thoughts as he made his way up to the loft of the great towers. Julien jumped from his desk to meet Claude.

"I'm so glad to see you," he called out eagerly.

"Hello, Julien. Have you finished your lessons for the day?"

"Yes, Master. Here is my writing." Julien hurried to gather some papers from desk.

Claude grabbed the jumbles of paper and skimmed over them.

"It would appear as though everything is here, but I will look over it all later. I'm sort of in a hurry tonight, I must get home."

"Yes Master, I watched the sentences today. There were many so I understand you need rest."

"Yes, the gypsy illegals are growing in number. My men catch as many as we can, but it gets a bit overwhelming at times," he sighed.

"Would the king not understand if you took just a day's break? You seem weary and troubled."

"I will be fine, Julien. The king has his phobias of the kind and refuses to let anyone rest until we find this leader who is organizing the gypsies to rebel against him, especially myself."

"I am sorry to hear this, it must be very hard on you. I know it's not much, but I will make sure your supper is very satisfying and puts you at a bit of ease for the evening. Rosa promised to let me help her cook if I had done all my lessons."

"It's really not a good time." Claude didn't feel like having a house guest as he had planned, but remembered his promise. He hoped Julien wouldn't push the subject.

"I understand, but I swear I won't be a bother. Please?"

Claude was reluctant, but he had very little energy to argue.

"I suppose. Pack your things. We leave now," he instructed as he snuck Julien into his carriage. Claude was grateful the ride had been quick; he wasn't in any mood for small talk.

When they arrived at his home just after dark, Julien immediately jumped from the wagon and ran through the door. He was thrilled to see Rosa again and ran into her arms. She hugged him tightly.

"I'm glad to see you dear! I take it your lessons went well this week?"

"Indeed! I finished writing my scripture quotes, and I've memorized my Hail Mary's," he cheered. He always loved sharing his accomplishments with her.

"I'll have to hear it soon." She grabbed his hand and led him to the table.

"Master has begun to teach me subtraction."

"That's amazing! Well supper is ready, and we should eat it before it gets cold."

"Say the prayer Julien."

"Yes, Master." Julien folded his hands. "Dear heavenly Father, Thank you for all of our blessings. Thank you for this food. We pray You bless and enrich our lives deeper in you. In your name, Amen"

As they ate, Charles barged into the house and shouted, "Claude! The people are rioting at Notre Dame. They're burning the new laws posted. It's chaos!"

Claude jumped from his seat.

"Damnit! I should have known these people would overreact. I'll get my carriage. Do you have the prison wagon with you?"

"Yes. I brought the large one with extra rope and horses. The other soldiers are already there with theirs." Charles informed him.

Claude looked to Rosa. "Will you be alright with," he nodded his head towards Marie's room while eyeing Julien, "everything here?"

"Of course, sir, I will take care of anything that should come about," she assured him.

The two men left in a hurry, which pleased Julien. He loved Claude like a father, but always had more fun when he could just relax with Rosa. He quickly ate his supper and then sprawled across the floor near the fireplace. As he stretched about, he noticed the door to the cellar had a new lock on it. He'd been taught that it was impolite to be intrusive about matters that did not pertain to him, but nonetheless, his curiosity won.

"Why did Master put that lock on there?"

Rosa briefly stopped from her chores to look back at the door; she had prepared for his inquisition.

"He is storing some very valuable artifacts and heirlooms he recently acquired, and he wants to keep them safe," she explained.

"That's a shame. I enjoy playing in there sometimes."

"You're much too old to be playing down there like a boy. It's time you learned useful tasks. I think we should bake a nice pie tonight," she proposed. Julien could tell she was attempting to distract him, but he didn't think it an important subject to bother with as he followed her into the kitchen.

"Pies are my absolute favorite! What kind should we make, Rosa?"

She looked around the countertop and rummaged through the pantries before finally returning to the table with handfuls of fresh fruit.

"Well... I have some apples, but I also have a few peaches," she showed him.

"Peaches are my favorite! My mouth is watering just thinking about it." Julien became very excited.

"Very well then. Let's get started, shall we?"

Together they cleared space on the table and counter and immediately got to work. The pie came out almost perfect, but it left a giant mess. After they finished eating their fill, Julien helped her clean up.

"I've got it dear. You should get some sleep." Rosa helped him get ready for bed and even tucked him in before returning to work in the kitchen. He fell asleep within minutes but woke to a rather large creak a few hours later. He saw Rosa at the doorway to the cellar and pretended to be asleep as she looked to see if she had disturbed him. When it didn't seem as though she had, she placed the lock back on the door, and quietly snuck into the kitchen. He found it suspicious but couldn't keep himself awake long enough to truly think about it.

It was nearly dawn when Claude finally arrived at home. He woke Rosa, and she began making breakfast as he sat at the table to discuss the night with her.

"Were there many arrests made?" she asked.

Julien woke up to the sounds of Rosa's cooking but didn't move. He was curious about what Claude and Rosa would speak of in private.

"Yes, but I won't deal with all of them this week, especially not today," Claude told her.

"Of course not. What kind of day is scheduled for today?"

"Just assigning sentences. I will postpone any evidence hearings until tomorrow. I don't have the energy to sit in the courtroom all day."

"That's understandable," she told him as she served his meal.

The conversation was plain and dull as always, and Julien decided he would be on his way to join them when he heard the downstairs room come up. He quickly stopped himself before he could be seen.

"He didn't get too curious, did he?" Julien heard Claude ask Rosa. He pressed in closer, he'd hoped they would mention what the lock was hiding. He listened carefully, but Rosa's explanation to Claude was the same as she'd given him.

"And you believe he won't go snooping if I have to leave again?"

"No, I believe he is smart enough to know the consequences of that," she assured.

Julien was disappointed. He knew there must be something important down there. He didn't like secrets or surprises and smiled as he realized the door had been left unlocked. Rosa must have gone down there while he was asleep. He tip-toed over to it and quietly opened the door to sneak inside.

# Chapter Eight

09 April 1796

It was clear there was a stir amongst the people, but no explanation as to why. The king added pressure on Claude, who began putting more tension on his own men. They worked diligently both night and day to keep order, but Claude still felt no closer to finding the people responsible for the troubles they faced. It began to worry him as they passed more restrictive laws that affected even the innocent civilians of the city, but he knew in his heart that his men were doing everything they could.

He arrived home early one afternoon. It had been an exhausting week, and he wanted to be away from his work and the stresses of everything that had been going on. He sat in his favored seat and stared into the fire as Rosa came to his side.

"Do you wish me to get the girl for you, Master?" She had grown accustomed to asking. It had become routine to both everyone in the home.

"Not now. I..." Claude seemed anxious.

"Sir?"

"Nothing. It's nothing, you can get her ready." He wasn't sure of what to say. He doubted Rosa could relate, but she was very intuitive. She sat next to him as she instated he talk to her.

"It's just... she resists me. I don't know what I am doing wrong. She has been here for weeks now. I look at her, but when I touch her... it's like she shuts me out. It infuriates me, and I lash out. I feel like we should be past this by now. She makes me angry, but then I always feel guilt and regret after. I don't mean to hurt her."

"You're beginning to see her as more, maybe feel something for her." Rosa made the statement but questioned Claude's feelings for the girl.

"I'm not sure what I feel. Well, besides feeling overwhelmed. The things I have gotten myself into, I'm struggling between what's right and my morals."

"It can be hard to understand. But if she is to stay here with you, you must try to learn it. You have to try if you want it to work." Rosa advised.

"But I don't know how."

"Most girls want a man to show her affection, be gentle. Marie is young and impressionable, she could learn to trust you if you gave her a piece of yourself to feel secure. She resists you and you lash out for the same reason; you have not connected with each other."

"And how am I supposed to connect with a girl who hates me?"

"If it's not over-stepping my bounds, sir, you can't hope for a relationship with her if you treat her as a slave for your own pleasure. She will never trust you."

"Thank you, Rosa. Can you please leave me for the night?"

"Yes, Goodnight."

He stared into the fire. He wanted Marie to be his and to not resent him forever for it. If she only knew what she possessed in her that he desired so much. He felt they were meant to be together and cared about her happiness in his home. He sat for over an hour before he slowly made his way to her room to unlock the cuff around her wrist. Marie looked up to him, confused. He had considered Rosa's words heavily and insisted she come up without it.

He reached out for her hand, and she let him lead her up the stairs to his room. He shut his door behind him and turned her to face him. He put his hand behind her head and kissed her as gently as he could.

Marie pulled back and put her hand to her lips. They felt odd.

"What is it?" Claude inquired.

"You've never done that before."

"I kissed you when we first met, and I'm sure I've kissed you other times."

"Not like that," she insisted.

"I understand this is strange to you. What's strange to me is how when I am not here, I think about you. Some days I simply want to see you, not just touch you."

"That is a very strange and curious thing," she whispered. She stared into his eyes and reached her hands around his neck to kiss him.

He lifted her up and her legs wrapped around him. The past had always been about him and his needs, but it felt as though the world shifted to be about her. She felt a flutter in her stomach. This was different than all the other times he'd been with her. He looked at her, touched her body, and grabbed her thighs tightly. She looked unsure of how she felt about it, but she smiled. She wasn't as resistant as she had been, and he could feel her body move with his for the first time. He kept kissing her as both of their emotions seemed to finally connect.

When his tongue moved in her mouth, she caressed it with hers. She remembered a girl from the school had shown her what to do. The girls in her class always snuck around with boys to kiss, but Marie wanted to save such things for the right and special time. She could feel Claude hard on her thigh, but instead of forcing himself inside, it was as though her body had welcomed him in, like it wanted him there.

As he moved inside her, she felt shutters in her stomach, kind of like a small tickle that she wanted to feel over and over again. Her lips tingled every time he kissed her neck. When he moved back, she pulled him in closer. Her legs wrapped around him, making him thrust in shorter yet faster movements. The faster he moved, the more amazing she felt. She let out a gasp. It was small and her voice was soft yet erotic. He put his hand on her chest, and untied her corset to expose the skin. He had never seen this much of her before and regretted never taking the time to truly appreciate her beauty. Her skin was soft. He moved his hand over her breasts to her stomach. She had a slender frame but the muscles in her stomach were strong and accentuated her beautiful curves. He kissed her neck and chest, squeezing her arms until he was finished.

Instead of getting up and making her leave like every other night, he moved to the far side of the bed and got under the covers.

"Come lay beside me, Marie," he commanded. His voice was gentle, but imperious.

"Are you sure? You need sleep I'm sure."

"Come by me." He was firm in his request.

She nodded and climbed onto the bed. Claude pulled her closer to him and kissed her. He wanted her to feel comfortable around him.

"Are you feeling alright?"

Marie was unsure of how to address him.

"Yes...sir...uhm," she stumbled.

Claude decided to truly take what Rosa had advised him to heart. He began to feel something for the girl, and he wanted to show her.

"James," he said softly.

"What? Who's..."

"Just say it," he commanded.

"James?"

"Yes. Now once more. Slowly..."

Marie took a deep breath. She could sense that he wanted something from her. She shifted on the bed to face him. She looked into his eyes and touched his face.

"James," she smiled at him.

"I've heard that name called many different ways, but the way it flows from your lips..." He stopped to ponder what he heard. "You will call me James. That is my name."

Marie was confused. She only knew him by Judge Claude Fontaine. Calling him Master was an adjustment enough, but to call him by a name unknown to almost everyone he knew? She felt strange. Maybe there was more to the judge than she had originally expected.

"My given name is James Claude Fontaine. The people know me as Claude, because that was my Father. Claude Augustus. It is a family name and my father believed it was a name people would fear when I assumed his role. Only a very few people know."

"James is a very nice name, sir."

"My mother thought so as well."

Marie was unsure of what to say next. The two of them had rarely conversed and never in the bed. This was usually the time when he would be gone on his way when he was finished with her. She looked around his room and began to hum a soft tune. The sound played in her mind repeatedly, and it always helped relax her.

"That's a beautiful melody. I could swear I've heard it before."

"It was first introduced at the Yuletide Concerto in London. I heard it many times when we lived there."

"I remember now. A young cellist played that evening."

"Victoria Vincent."

"She was quite the prodigy. Did you ever see her play?"

"Yes. So, tell me, have you always wanted be a judge?"

"My father always expected it of me. And... I did always believe the rules were extremely important to maintain order. God set commandments for his people to follow. I want to keep order and will achieve it by any means necessary."

Marie knew the things he had done to so many people in the name of justice, although she was losing sight of what was truly right or wrong. Life had become unclear and morals were clouded. It was all too confusing to even talk about anymore that night. She leaned over to crawl from his bed to leave him for the night, but he stopped her. He held her hands in his and looked down to them. He fidgeted with her small fingers as he attempted to speak.

"I was thinking ... Would you like to stay in here for a bit longer? With me? Just for the night."

"Really?"

"You've been here over six weeks," he recounted.

"You know how long I've been here?"

"I told you; when we are not together, I think about you often. I remember the day I brought you here quite clearly. You may roam the house while I am here and awake, so long as you stay away from the window and door in the kitchen," he told her. He put his arm around Marie and pulled her close. He kissed her head and continued, "I regret hurting you. I hope one day you can forgive me."

She pulled her knees up almost to her chest and rested her head on them. He had done cruel things to her many days over the last few weeks. She remained silent but gave him a small smile. She may not have it in heart yet to forgive, but she didn't want to offend him by letting him know that.

That morning Charles arrived at his home for breakfast. As they ate, he informed Claude that the king was anxious to meet with him immediately. The men quickly finished their meal and left for the palace.

"I called you here to inquire as to the progress of your search," the king muttered as he paced about.

"We're doing our best, but these things do take time."

"That's not good enough! I know they're organizing a rebellion. This gypsy leader has been supplying them with food and weapons. They're growing, bringing in more people. We need to find where they're hiding their army ants and weapons! I want to know who their leader is. We must cut them down where they congregate and destroy them all!"

"We just caught one of the rebels passing supplies a few days ago. I will interrogate him personally to the fullest measure. He may can lead us to the leader. If at best, put us on the right track."

"Do what you will with him Claude, I trust you to get what we need."

"Yes of course, your Majesty," he nodded as he prepared himself to toughen his crusade and push his men harder than ever to achieve their goal by any means necessary.

# Chapter Nine

06 May 1796

The weeks were the worst they'd been in years as Claude followed his orders from the king. He began to feel like two different people: James at home and Claude at work. When he was on the field fulfilling the kings wishes, Claude easily repressed his personal life. He felt it was absolutely necessary to uphold his reputation, but that often left his career to bleed into his home life. He began losing sleep which was highlighted by his attitude towards others. He desperately wanted to lie down when he returned home early one morning after a long night of patrols.

The previous night's shift was unplanned, and he still had to be in court that day. He let Marie have some time out of her room before he left to allow her to help Rosa cook breakfast.

"Can you get me the large pot from the cupboard?" James heard Rosa ask her.

"Yes." Marie said as she passed by the front door. She could feel the sun's warmth. It had been over two months since she had truly seen or felt the sunlight. She began to daydream as she leaned into the doorway, but James walked into the kitchen at the same moment.

"Rosa, where's my..." but before he could continue, he noticed her at the door. His thoughts jumped to what may be just outside and who may see. He lunged toward the girl and gave her a hard strike on her arm with his cane.

"Oww!" Marie turned quickly. "I just wanted to feel the sun for a moment," she cried.

"I won't risk you being seen," he scorned as he peered through the door to see if anyone was around.

"That's not fair! Just because you're ashamed of-" she began to argue, but James slapped her as hard as he could before she could say anything else.

"Be mindful of how you speak, child. You will not disrespect me again, or I'll lock you back in your room and never let you up here again to even remember sunlight. Do you understand me?"

Marie held her face and nodded, but James grabbed her to look at him.

"Your foolish brain is not made of rocks; I can't hear it rattle... Speak when you are asked! Do you understand me?"

"Yes, sir," she cried while wiping the tears from her eyes, "I'm sorry."

James pushed her down hard. When she fell to the ground, she stayed there to avoid him hitting her again and held her breath to contain her cries.

"I will be gone all day, Rosa. After my last meeting with the king, things are under more pressure than ever. I have some business to deal with. Lock her downstairs. I can't deal with that right now."

"Yes, Master. I will take care of it." she responded as she helped Marie up and led her downstairs.

Claude hurried to the courtroom. He was running late, and everyone was already waiting to begin. He quickly composed himself at his bench, trying desperately to fight past the fatigue. His chest felt tight, and his eyes were pained from the strain of forcing them to stay open. There was a spot on his head that ached down to his neck, but he had to force himself to focus.

"The honorable Judge Fontaine," the bailiff announced.

"Thank you." Claude took his seat.

The prosecutor approached and began to speak. As he presented his evidence for the court, Claude darted his eyes around the room. There were so many familiar faces. Had no one learned? Was anyone even taking him seriously, or was he a joke to them? The king demanded results, and he was beginning to feel like he was failing. His father would have never let things get this out of control. He needed to get a hold of his city for his father.

"Stop," he interrupted.

"Your Honor?" Anthony, who was standing to the right of Claude, looked up.

"What is this person in here for? Haven't we seen most of these on more than one occasion?"

"Yes, your honor. These are the rioters we broke up recently. There are a few here that have been previously convicted of small crimes and rioting."
Claude was becoming furious. He wondered if any of them even cared.

"Let me ask you people; do you feel like you are just in your cause? Do you feel right in opposing and rebelling against the king?"

There was an uncomfortable silence amongst the prisoners.

"Very well then. I am done hearing trials for rioters and repeat offenders. From this moment on, if anyone is caught disobeying the laws, the punishment will be without delay. These trials are a waste to everyone involved. These criminals have no remorse for their actions; they behave worse than untamed dogs. All who are arrested, beginning today, will be counted as guilty and put in the sentencing hold right away. A list will be put together accordingly, and no mercy will be shown to anyone."

"You can't do that," one woman stood and shouted!

"Excuse me? I am the law under the king! Dare you to tell me what I can do?"

"We have right to a fair trial," another man screeched.

"I am done hearing this now! Under the king, criminals no longer have rights."

"The king is a coward and a disgrace to the throne," a man shouted as he encouraged the other prisoners into a disturbance.

"You will not disrespect the King of France! Officers, arrest this man for contempt of court."
The prisoners stood to fight back. Their voices raised in anger to the judge and his men. Some began to fight; others just shouted and began to get more excited. Chaos grew in the courtroom and the guards were losing control. The guards knew they were outnumbered but continued to settle the prisoners. A panic grew

over the courtroom, and Anthony looked to Claude who sat frozen. His eyes focused on each convict, and he knew he needed to act immediately.

Anthony raised his gun and shot into the ceiling, and the prisoners fell to the ground. Shocked and afraid; they stayed quiet. Guns were rarely used, so it surprised everyone. Even Claude was shocked by his actions, and he questioned his deputy's sanity in resorting to such measures.

"Anthony have you gone mad?" Claude questioned. The deputy simply looked at him and smiled. He then turned to address the court.

"You will all get in line and obey! I will not hesitate to shoot you for resisting arrest. Under command of the king or not, I will get order in this courtroom right now! You will show respect to our king and our judge. Is that understood?" he shouted to the prisoners. Anthony continued to scream at them until everyone jumped to their seats in silence.

"Thank you, Anthony. Now, we may adjourn for the day. All here today can be brought to the sentencing hold. You are dismissed."

Claude left the court and announced the new law to the public. Soldiers came in multitudes to surround the people and ward off any resisters. Claude wanted to warn the city of how serious matters were becoming, but as he stood, the first protester emerged.

"Pigs!" a man shouted from the crowd.

"Who dares insult..." Claude became even more angry. "Show yourself!"

The man stood up on the stage behind the crowd. He was young, maybe twenty-five or so, but he was no mere boy. This man was confident, too confident, and it concerned Claude.

"These are my people! Our kind has done nothing to deserve such treatment! This judge you have elected is a corrupt man along with the king! His crusade is led by bigots such as Fontaine. I will do anything to tear down your empire of greed and debauchery! The Directorate will crumble!" the bold man professed to the people.

"Those are such big words, are you sure you understand them? What is your name, or are you too coward to stand out honestly against the king?" Claude challenged him.

"My name is Nikolais! Nikolais Quinn, and I am not afraid of you or these swine you claim to be soldiers! You're a criminal and a hypocrite!"

Claude felt a pain in his chest. The man's audacious claim was worrisome. Could it be possible someone knew of his transgressions? His paranoia grew to rage, and he ordered his guards to arrest the man. He wanted to set an example, and Nikolais would be the first to fall.

As Claude attempted to defend his name, Nikolais reached in his bag and threw rotting food at the judge. The guards charged at Nikolais who ran around the square as if he was playing a childish game. After a few moments of leading them around, he ran back up to the stage and finally stopped.

"Alright! Alright! No more games. Come and arrest me officers!" Nikolais reached out his hands, but as the guards approached, he let out a laugh. He threw down a small vial, and a blue smoke surrounded him. The guards charged in chaos and tried to catch him, but he had already disappeared.

"Find him! Put out an alert of this man. He is now wanted! I expect a sketch of his face on every post. I offer a bounty for any that brings him to me dead or alive!" Claude shouted as he shoved his way through the crowd and went back into the building. His pace was quick and heavy as he rushed down the stairs to the interrogation room where Charles had been beating a prisoner. Joseph was sitting quietly in a chair toward the back of the room observing.

"Has he said anything yet?" Claude asked as he put his things down.

"No, sir. Not yet anyway." Charles smirked.

"Then is he secured in that chair?"

"Of course. I've tied him and given him a well-rounded warm up. He's secure."

Claude crouched down and got close to the man's face. "What's his name?"

"Bryan," Charles answered.

"I tell you what Bryan, I may be inclined to not kill you if you tell me about your leader and where Nikolais Quinn hides."

"Even if I did know, I'd hang before telling you."

"Claude, if I may?" Joseph asked as he put his notebook away.

"We've been at this for hours... Do you really think you're any more likely to get him to speak than I?" Charles whined.

"I always get them to speak," Joseph sneered.

"Very well," Claude smiled, "do you know of my good friend, Joseph?"

Joseph grabbed his bag of surgical equipment and began to set everything up on a table. "Yes, we met earlier. I was simply an observer then." He put his hand on the head rest of the chair and put his face close to Bryan's. "Hello."

"He's a very well-practiced doctor. He can remove your spleen while you scream and squirm and you'll not only live through it, but you'll endure every agonizing moment of it," Claude informed.

Bryan nervously squirmed, "you're bluffing!"

"Claude exaggerates a bit. I can't assure you of survival, but I will try," he smirked. He grabbed a small knife and stabbed him in the thigh. The sound of the dagger penetrating the man's femur made Claude flinch. He knew it was necessary, but still wasn't fond of the practice when it escalated beyond his own comfort.

"But if that's what you think, if you think I'm... bluffing..." Joseph continued.

"I don't know anything!" Bryan cringed and then spit on Joseph.

"No, no of course you don't..." Joseph laid out a set of surgical knives. He grabbed a small knife and twirled it in front of him. he admired the instrument as if it were his oldest and dearest friend before he put it to good use.

"Did you know that sometimes the smallest pain can be the most unbearable?"

He walked behind Bryan in his chair and grabbed the man's hand. He smiled a bit as he shoved the knife under his fingernail. He commanded the man to tell him everything as he continued torturing the man.

Claude curled his fingers as the man continued to scream. Just imagining the pain the man had to endure made his own body ache, but he quickly shook off the sensation once more.

"God can't help you here!" Charles laughed.

"Tell the judge what he asks of you!" Joseph shouted as he tried to bargain with the man's pain.

"I know nothing! I was simply hired for delivery, no one tells us anything. We only distribute the goods already in the city. Someone drops the weapons at an undisclosed location and then picks a random kid to show us where it is. We never see them. They drop it off at night. We pick it up in the mornings and deliver it."

"Where? Damnit tell me," he demanded. He had to let go of any doubts. His men were the best at their craft. They were experts, and it showed as they progressed with their interrogation. It was beginning to work, Claude felt them getting a step closer.

Joseph laid the chair back and pulled up Bryan's shirt.

"Claude, I forgot my text but if I remember correctly... the spleen is around here," he pointed to a spot above Bryan's abdomen. "Hmm..." he thought for a moment, "however, the lung is right about here," he mumbled as he pointed to a spot within a centimeter or two away.

"Wouldn't it be quite a delight for us if you were wrong? The suffering he would endure!" Charles squealed with excitement at the possibilities.

"No matter... so long as I'm careful, I shouldn't puncture the lung," Joseph leaned in close, "because choking on your own blood does seem a rather unpleasant way to go." He pressed the scalpel into him and made a cut. The man's breathing intensified as he became more panicked.

"Please! Stop!" Bryan begged. He was losing his strength to fight anymore and couldn't stand another agonizing moment. Charles laughed, "It will only get worse!"

"I'll tell you!! I'll tell you! Please!"

"Go on... I'm losing patience," Claude pressed.

"To the people with marked homes."

"How are they marked?"

"Please...No!"

Joseph stabbed the scalpel into the man's stomach. He jumped in his straps, but couldn't escape the inhumanity. Joseph was careful not to puncture any major arteries or organs and continued.

"Please! I'll tell you," the man cried.

"Get on with it then!" Joseph shouted.

"A mint leaf talisman hung by a purple ribbon!"

"Very good. Now tell me who your leader is! Is it Nikolais? He has made his intention of destroying Paris known!"

"I don't know, please stop! God save me!"

"The judge asked you who the organizer is. Who tells everyone what to do? Tell us now!"

"I really don't know! Nikolais is nothing but a kid with no money, I don't see him organizing anything, and he's not even that smart!"

"If you don't know then I have no more use for you. Charles, instead of bringing him to back to the hold for those awaiting sentencing, move him with those to be hanged in the next rotation."

"Gladly."

"No wait! Yes, it's him!"

"You just said you didn't think it could possibly be him. Your change of heart wouldn't be a lie to save your own skin, would it?"

"No, your Honor. I swear it! Honest to God," the man pleaded.

"Thank you, I knew you would see things my way." Claude smiled and gestured for Charles to take him. "Charles, as we discussed."

"Wait, but I gave you what you wanted," the man pleaded. He squirmed and tried to fight away, but it was of no use.

"You did, and I am forever grateful, but we never made a deal."

"Please have mercy! I helped you!"

"All you did was give up one of your own, you squeamish little rat...nothing else you spoke of even makes any sense. Take him," Claude instructed.

"Just one moment, Charles hold him." Joseph told them as he laid the man back in the chair. He pulled the man's tongue out and ever so quickly sliced it off.

"Oh dear. You're having all the fun," Charles smirked as he anxiously watched.

Claude was stunned as he watched the man squirm and scream in the chair. This was true torture. The sight of all the blood was not only torture on the man, but it made Claude sick to his stomach. Without another thought, he ran to the door. When there was nothing left to come up, he dry-heaved until he could finally settle his stomach. Upon returning to the others, he watched as Joseph stitched the man up and explained to them that there was time before his hanging. He was insuring the rat wouldn't be able to warn other traitors with marked homes.

He was impressed. He realized this was what his job was: his mission. He had to get results at any cost. He needed to gain the stomach to execute whatever move necessary for the sake of their cause.

"Good thinking, Joseph. Charles, send out guards to find these marked homes. Burn them and arrest the owners. They are now traitors of the king! We will get to the bottom of this."

James returned home late that night. The situation he was in finally became real: he had gotten himself involved in things that were truly disturbing. Seeing Joseph cut out that man's tongue as torture almost seemed extreme to him. He had ordered Charles to burn down people's homes. Innocent children could be involved, and they would suffer at his command. Would God really want things this way?

The world was turning into a giant grey area. His mission was no longer clear. He was losing sight of right and wrong but remembered his father and the hurt of what had happened. It angered him even more: he had to snap out of this way of thinking. He was clear about what should be done when his father died, and he was certain of it now. The passion he'd felt was reignited as he decided to push his anxieties aside. There was no room for doubt. He straightened his posture and ran down to Marie's room. He unlocked her cuff and rushed her upstairs. He hardly remembered walking down the steps or how he had even gotten home, but he was sure something had brought him to the girl for a reason.

"I've had a very long day again, and I'm very tired," he vented to her.

"I understand."

"Today I was especially harsh with you. I do regret it. I told you I would be better, but I haven't. The king is pressing hard on me for results that I'm struggling to deliver." He touched her face; rubbing a bruise with his thumb, and then pulled her close.

"You are so beautiful," he remarked.

"Thank you, sir...I-uh... James."  He smiled at her attempt to be endearing and gave her a small bag from the floor.

"I got you this. Rosa can show you how to do it," he explained as she pulled out a bundle of yarn and needles from the bag.

Her smile was sweet, and she nodded in gratitude. James felt pleased in his gift but took it and placed it aside he directed her to the bed. He pulled himself on top of her, but something felt different. He could only focus on the events of the day. The blood, it was everywhere. His hand was stained with a drop of it he had missed. The sight of it reminded him of what he'd done, and a chill overcame him. He looked down to the girl lying underneath him.

He saw in her eyes that she knew something was wrong with him. He could sense her judgements as she covered her mouth, seeming to hold back her own food from coming up. His anxiety grew as she took a rather deep breath and then looked up to him. She seemed to be holding something back, but she reached her small hand up to him to touch his face. Their eyes met and he didn't just look at her, he saw her. He saw his sin in her eyes and became flustered.

"I'm sorry, I can't do this," his voice cracked in his speech. He threw himself from the bed and paced around to the wardrobe. He found the warmest robe to wrap himself in before returning to his preferred spot on the mattress. He wasn't worried about satisfying his urge, he just wanted a moment's peace from the noise in his mind.

"I apologize if I did something to offend you, sir. Are you alright? You seem troubled." Her voice was compassionate, but James didn't respond.

"I will go get the cuff and leave you to your thoughts for a moment. I'll be back," she whispered.

Marie ran down to her room, but the cuff was locked to the chain. She ran back up to get the key from James but noticed he had already fallen asleep. She wasn't sure what her next move should be. She contemplated which would make him angrier: waking him, or allowing him to sleep yet remain unsupervised. Her best option would be to climb next to him and wait until he woke up, but she began to feel very uneasy. The sick feeling slowly crept back up and forced her out of the room. She sat in the chair near the fireplace to catch her breath. Rosa grew worried as she watched Marie struggle and knelt beside her.

"Are you feeling alright, child? Your face is as white as a ghost. What's wrong?"

"I don't know. I've felt very strange these last few days. It didn't bother me too much until James was on top of me just now. I felt quite unwell. I tried to cover my mouth and breathe, but I-" she paused. The feeling had returned worse than before.

Her body felt hot and cold at the same time and ached as she tried desperately to hold her last meal down inside of her. She had never been poisoned, but she imagined the feeling to be similar. From the tips of her fingers, through her arms and chest, and up her stomach grew an intensely sick feeling. The room felt as if it were spinning around her, and she leaned over the arm of the chair. A painful chill overcame her, and she suddenly became very ill.

# Chapter Ten

07 May 1796

Without hesitation, Rosa retrieved a rag and water to wipe her face. She brushed the girl's hair back with her fingers and tried to comfort her. Marie was embarrassed and wanted to help with the mess, but Rosa insisted she rest. She finished cleaning the area and brought her some bread and a glass of water. The cool air perfectly matched the warmth from the fire that night, and Marie leaned into Rosa as she ate slowly.

"James usually wants me locked up when he sleeps, but I can't get the cuff right now without the key. He's asleep, and I'm afraid to wake him. I can't stand if he gets angry right now. I feel so weak."

Rosa felt this was a genuine opportunity for Marie. She devised a plan that she felt could potentially make the girl's life easier.

"This could be your chance to gain his trust. Do something where he can see that you aren't going to escape. Let's try to be done with the cuff, shall we?"

"He brought me a gift today. He said you could show me what to do with it," Marie smiled as she pointed to the bag on his bedroom floor.

Rosa retrieved it and laid everything on the table near the fireplace. An excited grin spread across her face as she ran to get identical objects from her own room. Rosa spent hours showing Marie what to do. She struggled quite a bit, but they laughed and enjoyed the lesson together. Marie had never enjoyed being terrible at something as much as she did at that moment. She was having fun with Rosa, like they were good friends.

"What are you doing?" James inquired. He was freshly dressed and stood tall in the doorway. His clean clothes reminded Marie that it was nearly morning. At first, she was too afraid to move but then eagerly jumped up to show him her attempt at a sock.

"I've tried my best at your gift," she explained.

"I can see. Very well," he smirked.

"Breakfast is ready, Master." Rosa had been intermittently cooking while spending the dark hours with Marie, and it was finally done. The two sat together at the table, but Marie could see the subtle hints of light from the sun peek over the horizon and headed towards her room.

"It's still dark out, Marie. Come sit," James instructed. He stood to pull out a chair for her, and she nervously sat down.

She had always eaten meals with Rosa and could talk about anything with her. They could laugh and have a nice time. James often ate meals at a nearby tavern with Charles when they went out on patrol, so she rarely had a meal with him. The few they did have together were quiet, and not much was ever said. She didn't have much of an appetite, the sick feeling was returning, but didn't want to seem disrespectful. She fixed a small amount on her plate and tried to spread it around to look like she had eaten. She waited patiently until he finally finished and stood.

"I must be going. Come," he instructed.
He grabbed Marie's hand and led her downstairs. He found the cuff and locked it back around her wrist. It was cold and uncomfortable, but she realized he would most likely never trust her, and this was just how life would be.

He kissed her, and once he had gone, Rosa came down to join her.

"I noticed you didn't eat this morning. Eat this, to keep your strength," she said as she handed Marie a plate with some bread on it.

"Most foods lately have made me feel uneasy. I think it's the smell that gets to me the most."

Rosa thought. "Tell me dear, is… that time… regular?"

"It's never really been. The last I can remember… I had one maybe two weeks before I came here and only one since. You don't think-"

"If this continues, I will ask to send for the doctor, but I won't tell him anything until we know for sure."

Her eyes began to water. She was afraid of what James may do to resolve the problem of a baby. Rosa rubbed her arm.

"He may be cruel at times, but he is a God-fearing man, I'm sure everything will be all right. Now try to get some rest."

Marie prayed she was right about him as she curled up in her bed and covered her head with the blanket.

The days following that morning, Marie did her best to keep herself quiet and busy. Her spirits heightened when she practiced her knitting without end and began to improve her technique. Her symptoms soon faded, and she began to feel like herself again. She was oblivious to the world outside her new home but could sense things were not going well; especially for James. Marie could see how truly lonely he was. When she touched him, she could feel his anxiety over him like a weighted coat. She often listened in the shadows to whispers between James and his guests of the search for a notorious gypsy criminal who was impossible to apprehend. It was a problem that seemed to devour the city and its citizens. Other days she could hear his sadness as he would vent to himself of his failures and regrets when he assumed he was alone.

Marie could sense his exhaustion as she prepared her bed for the evening. His presence filled the room as he leaned in the doorway and called to her. His voice was tense and strained, but she followed him to his room. She wanted to please him, but he seemed more interested in rushing. She understood it was a patrol night, and their time was limited. She pulled him back onto the bed to kiss her, which seemed to relax him for a moment as he climbed on top of her.

In his hurry, James lost his balance, and his hand pushed into her stomach. That's when she felt it: the sickness had returned. It was far worse than before. She tried her best not to panic and push it back down as her body moved under his. She held her breath, praying again she wouldn't get sick on him. She wasn't sure she would make it through this time. When he finally finished, she quickly sat up. She could feel her supper making its way back up with a horrible acidic taste in her mouth. She put her hand over her lips and forced it back down once more. She didn't want to ruin his good mood. She had to get more bread or water, anything to settle her stomach and quickly dressed.

"May I please get some water?"

"Yes, I'll be right there in a moment."

She threw her hand over her mouth and skipped in a panic to the kitchen. The light made her feel even more queasy. She couldn't hold it down this time, but she didn't want to mess up the floors that Rosa had just cleaned. She noticed the door, it was nearly dark out. She didn't think, she just looked to Rosa and ran outside. This made her instantly feel better.

In the very same instance, James walked from his room. Rosa tried to distract him so Marie wouldn't get caught, but he had already seen her and had her in his hand. He grabbed Marie by the back of her neck and threw her to the ground away from the window. He snatched his cane from the wall and swung it at her. Rosa tried to catch his hand, but it was too late.

"Ow, Please!" Marie threw her arm up to protect her face.

"You know you aren't allowed outside!"

"It was an accident! She's-"

"Sick! I'm sick! I didn't want to make a mess on the floors. I swear that's all! I wasn't leaving or trying to be seen."

"Sick with what?" He raised his cane to intimidate her.

"Please no..." Marie was scared. She didn't know if telling the truth would make things better or worse, or if it would do anything at all. All she knew in that moment was how much she wasn't ready to find out and began to cry.

James slapped Marie's arm with the cane, less hard this time, as to merely get her attention, "shut up before you're heard. Someone could have seen you!"

"She is loyal to you, James," Rosa spoke softly, like an old friend. "Trust me," she said, "I was going to ask you to send for Joseph."

"What's wrong with her? Why Joseph?" James lowered the cane.

"You know why..."

He looked down at the girl, and his face went pale. Marie stopped crying and looked to him. their eyes met as they had many times before, but this moment was different. There was a look in his eyes that she did not recognize, but he quickly turned away from her. He checked out the window, grabbed his coat, and left without a word.

Marie felt stuck on the floor. She could feel the world's weight on her as her thoughts raced in fear. She couldn't recall standing, but her focus snapped back to Rosa pulling her from the ground. Her arms tingled with anxiety as Rosa held onto them, and she found herself heading to James's room. She stood in the darkness and climbed onto his bed. She was scared about what he would do. She pictured his face when he heard; he may be a God-fearing man, but this could change everything. She laid back, staring at the ceiling.

For the first time, she was in his bed, alone, but it didn't feel right. She wanted him to come back and lay next to her, or at the very least to have not run away like he did. Her mind flashed back, and she thought about when he told her his name. Something happened that night, and she would give almost anything to go back and stay there in that moment.
Rosa came and sat next to her.

"Let me brush your hair."

"Can we stay in here?"

"Of, course," Rosa smiled. Marie tossed her hair behind her, closed her eyes and leaned her head back; the brush felt amazing massaging her scalp.

"Rosa... Who is Joseph?"

"He's a doctor. One of the best in his age. There are few like him who have or even can do the things he has done. He is also one of the few to be as educated in the woman's body as he is."

"I take it he's also good at secrets? He won't tell anyone I am here?"

"He's done many things for me. The late Master Fontaine was close with his family. Over the years, the two families have hidden many secrets for each other. They had a lot in common with their work and could help each other out."

"How so?"

"Well... being a judge gives you a lot of pull in the justice system and with the king. Joseph comes from a long line of doctors. In cases like this, a friend in the medical practice is beneficial."

"You know a lot about all this. You always know what to say to make me feel less afraid." Marie was cautious with her next words. "Do... you... speak from experience? I apologize if it's not my place to ask. I don't want to impose."

Rosa took a deep breath as she thought on the words to tell her.

"I was young when my mother brought me here. My father was no longer around, and she needed to care for me. James's mother was ill, so my mother took care of the house and her every need until she died. Then she caught the illness but did her best to work through it. She died slowly for two years. I was thirteen when the Master Augustus took me into his own bed."

"I'm sorry I shouldn't have-"

"No, no. You need to hear this. I know it's impossible to believe right now...but James is a much better man than the late Master. That man was truly... I'm not even sure of the words to say, but if there was any explanation to the way James can be..."

"I really hope he can stay the better man right now."

Rosa pulled her close. She combed through Marie's hair with her fingers.

"He will be, because I know deep down that's what he wants," she whispered. She climbed down from the bed and covered Marie's legs with a blanket.

"I know it seems easy." Rosa added as she looked towards the extra set of gate keys James had left on the table. Marie came to realize something. As Rosa stood up to leave, Marie called to her.

"I'm almost certain my family is dead, and if not, they're dead to me... I'm not a child anymore, but I'll have one... alone if I leave." She laid back on the bed.

She tried to sleep but she couldn't wrap her head around whether or not she was doing the right thing. She desperately thought about leaving, about not being in pain all the time. *Was she making the right choice? How far could she run right now? Where would she even run to? Could she raise a baby on her own? Would she be safe?* She had to try to survive. She pulled herself up from the bed and tied her corset.

She grabbed the key from the table and went out the door. She stood at the gate for a moment. she observed the large brass lock. Her fingers rubbed over the embellishments on the side, and she held the key next to it. She was surprised by how anyone would take the time to decorate such a small piece of hardware, but these pieces even matched. She turned back to the house and leaned into the wall. It was dark, but she could see the outlines of the courtyard and its simple design. She could see the door and the life she would be leaving. Tears streamed down her face. She looked up to the moon and prayed once again for guidance, unsure of where life could take her.

Finally, she took a deep breath and turned to unlock the gate. She opened it as wide as it could go and took the first steps beyond the threshold. She looked to both sides of the empty streets. She recognized where she was and began to walk, shaking with every step. The ground was cold on her bare feet.

# Chapter Eleven

14 May 1796

    The manhunt for Nikolais was the largest France had seen in decades. Claude and his men exhausted all measures in their search. Paris had begun to feel like a very cold place and not like the home it once was. As Claude rode through the streets, he observed his neighbors entering their homes for the evening. They were cordial in their nods, but never spoke to him beyond such greetings. He wondered if they avoided him because they had no shared interests, or if it was because they suspected him. They could never understand the relationship he had with Marie. He could hide the girl, but even that was proving difficult. An infant in the home of an unmarried official would surely be the scandal that could destroy him.

    He tried desperately to ignore the disturbance in his mind as he hurried to his post, but he remained on edge and irritable throughout his patrol. He had a lot on his mind and was worried about how he would handle it. The thoughts were on the brink of overwhelming him when he heard something nearby. He led Charles to the source of the sound coming from behind a small house. A man and woman stood playful as they gazed upon the night sky together, completely unaware they had been spotted.

    Claude silently stalked as the two embraced each other in the shadows. There was a light between them that could be felt even in darkness. His eyes followed as the woman's hand slid up her lover's chest while his hand cradled her head. Claude's chest tightened as he watched the gypsy couple hold each other. Something in the way their lips drew to each other caused a sting in his throat. The air was warm, but he felt a chill overcome him. His muscles tensed as they continued, and it caused a snap in his being. He dismounted his horse and charged to arrest them. Charles was dumbfounded by his actions but followed his lead.

"We are near our own home. We only came out here for a moment. It's a beautiful night," the woman tried to explain.

"I feel like you people never learn. I've set the rules and even made examples and still you refuse to abide by my rulings!"

"But sir, we weren't roaming the streets, this is our property," she argued.

"I don't care. I announced there would be no clemency shown. This is on you."

Charles reached for the woman, but the man became aggressive.

"Don't you dare touch her. You're sick and twisted in the sight of God. I hope he shows you no mercy on judgment day like you've done to so many! You deserve hell's fire," the man scowled!

"Let's not pretend we worship the same God, devil gypsy! You defile him with your lies," Claude sneered as he pulled his sword from its sleeve. His nod to Charles established the plan; he stabbed the man's chest in the same moment Charles captured the woman. He held the woman and covered her mouth before she could scream or draw attention to them.

"Claude, while I do enjoy a good slaying, there were no laws broken here."

"I'm simply in no mood for insolence and disobedience tonight. Of all people Charles, I would think you'd be the last to have complaint of this."

"Oh no, I have no complaints at all. I was simply stating you seem a bit out of character tonight. Is everything alright?"

"I don't know," he mumbled.

Claude's hands began to sweat, and it made him even more anxious. He could feel himself becoming unwell. He didn't need to hear Charles's opinion to know he was questioning his character. If he let the girl live, she would surely spread word that he was going mad. The sweat began to drip from his brow as he considered his next step.

"Just do what you will with the girl and finish her. We don't need her running her mouth about any of this," he instructed as he left Charles to his work. He wiped his forehead and rode back to his post feeling constricted with anxiety. He worried he had let his fear get the best of him.

As Claude made his way back, Anthony came to meet him to tell him of a hiding place the private detectives had found. The other guards had begun arresting all the gypsies without papers and held the landowners inside for Claude to interrogate.

"Thank you, Anthony. I have been considering you a loyal deputy, and I think you are ready to step forth in our mission."

"Yes sir, I have and will continue to do anything for you and the king. Whatever you need of me."

"You've interrogated them yourself, am I correct? Would you find these people to oppose the king, acting as associates of the rebellion?" Claude inquired. He thought on what his future actions may bring in this moment. He reflected upon his career and the life he had at home. He would forever be split in two, and pondered the worth of making a few sacrifices.

"Yes, I would," he heard Anthony respond. Claude decided in that moment and called the other guards to announce the news.

"Soldiers! Let it be known that I reside as acting sheriff of this community and hereby appoint Deputy Anthony LeJeune as my new replacement. He has dedicated himself for years now and has proven faithful to the king and his mission. None is better qualified for such a job," he proclaimed.

"But sir, you have been the city's greatest sheriff by far. I could never compare."

"Anthony, I will still be here to help and guide you through everything. I've had multiple titles for nearly two decades now. It will be an honor to step down knowing that someone just as qualified would be taking my place."

"Thank you, sir, you will not regret this one bit. I will make you proud."

"Very good. Do you think these criminals even deserve our time in court just to be released and continue to do their dealings in the dark, or should we make an example of them?" Claude made it perfectly clear that he had an intention with his questioning of Anthony.

"I think the people need to know we are serious about the consequences of what they are doing. We should set an example."

"Guards, put all of the prisoners back in the home. They will all be under house arrest until trial. We have no more space in the prison."

As the soldiers brought the people back into the home, Claude lit a torch.

"Let this be the first example of what is to come if anyone should find themselves desiring to hide any unregistered gypsies. This will no longer be tolerated. If no one wants to learn the way things have been, they will learn it now. You are the new face of justice and the law now, Sheriff. Show them who is to be feared and respected here. This is your city now," he snarled as he handed the torch to Anthony and locked the people inside.

Anthony held it firmly in his grasp and stared at the home. There were women inside. There was even a child with them. He stared at the fire on the torch for a moment. He hesitated, but quickly realized that is what his new job would entail. It was what he was signing up for, and he was sure his king would not make him do anything that wasn't necessary for the greater good. He lifted the fire to the house and backed away as the home went up in flames. He looked to Claude for approval.

Claude smiled as he instructed the guards to post a notice of the criminals inside the home and be sure none escaped. He congratulated the new sheriff and invited him to the tavern to celebrate his promotion. They discussed Claude's new course of action along the way and recognized Anthony's achievement to everyone that attended the festivities. It had been quite an exciting night, and they all rejoiced in Anthony's first acts as the new sheriff of their parish.

It was just before dawn when James finally returned home. His eyes were heavy, and all he could think about was a nap. He'd almost forgotten many of his troubles when reality suddenly hit him. A fit of panic veiled over him at the realization that his front gate was open. Many things had distracted his mind the previous evening, but he was certain he had at least shut it before he left. He ran into the house and down the stairs to Marie's room. She wasn't there. He frantically ran back up to the kitchen and throughout the house.

"Rosa," he called out as he ran past his room and back. He nearly tripped and fell into the wall when he saw her in his room.

She was sitting on his bed and quickly jumped up as he caught his breath in the doorway. This was going to be a big moment. It could possibly mean terrible things for her, but she didn't seem to care. She had made her choice, and now, she had to deal with it.

"I'm sorry. I'll go to my room," she whispered. She climbed off the bed and reached for the door.

"The gate was open, Marie. I thought you-" James stuttered but walked toward her slowly. He was in shock and could feel the palpitations in his chest. He could see Rosa now in the doorway and watched as they glanced at each other nervously. Marie shut the door, turned around and leaned into it.

"I did... I opened your gate, and I'm sorry. No one saw," she promised. She took a deep breath, stood straight and led him back onto his bed. He sat on the edge as she pushed closer to him, standing directly in front of his face. He didn't say a word; he couldn't even speak. He was certain she would have escaped since she hadn't been locked up.

"For just right now though, can we forget everything about today?"

James nodded. He stared into her eyes. They were dark and full of hopeful sadness and pain.

"I'm going to be so bold as to tell you, James. That despite the fear I feel about what may very well happen, and despite the horrible things you have done, I can't go back now. Here, this place, it feels right. I couldn't begin to explain why, but I want to be here." She kissed him as she climbed up and straddled him.

James felt confused but stared for a moment longer. She smiled when he touched her face. He put his hands around her waist and kissed her. She felt anxious, but excited. He struggled to unbutton his pants.

"Here, let me help," she offered as she went down to do it for him. He grew nervous as the girl reached in to not just touch it, but instead, kiss it. It took him by surprise, and in his shock, he pulled her up to kiss her. He'd planned to behave as they always did, but this time she was making all of the first moves as she straddled him and slid it inside of her. She pulled his shirt open to expose his chest and kiss him there as well. She tried to steady herself on top of him, but it proved to be a little more difficult than she thought. She tried to move around but lost her balance sitting so straight up and fell into him. It was unexpected, but James couldn't force his gaze from hers.

"Where did you learn that?" James had never experienced such things. It felt amazing. This is exactly how he had wanted to feel with her.

"My roommate at the girls' school would sneak a boy into her bed many nights. There was no divider between the beds, so I could see everything they did. She always moved with such ease, and the boy was always pleased and came back for more. That's what I wanted, so I tried to mimic everything I could remember seeing. If you don't like it..."

His hand slowly crawled up from her cheek to her neck. He caressed her ear and then held her head as he pulled her in close. He could think of nothing he wanted more than to kiss her beautiful red lips, but her hair cascaded over her face and tickled his chest. They seemed to be connecting for the first time. He liked her like this and wanted to keep her happy. He rolled over on top of her and held her hips to push himself deeper inside of her. It was an amazing sensation.

He grabbed her arms tightly and began to tremble for a moment but suddenly realized what he was giving into. The thought of her having his child and what it could do... If the people around him didn't suspect something was happening in his home by now, an infant would certainly ensure they did. He couldn't look at her any longer. Marie also seemed to snap back to the reality of it as she slowly crawled from his bed.

"I'm sorry. I'll go to bed now if that's what you want."

He simply looked at her but couldn't speak. As she turned to leave, his arm reached out and his fingers combed through her hair. She didn't look back as she disappeared into the darkness of her room.

"I'm curious as to how she got the key to the gate," he questioned Rosa as he sat for breakfast.

"She couldn't stay here unless she realized that she wanted to."

"And if she hadn't? What if she left?"

"I guess we won't know, but I can tell you that she's let go of what's outside of these walls. She's more afraid of what's out there not awaiting her than of what could have been awaiting her in here."

"Is that what's kept you here?"

Rosa sat down next to him at the table to join him for the meal.

"I've known you a long time. I've kept everything for you. I'm not sure you would survive without me," she teased.

He laughed as she nudged his arm. He smiled, "you may be right," he joked, but his tone quickly changed and became serious.

They sat in silence for a moment before he insisted she find Joseph, and she ran to the stable to ready her horse.

James finished his breakfast and cleaned the table. Afraid of what was to come, Marie sat frozen on the steps. She couldn't bring herself to move, even as he walked toward her to grab his coat. He stood tall above her, and she could feel him glaring down at her. She forced herself to face him, and their eyes met. His disappointment in her being there was apparent when he grabbed her hand and pulled her down to her room. He secured the cuff around her wrist. A heaviness fell over her chest and a burning behind her eyes.

"Please don't do this. Don't leave me here," she begged.

"This is overwhelming for me, Marie. I can't be here now. Rosa will take care of you when she gets back." He couldn't even properly acknowledge her as he quickly left without another word.

"When will that be? Please, come back," she called out, but her cries were completely ignored.

She was terrified and angry. She could feel her chest rise and fall as her breathing intensified. She couldn't explain the emotion she felt, but it seemed to take over her. She noticed the notebook he'd given her and threw it across the room. Screamed into her pillow, but it didn't help her to feel any better, so she tossed it as well. Her frustrations only seemed to grow as she paced around the bed. She was exhausted. She couldn't think or focus. Her face burned with rage as she questioned herself and the choice she made. Tears pushed through until her vision was no better than a blur. *Should she have run? Did she underestimate how much he cared about her?* The thoughts danced in her head, and she lost focus of what she was doing when she stepped on the notebook. The paper slid from under her foot and jolted her balance. She tried to brace herself but missed the bed and couldn't stop herself from crashing into her table and hitting the floor.

# Chapter Twelve

15 May 1796

When Rosa was a small girl, her mother worked as a private nurse in the city of Lille. The Beauchene Hospital had been established there for generations, and everyone, including all great kings of France, would travel to this hospital in times of need. The physicians were each at the top of their classes, and none were short of the best. Medical practitioners of all studies would compete from all over the world to be considered worthy of practicing medicine under the Beauchene legacy.

When Joseph finished his studies in England, he returned to find that the hospital was no longer large enough to accommodate the multitude of doctors and patients in France. Hundreds of people would be forced to travel for days to be seen, but many couldn't survive the journey. When he was just twenty-one years old, Joseph decided to open his own practice in Paris. It was a more centralized location that could better reach those in need, and Rosa had always admired him for it. Her mother's patient was from Paris and was thrilled to be able to return home to her family. The woman loved Rosa and her mother dearly and refused to return to Paris without them.

She pushed her horse as hard as she could, and it wasn't a long ride before she arrived at Joseph's home. It wasn't extravagant, and the courtyard was only mildly kept with simple and efficient décor. Rosa had known Joseph to always live within a reasonable means that required minimal staff. His parlour maid answered the door and informed her that Joseph was back in Lille helping his father for a few weeks. His father lived on the northern-most end of the city. It was almost a day's ride away. She worried about leaving Marie for so long, but she needed to be seen sooner rather than later.

She was diligent in her quest, but spent the majority of her travels in deep thought. She pondered what her family had been as a child and to what it became when her mother passed. She recalled the day Julien had come into her life, and the hardship that once came with hiding a baby in the home. She also considered the fact that Julien tried to sneak down to the cellar and had almost found Marie on his very first visit after she arrived. Rosa was lucky to have caught him and prevented it for the time, but should a child at any age make even the slightest sound, Julien's curiosity would reignite and win for sure. She loved Julien like a son, but worried of his ability to keep quiet about certain matters.

She arrived at the home just after dark. This house was very different from Joseph's. It was a home beyond luxury and was everything Joseph intended his not to be. It was filled with staff and often hosted parties and galas. The butler answered her knock, but Joseph was only a few steps away when he realized who was at the door. He promptly greeted her and invited her inside.

"It's always a pleasure to see you Rosa, but what brings you way out here?"

"Claude needs you as soon as possible. There's a problem."

"Business or personal?"

"Personal."

"Is he ill?"

"No. He is fine." She was shy to give too much information. She felt guilty for the whole circumstance and couldn't stand for Joseph to think of her as less for allowing it to happen. She looked up at him and knew he could understand. Joseph's father brought many women into his home over the years, and it was always typically the same story.

"How old is she? How long has she been there?"

"Only fourteen and a few months," she admitted. Rosa could see the look of dismay upon his face.

"Come, sit with me. We can discuss it over dinner. You look chilled," he insisted.

He commanded a maid to help her find a warmer coat, and they quickly sat together for a warm meal. He offered her a room for the evening before they traveled, but Rosa was uncomfortable with being gone for too long. She convinced him to leave with her immediately, and he sent for a boy to get her horse and prepare a carriage for them. The ride was quiet. Rosa told him about the girl, but words didn't come easily in the moment.

When they returned to the house, it was dark, and there was an eerie silence. Rosa led him down the stairs where they found Marie on the floor. Rosa tried to wake her, but she could barely move or speak. Joseph grabbed her hand; her wrist was bruised from the cuff. She sat up but quickly lost her balance when they noticed the side of her forehead was bleeding.

"What happened? Where's James?" Rosa questioned.

"It wasn't him. This was my fault. I don't know where he went, because he wouldn't speak to me," Marie said in a quiet mumble. Rosa looked around and realized she hadn't eaten in over two days.

"You must be starving; I'll go make you something," she told her as she ran upstairs. Joseph carried the girl to her bed and bandaged the gash. When Rosa returned, he gave her a serious look.

"She's very weak and feels cold. She needs food right away," he whispered as she rushed past him.

"Here, I brought you some bread." Rosa lifted her head and encouraged her to eat.

Marie quickly began to regain some strength and was finally able to really look up at Joseph. He had a kind eyes, and a gentle smile, but he looked upset, sympathetic even. He sat on the edge of the bed as Rosa introduced the two.

"Hello, Marie."

"Hello," she smiled weakly. Doctors had always made Marie nervous, but she felt she could trust him.

"Dear... Joseph is going to take a look at you and make sure everything is all right. I promise, it may seem scary, but you're in good hands. Just lie back and I'll be right here for you," Rosa's voice was soothing as she eased Marie back and held her hand. Joseph uncovered her. He began to examine her and lifted up the skirt of her gown, but she jumped back.

"No, no! It's going to be alright," Rosa tried to calm her anxiety.

"I promise I'm only trying to check on you. I don't want to hurt you." Joseph thought for a moment, "I will just look and work very slowly. If there is anything I do that becomes too much for you, just tell me, and I will go slower. I can stop at any point to give you a break should you need it."

Marie nodded and laid back. She understood it was his job. She laid back and stared to the ceiling. There was solace in the familiar habit of counting the cracks above her. When Joseph was finished, he nodded for Rosa to follow him upstairs to allow the girl some much needed rest. He began to explain his concerns when they found James sitting at the table.

"Where have you been? Something could have happened to her!" Rosa demanded to know. She cared about Marie and was very angry. She felt like James should take responsibility for the girl he forced into his home. He made many promises, but she felt he was falling short of what he was capable of.

"Please, Rosa. Leave us to speak." Joseph sat down next to him.

"Claude, the girl is weak and malnourished as I'm sure you can see. She's cold and bruises fairly easy. If I had to give it my best guess, I would say it's anemia. It can happen from being pregnant."

"So, she is indeed with child?"

"I would say she's in the early stages of pregnancy, maybe six to eight weeks by the swelling in her uterus," he estimated.

"And there's still time?"

"If you're about to ask me what I think you are, I don't believe she could survive that in her condition."

"I can't have her making babies every year-"

"You do understand how this happens, don't you? Why didn't you send for me sooner than now? If she had been healthier, I could have prevented this! Killing that baby could kill her."

"Then we'll wait till after. This can never happen again."

"Very well, but you must do exactly as I say in the coming months, or there won't be anything I can do to help. This is very serious," Joseph warned as he gave Rosa instructions on what Marie needed to regain her health.

"Thank you." Rosa smiled at Joseph, he nodded and smiled back.

"I'll be back as I can to check her progress." He left for the night but returned regularly to ensure she was getting keeping up her strength. He had many patients in the same circumstance, but there was something about Marie that affected him so much more. He spent extra time doing whatever he could to make her as comfortable as possible throughout her trying pregnancy.

James began to realize how much he had put Marie through. He told himself he truly cared for her, but his affections fell short when he continued to treat her as just another gypsy whore. That wasn't who Marie was, and that's not how he wanted her to feel about herself. He knew something needed to change: himself. He vowed to do better, but the kind of change that was needed wouldn't come without a price, and someone would certainly pay that price.

# Chapter Thirteen

27 December 1796

     The months passed by slowly, and Julien continued to grow. His build and features were distinct of his Romani heritage, but he was much taller than most gypsies. His eyes were lighter as well, and it sprung curiosity in him of who his parents were. As he aged, however, he felt he had all the family he needed. He cherished them, and in the recent weeks noticed that Claude was visiting much more often. He didn't know what could be happening, but it seemed to him that he avoided his own house. He would frequently come before and after patrols, but Julien was rarely allowed to return home with him.

     He missed Rosa, but was happy to have his master pay so much attention to him. Claude was strict and less endearing, but Julien knew he loved him. He thought of him as a father-figure, a teacher, but first above all, his master. There were other people around the church, but none paid him any attention. The clergy and nuns rarely associated with the workers of the church, the other servants were much older, and he was prohibited from going outside, so Julien grew used to being alone. He wished he could go into the city to make a friend, but knew it would not be allowed and turned to his dolls to fill that hole. He had perfected his art and found new ideas for features and appearances, and even began making furniture and accessories for them. When he wasn't consumed in his studies, he spent the rest of his free time playing with them.

One afternoon Julien had finished his independent studies early, and noticed a few of his projects could use a bit of attention. He laid his tools out gently on the table and began to work on things as he could. It was calming and gave him a sense of peace and purpose as he shaped the clay and worked the molds. He became so engrossed in his work that he had completely lost track of all time until he heard a knock at the door. The monsignor was paying him an unexpected visit, as he occasionally would. He would come to check the workshop, and always seemed so fascinated by his collection.

"These are absolutely beautiful. You're improving on your fine detail in the face. I can see you practice, but I really think you should sign these. Claim right to your art," he encouraged.

"But no one ever sees them. They're just for me to pass time."

"Have you ever thought about making a few to sell?"

"Sell them? But they're all so special." Julien had never considered parting with his creations. They had names and personalities. They were like a family. To just give one away to a stranger felt almost inappropriate to him, but the monsignor assured him they could be a special little girl's best friend. He'd never considered it that way, but recalled seeing many unfortunate girls running around the streets with sticks or poorly made moppets. It saddened him, and he realized they would most likely love to have one at a more affordable cost than what the popular boutiques currently offered.

"You will be nineteen in a few months. You should start working towards a business. You could travel to London or Spain, but even the market outside of these walls are a good start."

"I've always wanted to see London. Do you really think I could do well there?"

"I encourage you to try and step out on your own. There's a whole world to see, and these dolls could take you there."

"But my home has always been here. It's my duty to serve in the church. I owe it to my family."

"I know the Arch-Bishop in London well. I can speak to him, and you can serve in their church if you would so desire."

"But how would my master feel about me leaving Paris?"

"The story you've been told is not my business, but you are a man now. Any sins of your parents are their own, and you should not feel so responsible for them," the monsignor advised as he stood to leave for the evening mass. "I've had many men serving the church with potential to do great things, but few with as much promise as you have."

"Thank you, Father. I will think on it while I get started and won't decide anything until a new set is ready."

"I really hope you do, because I know you can do so many great things in the world," the monsignor smiled and left him on that thought. The father's kind words always brought a good spirit to his heart and made him feel more confident in himself.

Julien smiled and continued in his work as the man seemed to trade places with Claude, who appeared in the doorway as quickly as the monsignor had gone. He happily greeted his master but could see the look of disgust that covered his face.

"I can't believe you would bring a guest here in the condition this place is in. This room is a complete mess, and no matter how much I teach you, you never learn," Claude grimaced.

"I'm sorry, I was in the middle of a project. I wasn't expecting him to come by."

"You should always be prepared for a visitor. You've only been allowed to use this workshop, but it does not belong to you," his master snapped.

"I really do apologize." Julien's light and pleasant mood faded as his master took a seat across from him and gestured for him to sit as well.

"Anything you would like to start with before we begin?"

"The monsignor had come to see me about my art. He seems to really like it and thinks I should do more with my collection," he shared. Talking about his work was the only thing he knew that made him feel good about himself and the things he did.

"You are getting better, but I think there are more important things to concern yourself with right now. How about we start with you telling me the lesson we learned just the other day, shall we?"

"We learned my dictation and grammar," he tried to say as he shifted uncomfortably in the hard chair.

"No, Julien. I'm referring to the lesson you had to learn because you failed in such subjects." His voice was calm and monotonous, which always made Julien more nervous to speak.

"Oh... I..." he choked back the words. The embarrassment began to overwhelm him as he looked to each of his dolls: their eyes all directly upon him. He could feel the heat in his face begin to turn his cheeks red, and he stood to cover them.

"I told you to explain your lesson, or should we go over it once more?" Claude grabbed his arm and placed him back in his seat before he could get to the doll cabinet.

"No, Master. I'm sorry. I did not study diligently in my dictation, and my spelling was, as you called it, appalling. I did not pay attention during my lesson and failed my examination."

"And what happened because of it?"

"I...uh... had to be..." he stuttered nervously.

"Speak up, Julien! I cannot hear you. Tell me about what happened when you failed in a simple quiz of your lessons: a test you receive weekly and should have not been so surprised by," his master scorned.

"I received a caning for my inadequate behavior. I am very sorry," he sighed.

Julien began to shake. He could feel each of the dolls staring upon him as he recalled the event. A vision of his hands on the desk in front of his nose crept to his mind. He remembered laying his head down upon them and peered over to the cabinet that held his figurines. His memory haunted him with his reflection in the glass as he was bent over his desk and forced to expose himself for such an embarrassing ordeal. His fingers curled under the chair as he sat painfully and relived the moment as if it were still happening. He began to perspire in his attempt to distract his thoughts, but he knew this was what his master wanted.

Julien's lessons always required him to return to that feeling once again, to remember the pain with each strike he endured across his bare skin, and the shame he felt as he was boyishly punished for his incapacity to do well. Such events had taken place many times throughout his life, but hearing the monsignor refer to him as a man now made it all the more humiliating to him.

"And how have you rectified your actions since then?"

"I put aside my hobby all week and focused only on my studies. I will be sure to not fail today."

"I'm certain you won't. So, what else did we go over in last week's lesson? It's been a long few days."

"We made a multiplication table, and you showed me how to use it. I've memorized up to '5x8' without having to look," Julien reminded him.

He pulled every positive thought he had to his surface. It did no good to hold on to the hurt, and he was very enthusiastic about this lesson. Arithmetic was his favorite subject, and he never made bad marks in any of the materials he covered with his masters help. Claude placed a paper on his desk and nodded to begin. Julien concentrated on the test before him and did his best to relax. He knew that he sometimes would become too excited and fail, so this time he was sure to calmly focus. He handed in his paper and felt confident as he sat silently to watch his master grade his work.

"You did well, Julien. By next week I want you to know up to the twelves. The tens and elevens units are very simple as you can see, but the challenge will come after that. You won't be able to use the table, you will have to use the method I showed you when we first began. Do you still have those notes?"

"I do," he answered as he eagerly glanced over his work. He'd done his best and felt proud as he placed it on the shelf.

"I think that will be all for now. The night patrols have been daunting, and I don't have the energy to do anymore this evening. I plan to rest tonight."

"I understand," Julien nodded as he began to pack his things.

"What are you doing?"

"It's Thursday. I usually visit on Thursdays."

"I'm not sure that tonight is really a good time."

"But I've worked so hard this week, and I didn't come last week. I promise I have learned my lesson. Can I come?"

"The word is 'may'. May you come?" he instructed.

Julien repeated the question properly and was allowed to return with him to see Rosa. They arrived back just after dark. He ran in to hug Rosa as he always did, but her embrace was different. She appeared nervous and quickly directed him to the table near the fireplace before insisting on speaking with the master alone. His curiosity grew more as the two seemed to whisper to each other of important secrets. He wanted to know, but didn't want to risk getting caught. The pain he felt in his seat reminded him to be more cautious during his stay, but Rosa seemed very concerned as she spoke to the master. They whispered and mumbled to each other. Julien tried hard to eaves drop, but the words were inaudible.

"Alright, Julien," he finally heard Rosa say as she looked back to him, "would you please set the table for me, darling?"

"Yes, of course," he quaintly responded, but by the time he made it to the table, they had finished speaking and went their separate ways.

The remainder of the evening was like any other. They ate their supper, enjoyed a sweet treat together and read by the fire before bed. Julien played with a new set of tools Rosa had bought him, and Claude seemed to be in a content mood. Julien had missed nights such as this and leaned into Rosa as she read him a chapter from his favorite novel. She caught him before he fell asleep and directed him to their room. She kissed his forehead and tucked him tightly under his covers, which always seemed to put him straight to sleep.

It didn't feel like any longer than the snap of a moment before Julien was awaken by a strange sound. He could see Rosa come from the cellar door. He wanted to finally go to her and ask about it, but his master was there as well. The look on their faces assured him that something serious had happened. He couldn't hear their words, but was able to see Rosa's lips mention sending for Joseph.

Rosa immediately turned to her room to wake Julien, but he was already sitting up and waiting for her.

"We have to leave. There are massive riots near the courthouse and he won't be back by the time he would need to bring you back to the church."

"Rosa... I heard a peculiar noise. What happened? Did it come from that room?"

"Hush before the master hears you. You haven't woken enough to think properly. It was just your imagination. I need to get you back immediately," she whispered as she pushed him to the carriage. Julien knew he wasn't imagining things, there was something suspicious going on, and he wasn't willing to give up on an answer that easily.

"Rosa please tell me what's happened. I know there isn't a riot, you both have been very strange for quite some time, especially this night... What's down there in the cellar?"

"I can't tell you. I don't ever want you lying, so it's just better that all I tell you is that there is something down there he wants hidden. For the sake of everyone, I suggest you never talk about this around your master," she warned.

"But I don't understand why..."

"Will you just trust me. You know I only want the best for all of us, my darling."

Julien nodded but turned his head from her in disappointment. His curiosity grew stronger, but he knew he would never find answers from Rosa. He desperately wanted to know, but it was nearly impossible. He knew his master would never be hiding rebels. He assumed it must be something for the king, but his lack of knowledge involving things that occurred outside of the church limited his imagination. The only way to discover his master's secret would be to keep at his studies and come back again with more caution. He had almost been caught sneaking around once and dreaded even the thought of being caught by Claude. He would have to wait for just the right time. He didn't like it, but impatience would get him nowhere this time.

Rosa quickly tucked him into his bed at the church and returned to find James waiting at the table near the fireplace while Joseph was downstairs. She could hear Marie screaming and went down to hold her hand as Joseph delivered her child.

"I've got the head, just keep pushing," he encouraged.

"It's almost over, sweet girl," Rosa assured her. She pulled back the girl's sweat soaked hair and wiped her blushed face with cool water. She looked to Joseph, who looked back in agreement: they both believed she was a very strong girl that could handle more than most her age. Together they reassured her that she would make it, even in her doubts.

"I can't... I can't do anymore! Please, make it stop," Marie cried.

"Just one more big push and I think I can get it. You have to push! It won't end until you do," he cheered as he prepared himself to catch the infant. She screamed as she pushed, and Joseph quickly pulled the baby from her and wrapped a blanket around it.

"It's a girl," he spoke softly as he handed Marie the baby, but James abruptly grabbed it from her.

"Say goodbye. She can't stay here."

"No, please don't take her! What will you do to her?"

"She belongs in a children's home where she can be cared for properly."

"I can do that; I can take care of her like any other woman could."

"We cannot accommodate a child here," he insisted.

"Please, you let me bring her into the world, so I know you feel something."

"For you. I only let her grow to save you."

"Just look at her, please. We can't abandon her. She is ours, and we must raise her here," she pleaded.

"I will help her," Rosa assured him. She didn't want another baby to be lost as she thought on her own sadness and misfortune of the past. She thought of Julien and the light he brought into her life. She encouraged James to look down at the beautiful child in his arms, and he did. She was sweet and peaceful. She yawned and her tiny golden-brown eyes looked up to him. Her little hand grabbed his finger, barely wrapping around it. Rosa could sense a shift in him, but the feeling quickly faded as he walked over to Joseph.

"She's had a good delivery. The bleeding will only last a week or two. I'll come back then to check on her, and in a few weeks, as long as she is taken care of and heals properly, we can proceed with our plan," he warned James. Rosa backed away as they finished speaking, and James handed the baby back to Marie.

"You have three weeks to wean her, she cannot stay beyond that. I wouldn't even bother naming the child," he snapped.

# *Chapter Fourteen*

08 February 1797

It was cold, and the city was lacking in spirit. The days seemed to wither away, and the dark was taking over the people's lives. Winter had come, and it brought with it the most brutal chill that turned Paris weak with sickness. Claude could feel a change coming and was certain the gypsies were taking advantage of the city's despair to strengthen their army. He was quickly losing his best men in the fight and knew it would soon take a more dated approach to regain order. His methods could even be described as barbaric, but little choice was left with the king's ever-increasing paranoia. He traveled the long distance to the Beauchene hospital immediately after court one day to seek Joseph's expertise.

"There is more pressure on me than ever to find who the leader is. The king is not completely convinced some poor kid like the Quinn boy could truly be responsible in conducting such a complex organization. Honestly, I am just so tired from all of this. I want to step down more, but I feel stuck, Joseph."

"Maybe now is the time to consider the fact that you are not serving the king's will on your own. You have others that should be sharing in some of the responsibility as well," he reminded.

"I suppose Anthony has proven more than capable. Maybe if he can handle it, he could take over a few more jobs. It would greatly benefit me to focus my attention on the courts and only a few patrols per week. I will continue to oversee everything, but with all that is going on, I'm spread too thin," Claude complained.

"A break might be just what you need. Bring Anthony tonight, and we will see how he does. An interrogation would be the perfect way to test his endurance and skill," Joseph added.

He thought on the proposal and sent word for the sheriff to meet in his court chambers just after the sun set. He was pleased by Anthony's quick response and loyalty in heeding the call at any moment. They greeted each other and then Claude promptly led him to the room where Charles and Joseph were waiting.

"What is this place?" Anthony was amazed by the mysterious room. He had never known anything to be hidden under the courthouse, and Claude could see that he was enthralled by the things he was certain to learn there.

"Anthony, there are certain aspects of the job you have taken on that I must show you how to do on your own. My techniques are both efficient and effective and give you the best results."

"What aspects would that be?"

Claude turned his attention to a man tied down to a chair between his partners. He pulled Anthony closer and leaned in to quietly share in his plan.

"We arrested this man last week for leading a riot near Notre Dame. We suspect he may have information that can lead us to the whereabouts of Nikolais."

"So, we're going to try and extract that information from him?"

"Yes, but we must do it properly. I have called Charles and Joseph to help us, because they are the best at extracting what I need from people."

"I see. What would you like me to be doing?"

He sensed Anthony wasn't confident in his abilities to hurt people to get what he needed, but Claude also knew he desperately wanted to prove himself to them.

"Not much, just keep encouraging the person that you can stop all the pain if they only help you. You must appeal to them if you can, make them believe you will be on their side if they give you what you need. We'll start there and see where the night takes us," Claude instructed quietly as he signaled for Charles to begin.

As Charles and Joseph tortured the prisoner, Claude guided Anthony through his role. The process was slow and steady, and Anthony was gaining confidence and momentum as he did more. He followed under his command perfectly and without hesitation.

"Where does Nikolais get the money for the weapons? Does he use witchcraft to elude the soldiers?"

"Just one question at a time, Anthony. It draws out the process and wears the prisoner down. It makes him more likely to slip the truth," Claude whispered to him.

"Oh, I understand."

"You're doing well for your first time," he encouraged.

He showed Anthony new tricks and allowed him to practice his favored techniques on the man for over an hour. Anthony even helped as Joseph guided him in cutting off one of the man's fingers, but the night was quickly passing without any true progress. Charles impatiently gagged the man as he complained of the headache his screams caused. It was unlike his typical behavior, and Claude could sense everyone was growing tired. It was necessary to finish for the night.

"Very good, Anthony, I would have taken you for a weak stomach, but you truly surpassed our expectations tonight," he congratulated.

"Thank you, sir."

"Now, go home to your wife and son. We will clean up here."

"But he didn't tell you anything," Anthony muttered disappointedly.

"Not all do, and that's alright. He will be taken care of, and we will find another," Claude assured him. In his excitement, Anthony rushed to clean himself and ran from the courthouse for the night.

"And how would you have me take care of this one, Claude?"

"End his suffering. Cut his throat, and let's be done for the night. I think we could all use the rest before morning," he grumbled.

"You didn't want Anthony to take part in that as well?"

"He's not ready for such ordeals. It's best we progress him along slowly, I intend on nourishing his loyalties and making them grow stronger. He must take my place, I have so much else to deal with."

"Yes, I was going to inquire about that. How has everything been at home? It's been over four weeks, and she should be healed enough to proceed as we agreed."

"I've done a lot to keep busy and give her the space she's needed. Rosa has been strict on your instructions. It would be nice to have one less burden upon the house."

"I have some patients that need attending to first thing tomorrow, but I will more than likely be done by mid-afternoon. Shall I stop in around that time so I may check her? I can have her finished up just after nightfall."

"Thank you. I will clear my schedule and be there. I do appreciate everything you have done for me, both business and personal."

"And you are absolutely sure you want to go through with this? There is a very real risk I must warn you about. She-"

"We will proceed as planned. I want it done," Claude demanded.

Joseph shared in a faint smile as he cleaned his tools and placed them individually in their proper order within his case. Claude admired the organization and almost compulsive care put into the way he would prepare his equipment for each interrogation.

Alone in her room that very same night, Marie kneeled next to a small cradle and hummed softly as she rocked her daughter. Exhaustion and dread of her future began to wear on her, but she continued to keep a watchful eye on the infant. James had never returned since the night she was born, and she was certain he had locked her in and abandoned them. She felt alone, and her body ached. Her face began to burn with the pain in her mind. She felt stuck and unable to escape her cursed life.

The baby began to wriggle in her bed, and Marie held her breath in a panic. She feared every moment they could finally upset him enough to come down there. When she finally felt safe, she took a breath of relief and despair. She began to cry as she thought of the torment a child would endure if she was required to live in such a dark and horrifying place. She stared down at the beautiful sleeping cherub and gently touched her face. Marie knew that James would surely destroy and oppress such a precious and innocent soul and put her hand over her baby's face.

# Chapter Fifteen

08 February 1797

The night was quiet as Rosa finished cleaning for the evening. She stood at the window as the wind blew through the city outside. It whirled through the trees, streets, and around the homes when it seemed to quickly silence itself. A grim presence fell over the home, and she knew something was not right. She headed to her room when a faint whistle caught her attention. It led her through the home, and she followed it to the cellar door. She stepped inside and the sound deepened and turned to a sorrowful humming. She didn't recognize the melody, but its tone was ominous and pulled her down the stairs slowly. She could see Marie leaning over the cradle, and suddenly realized what was happening.

"You should live happily in heaven's light rather this dark and horrid cellar," she heard her whisper. She didn't have a moment to think, she simply acted and pulled Marie away. She held her breath in fear, but a great sigh of relief came from her as she heard the infant scream; she was going to be alright. She picked her up and cradled her in her arms to gently soothe her. Marie collapsed to the floor, but she had to force herself to stay strong as she comforted the baby. Her heart began to break as she witnessed the girl pull at her hair as she muttered nonsense through her tears and sobs.

Rosa could see the hysteria and delusion in her sleep-deprived eyes. She rocked the infant back to sleep and gently laid her in the cradle. She knew Marie wasn't thinking rationally and wanted to help her. She had aided the midwives for years and saw many women in despair, but she realized that many things were far from normal for this particular new mother. She knelt to the floor and held her tightly. She wanted to comfort the young girl until she was calm enough to finally speak.

"I'm the worst mother. I nearly murdered her! An innocent soul! What is wrong with me? I belong in hell for what I've done."

"Marie, stop! I know it's hard to believe, but many babies die at the hands of their own mothers soon after birth. I believe many would rather get rid of them before they ever breathe life if they could pay the price, but that can be dangerous too. Most would be hanged a witch, so they resort to measures such as you almost did. I'm not saying it's alright, but you deserve to know that you are not alone. A new baby is not easy, and you're enduring this under special circumstance. It's a terribly hard thing."

"I honestly don't know what I was thinking. I can't even recall putting her in the cradle. I was rocking her on the chair... I don't understand," she cried hysterically.

"When is the last time you slept? Have you even been to your own bed?"

"I can't. If she cries and upsets him... I don't know what will happen. I just can't. I should have let James take her right away. She would be better off at the children's home."

"That's not true. I know that you love her more than anyone could. These feelings are not your own, just demons that crept into an exhausted mind, love. You don't want to be rid of her."

"How do you know?"

"Because I raised a boy once. He wasn't my own, but I loved him as though he was. I gave him up, and even though I see him often, it isn't the same. I will always regret letting him go."

"You must think me a horrid person."

"I could never think that. I want to help you and this precious little girl."

"I'm sorry. I'm so weak. I really never wanted to hurt her."

"I know that. You should get some rest. I will keep her quiet with me tonight, but you must get sleep. I will help you through this," she promised. She hugged the child and tucked her into the bed. She kissed her forehead and smiled as Marie seemed to finally take a breath. It was the first time in weeks she had slept, and she didn't wake up through the entire next day. Rosa cared for the baby and kept her happy as promised. She left her to rest until the evening when Joseph arrived and led him downstairs.

"I'm sorry it took me so long to return, I wanted to make sure you were completely healed. These are my best nurses behind me. They are going to help us today," he told her as he set his things on the table.

Rosa had known them for many years and eagerly greeted the women. They were all of similar age and had travelled together from Lille when the new hospital was constructed. She showed them the new baby, and the three women admired and played as they checked on her health and growth.

"How is everything with feeding the baby? Any troubles?"

"It was hard at first, but we're starting to get it," Marie admitted.

"Well, my nurse has helped many new mothers when they've struggled. She's very experienced. Should you have any problems or questions, Rosa can send for her any time."

"Thank you."

"And how is your favorite patient feeling now, Joseph? You seem pleased with her care," James interrupted as he skipped down the steps to her room.

"She is in remarkable health. I believe she's ready," Joseph briefed him. James nodded, but Marie was confused.

"Ready for what?"

"You haven't told her?" Joseph was surprised and pulled James aside. "I thought she had just accepted long ago that this was her fate. How did you expect me to do this without her knowledge? I'm not comfortable doing such a life changing thing to an unknowing young girl," he mumbled to James furiously.

"I haven't even seen her, because you told me to leave her be. I did as you asked, but I didn't think it was important either way. This is not her choice," he replied loudly. It was clear he wanted everyone to know his concern for her freedoms in his home.

Rosa sat next to Marie, who appeared very afraid. She knew the girl couldn't fully understand what was to come and hoped to ease her concerns before she panicked.

"Cherish the child you have. She will be the only one."

"Why? What is happening?"

"Joseph has to take your womb from you so that you don't carry another," she explained.

Marie didn't fight; she knew there would be no point. James was right, and it was not her choice. Rosa watched as she slumped into her bed, but then something instantly changed. It was as if it had truly struck her: she wasn't simply giving up a womb. She stood speechless as the girl grabbed the baby from Joseph and jumped from the bed. Marie couldn't be sure which of the many emotions inside of her had surfaced, but whichever it was, it startled James. He nearly stumbled as she pushed past the others to force herself in front of him. She stood tall, her eyes almost level with his, and her next words were spoken in a low, dominant tone.

"I will do this for you, James, but you *will* let me keep my daughter."

"That doesn't sound like a polite question, girl," he retorted.

"It isn't. I will give her a name, because she is mine. You can take this from me, but not her. You will not take her from me as well," she challenged.

"You're getting very brave; do you realize that?"

"She is our daughter, and she will stay with us. Look down at her. I want you to really *see* the life I hold in my arms," she begged.

Everyone in the room watched intently as James finally broke his composure to look down at the child and witnessed his hard-exterior crack as he faintly smiled at her. He touched the infant's hand, and her finger instantly grasped his; she was now wrapped around his finger as any daughter was.

"Very well, but she must stay down here. Her presence must remain unknown to anyone, do you understand me, Marie?"

"I understand perfectly." Her voice was confident, and her glare was unshaken.

"I think, before we go any further, Marie needs to give her a name," Joseph interrupted.

Rosa rubbed her arm as she looked to James, longing for him to be a part of the moment. She nodded to him for a suggestion, and he seemed to choke back a thought before he finally spoke.

"My mother's name was Anna, and I would like to see it fit with a name you like as well," he muttered.

"I've always liked the name Grace. Should we call her Anna Grace?"

"I would rather see Grace be her first name. It's very lovely."

"Then I shall go get little Gracey Anna cleaned up and ready for bed then," Rosa giggled as she reached for the tiny angel in Marie's arms.

"Wait! That! That is her name," James called out to her, "Gracianna, as one name. It flows beautifully, don't you think so?"

"I like that. Gracianna it is," Marie agreed. She kissed her sweet Gracianna as she handed her away and got back in her bed.

As James and their daughter left the room, Marie slowly inhaled and calmly exhaled to prepare herself for what was to come. She nodded to Joseph, providing him with her consent to continue with his plan for the night. She knew he didn't need it but could see in his eyes that he wanted it before proceeding. He set out his tools, and his nurses began work to make her comfortable.

A strange sensation overcame her, and she began to feel as if she were in a dream. She could see his knives, the nurses' masks, and all of the terrifying equipment. She wanted to run, but whatever Joseph had given her prevented it. She could no longer move, and her body no longer ached. She could feel herself slipping, and her heart raced. She couldn't recall if he explained this was how she was supposed to feel or if her choices were now killing her. Her mind riddled with questions, and tears began to blind her to the things Joseph was doing. Dizziness and confusion took over, and she suddenly felt very tired. The world went black around her as her vision narrowed and seemed to drift.

# Chapter Sixteen

20 January 1798

      Over a year passed, but Claude often thought on that night. The girl in his home had truly changed his life and perception, but he was careful to not let it show. He retained his typical composure as he conducted his household. His child secretly grew in his home with her mother, but he often kept his distance. He had grown to care for his daughter as Marie predicted, and he wanted to only let her see the best of his moods. They were hidden and safe, which only helped Claude with his current predicament.

      The pressure was rising to conclude the search for Nikolais and destroy the self-proclaimed revolutionaries. He tightened the laws, and restricted the people more than ever. Soldiers were posted at every corner of the town to enforce the laws and curfew, and brutal interrogations continued to find criminals. He was at a crossroads of what the king demanded of him and what God would want him to do. Claude had become a hero in France and one of the most feared men in Paris. It was hard for him to truly consider the well-being of his soul when there was so much to do to keep the city civilized and at peace. He prayed God was understanding of his commitment to do whatever was necessary as he hurried to the king's meeting room. Claude stood quietly and listened carefully as the king paced about and vented his every frustration upon him.

"I want to know why the Quinn boy hasn't been caught and arrested yet. I don't want to do this, your father was dear to me, but if I need to find a new official who will get it done, I will not hesitate to do so," the king threatened.

"Your majesty, with all due respect, I am one of the few that truly knows what you are really after with this gypsy witch hunt, and I have done everything to make your wishes a reality. I've given up my own life outside of this career to please you. You will find none more dedicated than I."

"I know! It's just this criminal has me on edge. He uses witchcraft to torment us and disappear. I need you to get more men and make more arrests."

Claude could see that the king was oblivious to what the search was taking out of the city, even with so much support from the people. He knew he had to find a rational solution that would make the king understand.

"Sir, we have all the men we can at every corner. We've met the quota for arrests and done all we can that's possible. If we just start ripping civilized, law abiding, legal gypsy families from their beds, we will surely lose the people's trust in our mission."

"I have faith in you, but I am raising the quota. I want tighter laws regarding protest, don't even allow them to stop in the streets and congregate. I want my home back to the pleasant way it once was."

"As you wish," he mumbled as he stormed from the palace.

In his frustration, he decided to leave his horse and walk home. He realized how much he had sacrificed for the king and what his life was becoming. He had never given much thought to his actions in the recent years, but it was beginning to concern him. He strolled through the market to clear his mind when the loveliest gown caught his eye.

The top's lace was soft and blended beautifully with the silk of the skirt. The color was light with shades of pink and white. The mannequin didn't do the dress justice; there was only one girl he could picture in it. The colors would accentuate her complexion, and he could just imagine her beautiful hair cascading down over it. He requested the vendor discreetly wrap it as a gift and brought it home. He handed Rosa the box and whispered instructions to her before running down the steps to Marie and their child.

He quietly stood in the doorway as he watched her play with Gracianna on the floor. She had recently learned to walk and took to it well. She was quick and always moving and had the sweetest laugh when she wanted to be chased around. James sat next to Marie and played along with them. They began to play a clapping game together, but James simply watched Marie. Her smile was beautiful, and he could see her happiness as she enjoyed every moment with her daughter. She was irresistibly lovely, and he kissed her cheek. She seemed to be caught off her guard, but she simply looked at him with a smile. Her eyes stirred something in him, and her small hand reached up to his neck as she grabbed him to kiss his lips. He could feel her passion but wanted to stop her before they did anything more. He unlocked Marie from her chain and picked their baby up from the floor.

"I'm going to entertain Gracianna while you go upstairs. Rosa has something for you. Now, relax for a moment and wash up. There will be something else for you after."

She pulled herself up on her tip toes and kissed his cheek. She thanked him and ran upstairs to find Rosa had drawn her a warm bath. She helped her get cleaned up and fix her hair. She braided Marie's long locks and randomly placed small pearly pins throughout. She smiled as she admired her reflection, but Rosa could see her confusion and led to into her room.

"He brought you this as well," she eagerly shared as she handed the box to Marie. She quickly opened the gift and held the dress in front of her.

"It's so beautiful! I've never even seen a dress this elegant. What is it for?"

"James wants to take you out of the house when it's dark, but I don't know his plan."

"It will be so nice to feel fresh air again. I miss the sun, but the moon is perfect too," she reminisced. Marie was thrilled and quickly got herself dressed to leave with James.

The carriage quietly strolled through the woods outside of the city to a field about twenty minutes away. He laid a blanket down and put a basket with wine and some fruit down on it. The moon was bright and provided the perfect glow for them to enjoy the night together. He pulled her close to him and wrapped his arm around her. She had been in his home for quite some time, but he never took the time to know anything about her. He put his career first his entire life, and it got him nowhere. For him to be happier in life, he realized he needed to change something.

"I know I've been harsh, and this is not exactly the life I'm sure you dreamed of, but I don't always mean to be cruel and unfair. You're a special girl, and you deserve things that are hard for me to give you. The rebels are rising, and the king expects me to control the whole situation. It makes it nearly impossible to make life any better for you. I wish I could just make the gypsy problem disappear like they do when the guards try to capture them. I brought you here to show you that I want to change things."

"My father might have been one to help you. He loved my mother, but he also believed that her people weren't above anyone. He thought all should fit into society and certainly not run it. I don't know the whole story, but I think it had a lot to do with why we left England. You both had similar views."

"What did your father do for a trade?"

"He was a blacksmith until he became ill. He even had his own shop."

"Vincent Adams?

"You knew my father?"

"I remember a blacksmith with three or four daughters; He was a good working man," he admitted. He felt a deep hurt as he thought about how he tore a daughter from an honest working Englishman. Guilt began to build inside of him, but not as strongly as his desire for her. He forced himself to not to dwell on things that may distract him from the good that night brought.

"Did you attend his funeral?" Marie inquired.

"That was after you came to stay with me; weeks after. How did you know?" He noticed that she didn't seem upset and wondered if maybe Rosa had told her long ago.

"I said my goodbyes to him. We went for a doctor the night you found me because he was at his last moments. I didn't know he held on for weeks after, I hope he did not worry too much of me."

"I'm very sorry. I completely misjudged you, Marie. I, at times, wish we could have come together in a different way. That it didn't come with so much hurt to you."

"It's no matter now, that's done with, and I've accepted this new life with you."

"I want you to be comfortable at home; it is your home too. As of tomorrow, you will have been here for over two years. I want you to have this," he whispered.

He handed her another small box to open. Inside it was a gold bracelet with charms attached to it. She noticed one of the charms was a small key.

"It's the key to the cuff I've made you wear all this time. I hate that I ever had to make you wear it."

"I didn't realize you remembered the exact date I came here…or that it had been that long. You must really care about me, don't you?"

"I have grown a feeling for you that I can't begin to describe. You are the most beautiful girl I have ever met, and you gave us a beautiful daughter. I don't put much mind into feelings, but I would say that I have a love for you that I've never felt for anyone."

"Did you just express you love me?" Marie touched his arm flirtingly.

"That's not exactly what I said," James snapped. He had never experienced a love like this, and he didn't want to lead her to think he did unless he really meant it. He cared about her and was happy to have her in his life. He had a vision in his mind of how he would tell anyone such a thing and felt it best to wait.

"That's alright, you don't have to." She stood up and danced around in the field.

He followed her and as she spun in the moonlight and threw his arms around her waist. She jumped into his arms and wrapped her legs around him. He fell back onto the blanket and her hair fell into his face. They laughed together as they touched and played. She moved her hair and looked down at him. They stared for a moment before she leaned forward and kissed him. There was a distinct passion building that was left over from earlier that day. He knew she wanted him, but he insisted on making her wait just a bit longer.

"Wait, not yet. We have one more thing to take care of before we need to make it home." He told her with a smile as he gave her one last surprise.

# Chapter Seventeen

25 February 1798

It was a cool night in early spring, and one to be celebrated. Julien delighted in himself for staying out of trouble and excelling in his studies in the recent months. He waited with anticipation for Claude to bring him home that evening after his lessons. It was his twentieth birthday, and he was going to be spending it with Rosa. She always cooked his favorite foods and baked the best sweets for him on his special day. He looked forward to it every day throughout the year.

Claude picked him up earlier than usual, and together, the three enjoyed supper and cake by the fireplace. Rosa surprised him with the gift of a sewing machine. It was quite large, but she assured Julien that he and Claude would be able to get it to his workshop without a problem. She told him it was invented for the use of leather and canvas but could be adjusted for his use to better make clothes for his dolls. Julien was thrilled to have received such a gift and was eager to use it for his work. He had been taking the monsignor's advice and started a collection. Should his dolls sell in the market well, this would be an efficient way to make their clothing.

They began assembling the gift when Joseph came to the door. He was out of breath and very worried. He told them there had been a mass riot and that many counter-protesters and

French were hurt. Joseph desperately needed extra nurses and requested Rosa's aide. She quickly packed a few things and left with him in a rush. Claude prepared himself to help his officers, but Charles had already barged in the home in a panic. The king was requesting their presence once more, and he could only imagine it was due to the riot. Julien knew there was no time to bring him back to the church, so he promised he could be trusted to stay home alone.

He sat on the floor as he tinkered with his new gift. He began mixing and matching the fabric swatches his master gave him and compared them to different textured buttons and trims. His excitement grew as inspirations struck for new styles and fashions. A few of his dolls still needed an ensemble, and this new gift would make that possible. He made himself cozy against the fireplace and lost track of time engrossing himself in drawing designs for his future projects. When Claude finally returned home, Julien realized that the hours had passed like a single moment and was surprised by how late it had gotten.

"I didn't expect you to still be up, Julien. Has Rosa returned?"

"No sir, she is still out."

"I was informed it was quite the mess out there with all those gypsy criminals."

"I hadn't heard; it's been so quiet here. How was your meeting with the king?"

"He's enraged and somewhat irrational. This gypsy problem is out of hand, and he demands I do more to eradicate the problem. Why are you still up?"

"I'm sorry. I was really enjoying the gift you and Rosa gave me. It gave me a few ideas."

"I'm glad to hear it, but you really should be getting to bed now. It's late."

"Before I do, I wanted to speak with you about something that has been on my mind lately... I know this is a terrible time, but I've just been doing some thinking..."

"Is that so?"

"Yes, sir. I was wondering..." Julien began to stutter. His master's eyes were piercing, and it made him even more nervous to speak. He began to feel a twinge in his gut, but he did his best to be confident and brave.

"What?"

"Well, you've said that this city has a serious problem."

"Where are you going with this?"

"I want to leave Paris. I've given it more than enough time to consider it, but I want to travel to London first and bring my work there."

"And what do you think is in London?"

"They have a richer class of people; I can sell my dolls there and make money to travel around. I have been working on a collection of dolls to suit any girl for a long while now. I want to visit the world."

There was a part of Julien that felt Claude would understand and support him in his quest to fulfill his life, but his glare assured him that he was wrong.

"No, you are a servant in the church. You have a duty and can't just leave."

"But the monsignor says I am good at what I do. He's the one who suggested it, and I can still serve the church there. He just thinks I should take this time-"

"The monsignor is not your guardian, I am!"

"I live under the monsignor at the church, and he thinks I should go," he argued. The frustration began to build, and the two were filled with annoyance and personal rage. Julien stood abruptly and began to raise his chest as if to challenge Claude.

"I am the one who saved you from the streets! I paid for your food and clothing and room all these years. I raised and educated you. You owe me for that life!"

Julien could see the anger growing, but for the first time in his life, he was not giving up. They quarreled back and forth, and their voices began to grow louder and deepen in their furious rants.

"It's my life! I'm twenty years old now. I am a man, and I *will* do whatever I want!"

"Oh, you *will*? You seem to not care for my role as your caretaker at all, is that right?"

"No, that's not-"

"Julien, the day has weighed heavily on me, and your stunt is even more distressing. I will not tolerate this blatant disregard for your authority. Age doesn't make you a man; your behavior does, and you're behaving like nothing more than a selfish boy. Now, put your hands on the table. Since you've convinced yourself that you *will* disrespect me, I *will* remind you of your place," he commanded as he unlocked a cabinet near the mantle. His glare was threatening, and he pulled a terrifyingly small cane from inside and presented it.

Julien's body began to give in. His mind was faltering, and he could sense his bravery slipping from him as he watched Claude scourge the implement through the air. This one had been known to him as the 'blood whip', and he could feel its sting before it even touched his skin. It had only been used one other time and was remarkable enough for Julien to know it was the last thing he wanted to endure that night. His fear paralyzed him as his master moved closer. His heart began to race, but when Claude grabbed his arm to force him into submission, he found himself pulling away. He jerked from his grasp and stepped back with confidence.

"No!" Julien shouted. He surprised himself at such an outright defiance, and by the expression on Claude's face, he was even more shocked. It was an empowering feeling, and his spirit was on top of the world. He took a deep breath and stood tall in his soaring courage as he readied himself to leave.

"Don't you dare walk away from me!"

"I'm leaving and not coming back. I've lived my life your way, and now I am a man. I deserve to do this," he proclaimed as he shoved past him.

Claude grabbed his shirt, pulling him back violently, and they began to push and shove at each other. He felt he had the chance to escape, but Claude punched his stomach. A strong queasiness halted Julien, and his master took advantage of his loss of balance. He kicked his leg from under him and forced him to the ground. Julien let out a cry; his leg throbbed with pain. Claude took the cane and struck him continuously across his whole body in his fit of rage. The pain was unbearable, and Julien's vision became disoriented and dark as he endured the brutal punishment.

"The only *will* you'll be bending to, Julien, is mine. Don't you ever forget that again," Claude scowled as he walked out the door and locked it behind him.

Julien's sight faded in and out, and he struggled to stay awake. He curled up on the floor and closed his eyes. The cold air blew through the home, and his muscles twitched as the winds pressed the fabric of his clothes into his wounds. He stayed there, motionless, until moments passed, and he woke to someone helping him to the chaise and onto his stomach.

Suddenly his body was overwhelmed by a powerful stinging. Whoever helped him was now cleaning the fresh cuts the switch left on his back. He could see small feminine hands through his blurred vision and let out a sigh of relief.

"Rosa?"

"No, now stay quiet and look down," the woman commanded him.

"Who are you?" His body began to shake with a whole new fear at the thought of what his master would do if he found out he had drawn attention to strangers in his fit.

"Never mind that. Now, tell me who you are, and what you did to upset the man who owns this house," she inquired.

"I am no one, just a dumb fool. We fought, because I am stupid and challenged his authority. I really shouldn't say any more than that. Are you a passerby? Did you hear me cry out?" Julien worried about getting caught and hoped the woman was the only witness.

"I am nobody as well, and I think the whole town could hear you. You carry on like a child. I understand how much it can hurt, but you need to control your reaction before you get yourself into deeper trouble one day. You should just stop screaming, and... men like him usually grant mercy when you concede. Now lie still and face down. The patriarch of this house could return very soon, and I know he wouldn't appreciate me in his sitting room."

"He doesn't like anyone to know I come here, so I'm sure you are right. Why can't I look at you? How do you know that will work?"

"Because, as it's quite obvious, I don't want you knowing who I am and telling anyone I came here. My master has done the same to me, and I'm certain he would do it again should he find out that I am not where I'm supposed to be."

"I won't tell anyone. You can trust me."

"I don't trust you," she snapped.

"I apologize, but thank you for helping me. I'm sorry to hear that anyone would put you through such a horrid thing. You sound beautiful," he whispered. He could hear a faint sigh from her and knew she must have suffered a great deal to be so compassionate towards him.

"Don't ever mention me to anyone, or we're both dead. Do you understand?"

"Yes, thank you."

"I'm done. Now lie your face into the pillow and count if you can. If not, sing a lyric you favor. I really don't care what you do so long as you keep your face down."

"Alright, if that's what you want."

"And I suggest you put a clean shirt on," she advised.

"Can I at least know the name of the girl that helped me?"

"I suppose there is no harm in sharing a common name. It's Marie. Now, please keep your promise," she demanded quietly.

"That's a lovely name. One…Two…" Julien counted as she requested, and when he looked up, she had disappeared. He wanted to know who she was and why she would help him. No one had ever come to his cries before. He ran to the door, but no one was outside. He was too afraid to go beyond the door, so he ran back to change like she had instructed and cleaned the mess from the rags she used to clean him.

His head circled with questions as he sat by the fire. He looked up and noticed the lock on the cellar was gone. Could that be the secret he had forgotten? Impossible. He realized he had not thought of that room in over two years. Nothing had happened since that one night that raised any suspicion, and he couldn't be sure there was any reason to question its relevancy now. Maybe it was a spirit, a guardian angel sent to finally protect him. He stared at the door wondering for what seemed like hours when he suddenly felt a hand on his shoulder.

"What are you still doing up," Rosa questioned, "it's very late."

"I'm sorry, I'll be off to bed."

"Where is the master? Has he not returned from the king?"

"He did, but then he went out again."

"Oh…" Rosa noticed the cabinet near the mantle had been unlocked, and watched as Julien dazed toward it. She shut its door and leaned into it. Julien's eyes looked up to her and he knew she could sense his pain. He felt shame, but his hurt changed as she opened her arms for him. He ran to her and cried as she cradled him gently in her arms.

"We really should get you off to bed before he returns, love." Her words soothed his pain, and he followed her to bed. She tucked him in as she always did and kissed his forehead. Julien realized he had no idea what it meant to be a man. He imagined men did not have their mothers, or any woman, put them to bed. He questioned his life, but it was the only one he had ever known. Claude taught him many lessons, but none of the world and how to survive in it alone. He did his best to get to sleep, but his wounds rendered him unable to even rest his mind.

As the light peaked through the window the next morning, Claude came to retrieve Julien before Rosa had woken up.

"You will get up, and we will leave immediately," he instructed grimly. Julien looked to Rosa, but Claude was terrifyingly firm in his command to not disturb her. He brought Julien back to the church, and together they carried the sewing machine to the workshop without conversation or even eye contact.

"I will allow you to keep this, but as an added punishment, you will not return home with me to see Rosa for at least a month's time. You will learn your place and where it stays. I never want to hear you speak of abandoning your duties here ever again. Am I understood?"

"Yes, my master," Julien let a tear fall, all he wanted was to run away, but he couldn't leave Rosa. She was everything to him. He would learn his lesson if that's what he had to do to see her again, but now it was more than that. He hoped to one day find the angel that came to him in the night. She was the only other person to have ever shown him any kindness, and he hoped to one day hear the voice of the sweet Marie again.

# *Chapter Eighteen*

04 March 1798

The week seemed to pass by quickly. Despite the last harsh winter and brutal morale of the city, there was one day every year that everyone would gather to celebrate their survival of the cold months. Spring was at its finest this year; the air was cool and provided the most calming breeze to counter the sun's heat. Light had barely risen over the horizon when Claude and Charles arrived in the king's meeting room.

"It's really too early to discuss business. I feel robbed of my rest, but this is necessary," the king complained.

"Charles and I typically are finishing our shifts by this hour, but I sent our strongest men home to rest in preparation for the day."

"It troubles me that we haven't found the leader yet. If you two can't handle this task…"

"We put our best men out to search for Nikolais. We will find the devil," Charles interrupted.

"It's been years! Over two godforsaken decades ago, when your father first led this crusade, Nikolais was nothing more than a mere boy. You can't honestly believe he's the only commander and wasting all of our resources on him," the king continued.

"His grandfather was a revolutionary, and his family was a part of the militia. We should have dealt with their offspring the way we dealt with them. It makes perfect sense the boy inherited the role, and that is why he is such a high authority in this rebellion. He leads every protest, and they protect him like he is their king. Who else should one suspect?"

"Then find him, damnit! We need to squash them. The city is crawling with these people, and I want this problem resolved immediately."

"And what would you suggest I do? We have done every single thing we can think of that is short of an outright genocide."

"I don't damn well know, Claude! That's why you are in charge of this! They have their annual celebration of drunks today. Cancel it! Give them nothing to rejoice in."
The king was growing in his paranoia, and ideas on how to solve the problem were becoming scarce. The queen, who often remained silent at meetings, stood up to speak.

"My dear husband, I disagree that is an appropriate way to handle this."

"You would," the king rolled his eyes as he turned to Claude, "Annalise loves lavish thrills and events, even when they are not her own."

"I simply think that the festival is the perfect way to draw out Nikolais. He finds excitement in provoking the soldiers as he can. Prepare for such a thing. A parade is the perfect event to taunt; many people and hiding spots. Wouldn't you agree, Claude?" She had an alluring smile when she looked to him.

"We have enough volunteers and soldiers for the event. Should he show his face, there will be no escaping," Claude promised.

She walked behind the king and reached her arms around him seductively, but as she kissed his cheek she looked up to Claude. She smiled, watching him intently. She did this often when he came to the palace, but she was becoming less subtle every time. She stood back and walked toward the door, staring at him as she left. It left an uncomfortable feeling in him, but the king didn't notice a thing. He dismissed the room to attend to the streets and proceed with the festival. Claude left feeling more under pressure than ever. Things had to change, and he had to work much harder to not fail his king.

He was quick to return home and eager to spend a moment with his family before the upcoming shift. As he opened the door, the entrance filled with the delightful scents of the kitchen. He could smell the fire from the oven cooking what was to be an early lunch and watched as Marie and Rosa prepared the meal. Gracianna, now just over two years old, played quietly with her doll.

When he sat down, she ran to him and straddled his foot as she eagerly slapped his shin to mimic riding their horse. He had brought the child outside of the city with him at night on a few occasions, and she loved riding in his arms. He lightly shook his leg and bounced her around just to hear her precious giggle. She was intelligent for her age and learned quicker than he had ever known a child to. Claude enjoyed teaching his daughter, and it was always a pleasant experience for them both. He lifted her up, and sat her next to him as he grabbed an illustrated book to read to her. Together they quietly flipped through the pages when a loud commotion grew outside. People were gathering and congregating in the streets as if they were getting ready for something.

"What's going on out there?" Marie asked, peeking out the corner of the window.

"The idiots' celebration is today. Now get back from there!"

She backed up, but was slightly confused. She didn't realize people still celebrated such occasions.

"It's the Bacchus Feast. It's a parade for everyone, but mostly peasants go above and beyond to celebrate," Rosa kindly explained.

"I remember it now. I miss things like that."

James struck her on the head with his cane, and she dropped the glass in her hand. She hadn't noticed he left the book to Gracianna and was now standing next to her. It startled her, but she more so seemed overwhelmingly annoyed.

"You've wandered in front of the window again. Quit day dreaming and do what you're told."

"Of course, Master..." she commented in a snide voice.

"I suggest you consider your tone, Marie," he glared, and she seemed to instantly regret her choice in a sarcastic tone with him. He was much kinder to her in the recent days, but she knew better than to push her boundaries too far. She looked to the floor at the mess she had made, and he kissed her head gently.

"I'm sorry, James."

"I know. Now, Graci needs to eat. Take her downstairs and make sure she gets an extra sweet from me," he smiled as he caught his daughter's curious glance. The child grinned back at him and continued in her story. Marie nodded and quickly picked Gracianna up and brought her to their room. When she was gone, James requested for Rosa to pack up enough food for him and Julien. It had been a few days, and he needed to check on him as well.

When he arrived at the church, Julien promptly sat at his desk. He was quiet and cautious as he spoke. Claude conducted his studies as always, and they reviewed his most recent lesson together. When he finished, he went to wash himself up, and Claude set their meal out. They ate without much conversation, but Claude had something on his mind that he wanted to share. He had waited for the right moment and even helped Julien pick up after lunch.

"I can see you really have been working on quite the collection of figurines," he began.

"Yes, sir. The machine has really helped the efficiency of making their clothes as well. I do appreciate it."

"You know, Julien, I did take your request into consideration. It's foolish to think you will ever leave Paris, but you do need to do something with all of these dolls."

"What would you suggest I do, master?"

"I spoke with the monsignor. He and I have agreed that you should sell them. We have set up your very own booth in the square. You may be a vendor during the festival," he told him as he watched his face brighten with excitement.

Claude had initially hoped Julien would remember he was not an affectionate man when he reached for an embrace, but he pushed past his discomfort and wrapped his arms around him. He could see his happiness and appreciation and sat him down to set a few rules before he was allowed to go. Claude went over their lesson on currency, pricing, and percentages one last time. He wrote everything down that would help and provided Julien with a list to refer to during the event.

"You must remember that you are a servant of the church. You may sell the dolls, but twenty percent of your profit will go toward the sanctuary. You will not move from your booth, and you will keep all conversations strictly professional, am I clear?"

Julien agreed. Claude was hesitant to let him out on his own, but trusted his control in Julien's decisions. He finished his paperwork and left Julien to prepare his dolls for transport to his booth.

Marie rocked Graci as she began to reminisce on her past life. She thought back on her memories of the festival her family used to attend. She remembered the wonderful food, the dancing and games, and the laughter of friends gathered in the streets. She began to miss it more than she ever thought she would. She recalled her mother selling handmade jewelry that she and her father would make together from the scraps in his shop. Her mother would create designs, and her father would do anything he could to make her visions come to life. She desperately wanted to experience that once more. She laid Gracianna down for her nap and quietly snuck upstairs.

Rosa was in another room cleaning, and there was no one within sight. She stood in the doorway as she watched the back of the crowd make way to the town square. The sun was warm and tempted her. The area was clear, and she was certain that no one would see her come from this house. She insisted on attending the festival and would be careful to stay hidden. She left a small note, and a rush of excitement filled her as she caught up to the crowd without being noticed.

# Chapter Nineteen

04 March 1798

The festival had grown in the years since Marie last attended. She was cautious in her search and finally spotted James in a booth near the stage. Certain to keep herself out of his line of view, she blended into the crowd so as to keep an eye on his whereabouts. The warmth of the sun filled her with an energy she had long been missing, and her nervous steps slowly transformed into a frolicking skip. She tried to keep herself hidden, but couldn't resist making the most of her day.

She tasted the foods, watched the street performers, and even let a kind madame dress her hair in flowers. The streets were beautifully decorated. There was music, and dancers in the street. Some people were selling their crafts like paintings, and sculptures.

"Some beautiful glass beads for the maiden? Try them on," a vendor offered. She admired them against her dress, but didn't want to waste the man's time.

"I have no money sir, I apologize. They are very nice though."

"Are you sure? They're quite the fine match for such a lovely girl," he complimented.

"I really shouldn't." She tried to return it but backed into another man in her struggle to get the necklace off.

"Those beads do suit you quite well," he told her as he handed the vendor a coin and nodded. His almond eyes caught hers, and she became flustered.

"Oh... thank you, but you really didn't need to do that." He was very handsome and had a friendly smile. His hair was thick and untamed, a nice change from what she was so used to seeing on the strictly groomed men she'd known. It wasn't long, almost to his shoulders, but it curled at the ends. His build was strong,

"I wanted to. The gold matches your eyes in the sunlight. I don't believe I've seen you around here, and I've been living in this city for years."

"I'm not really from around here." She walked with him, but did her best to not lose her sight on James.

"I see, that's probably best," he remarked.

"Why?"

"Gypsies aren't well liked around here."

"It's a bit frustrating when everyone makes assumptions about everyone else based on looks. I wish people would quit calling me that. I'm only half..."

"Really now? Mother or father?"

"Mother," she admitted.

The man smiled and brought his hand to his chest as he shared, "my mother as well."

"You're like me?" Marie felt like for once, someone may understand her. She wanted to know him more.

"It would seem so."

"I could have guessed you were Italian by those eyebrows," she teased. They were very thick and perfectly contrasted his face. He laughed at her silliness, and they both seemed to connect well.

"Is it safe to assume you are enjoying yourself this day?"

"Yes. It reminds me of many great times I had as a child. It's been so long since I've been to a festival," she continued as she walked closer to him. He was intriguing, and she began to get lost in their conversation.

"Niko my man! I'm going on now," a very small man yelled from in front of the stage.

They came together for a hug and the man introduced them.

"This is my best friend, Lee. A man his size makes for a good fool's entertainment. He's a big personality for such a small man."

"Very funny, jackass," Lee playfully shoved him, "help me on stage! I need to go introduce Natalya to the crowd. I'll see you in a moment, alright?" He waved as he made his way to center stage. His height and loud voice immediately caught the crowd's attention.

"Lee likes to think he's the show's ringleader," he told her as they watched the performance begin.

"Ladies and gentlemen welcome to today's grand event! Every year we look forward to celebrating the great Bacchus and his Feast of Indulgence with our fellow friends and family! We love life and all its small pleasures, but I know you aren't here to see my pretty face and listen to my lovely voice. I now introduce to you, the seductive, the mesmerizing, Natalya! Be prepared to lose your minds, men and women alike, at the movements of her body as you delve into her artistic performance."

Natalya pranced to the stage and began to dance around beautifully. She was mesmerizing to all, and everyone was staring at her. She moved with ease and grace around the platform. Wives in the crowd, especially the French wives were disgusted. She climbed onto the Official's booth and danced seductively around the post. James was appalled. She put her foot up on his arm rest to expose her leg and pulled a lace scarf from around her thigh. She tied it around him, who was mortified, then went back to the stage. He seemed shocked that she would do such a thing. Marie had never seen him so speechless, but seeing it made her uncomfortable. She tried to distract herself and enjoy what may be her only day of freedom, when he turned his focus back on her.

"What's your name?" He continued in his flirtation. His hands wisped and waved until a small yellow flower appeared between his fingers, and he gave it to her.

"Where did you get this?"

"Just a bit of magic," he smiled as she blushed. She wanted to share her name, but couldn't risk James ever knowing she had been there.

"My name is a secret," she whispered coyly. "I would rather you tell me your name."

"You don't know? See that sign over there? I'm famous!"

"Nikolais Quinn... That, sir, is a poster for your immediate arrest," she laughed, unsure if she should be nervous or intrigued.

"You can call me Nik."

"Alright," she giggled shyly as she looked back at the poster.

"Does that scare you?" His face was now close to hers as he stared into her eyes.

"I'm not afraid of you," she remarked as she shifted to nervously keep watch on James. This man made her much more comfortable than the one that would be waiting for her if she got caught.

Nik kissed her cheek and smiled.

"Well I hope you enjoy the show, I really must go, but I must see you again."

"I don't think that's-"

"I will give you time to think on it."

"Oh, no. You don't understand-" but before she could finish her sentence, he threw something down and smoke surrounded him. He disappeared. She gasped and smiled. She felt excited but then quickly snapped back to reality. She knew she would never see him again. She looked back to search for James but happened upon another face she recognized.

In the same moments, Julien was putting the final touches on his booth in a way that best accentuated all of his dolls and their things. He promptly began making sales. His shop was a success amongst the girls, and they all seemed to bring in their friends to get one as well. Many complained that the other toy shops and boutiques were far out of their affordability, but even those weren't as unique and well-made as Julien's work.

Each of his dolls came with a small hand-written certificate. They contained the name of the figurine with a short story of her personality or life to make each one special. The certificate contained a special number that could be found on the bottom of her foot. He also added the numbers of the doll's 'friends' so that the girls who bought them could make real friends as they searched for the owners of the other dolls. He had seen so many children playing alone from his window and wanted to bring them together. With his own money, he would even donate a few to girls that could not afford one. It brought a warmth to his heart, but he also began to grow hungry.

He momentarily locked up and went to find something to eat. He had never been to such an event and wanted to enjoy the festivities for even a moment as well.

"That smells so good, what is that?" He followed a scent that made his mouth water with hunger, but it was pulling him farther from his booth.

"Tomato basil soup, but what you're smelling is my fresh rosemary loaf. Try a piece," an elderly woman offered.

"Oh, yes please." He took a taste and used a silver coin he had earned to buy a bowl of the delicious dish he had just sampled.

"Did you enjoy the show?" A beautiful woman stood next to him at the table. She had long braids of thick, black hair tied in purple and gold ribbons and wore a bracelet around her ankle that sounded of tiny bells as she moved. He knew it was inappropriate for him to look, he thought of how his master would scold him for such behavior, but he couldn't help himself. Her dress lifted as she sat next to him, exposing her dark complexion. The bangle complimented her tone and looked so pretty dangling on her foot. He realized he was putting too much focus into it and forced himself to straighten up.

"I couldn't see much of it from my booth," Julien admitted.

"So, stand closer to the stage," the woman insisted. She flirtingly pulled him closer to her.

"Oh no, I really don't think I should."

"Here, have a drink with me. My name is Natalya, what's yours?"

"I'm Julien," he responded nervously. He had never had such contact with a woman other than the nuns in the church. They never paid mind to the servants, and were often strict and unfriendly, especially towards him. This woman was very friendly, and seemed to smile often. She had a light and happy expression that was contagious to anyone near her. She handed him the pint and moved even closer to him, their bodies almost touching.

"Thank you." Her eyes were a beautiful light hazel and green tint, unlike most gypsies who had dark eyes. Hers were exquisitely rare, and he couldn't force his gaze from them.

"I've never seen such pretty eyes on anyone before," he complimented.

"Why, thank you. These pretty eyes have never seen you around town before. Are you visiting?"

"Yes, I'm just a vendor today. I don't live in the city." Julien didn't want to lie, but he had made a promise. Nonetheless, she would never be allowed to visit him.

"What are you selling?"

"Dolls. They're made of hardened clay, but I paint them to look porcelain."

"That's amazing. Can I see?"

He didn't understand her excitement, but he brought her over and showed her. No one had ever looked so enthusiastic in seeing his collection or listening to the things he had to say about them. She read every certificate and seemed to really appreciate his work. She looked at them all, handling them with care and admiration. Her pleasant interaction surprised him, and he simply watched her smile as she browsed his small shop. She picked up a smaller one with an elaborately painted face and long black hair that had beads and bells on her dress.

"This one is my favorite. She reminds me of my younger sister."

"Looking at that one, I think of you. I couldn't imagine another human as beautiful as you. Is your sister a performer as well?"

"No, she died very young during a plague outbreak years ago."

"I'm very sorry. Here, you should have it as a remembrance."

"That's very sweet of you," she smiled.
A rather small man called her over, it was her time to get back on the stage.

"That's Lee, he may not be the ringleader, but he's the best at directing everything. I must get back, but I hope you enjoy the show," she told him as her eyes locked with his. Her smile was indeed contagious, and it spread to his face rapidly. She touched his cheek, which caused an odd sensation in his gut. His nerves paralyzed him as she leaned in close to his face, her lips almost touching his. His eyes widened. He didn't know what she was trying to do, no one had ever been that close to him. He wasn't sure how he was supposed to feel and stood frozen. She must have sensed his confusion, because she stopped and took a step back, smiling coyly at him. He felt an overwhelming energy from her and was nearly breathless as she danced away onto the stage.

As Julien watched her, he overheard a conversation behind him. A man was performing slights-of-hand to impress a girl and pulled a small yellow flower out of thin air. She seemed to be amused by his tricks, her eyes sparkled in the sun, and her cheeks blushed. They spoke for a moment, but just as Julien could see the two connecting, Lee called out from the stage. The man kissed the girl's cheek and threw down a bottle that surrounded him in a misty smoke. He disappeared as everyone gasped in disbelief, and the small group around them clapped. Julien joined in as he watched the girl in her confusion, but then their eyes met. She was very lovely but was giving him a strange look in return. It was as if she'd seen a ghost, and she quickly made herself lost to the crowd.

There was something very peculiar about the way she looked at him. He wanted to run after her, but he noticed Natalya on the stage and became entranced. He watched her every graceful movement as she twirled on stage. She grabbed his attention, and their eyes met multiple times as she danced. He had quickly forgotten the mysterious girl and searched for Natalya when she finished. He had to speak to her again; he wanted her to know how beautiful he thought she was.

"Lee, I need a break. It's getting hot out here, and I'm tired," Natalya called out as she went behind the tower through an alley to get away from the crowd, but another had followed her as well.

Charles stalked behind her. He began muttering offenses at her and grabbed her. She tried to push him away, but he pulled her closer and twisted her arm back violently.

"You are quite lovely in the way you dance. Tell me, do you move that way on top of a man?"

Natalya pushed harder in her fight to escape him, but he was an overpoweringly larger man than her. She bit his hand in an attempt to scream, but her efforts hardly affected him. Suddenly, another man approached the scene.

"Get off of her!" Julien punched Charles as hard as he could. He jerked him away from the woman, and she was able to get free. "Now, run! That way," Julien told her as Charles began to fight back. She ran to the end of the alley to catch her breath and could hear Charles yelling for help. The other soldiers hastily arrived to subdue him. Natalya tried to go back, but Nik had witnessed the trouble and stopped her. He showed her that they were far outnumbered and couldn't save him. Reluctantly, she left with him, and Julien was arrested and brought to Claude in the square.

The people became unsettled by men fighting across the stage, and Marie could see that James was angry. He was leaving his post, and his soldiers were beginning to fill the square. She struggled to push through the crowd, but managed to escape the festival unseen and ran home. When she got back she tried to sneak in, but Rosa was waiting nervously as she came through the door. Rosa jumped up and pulled her in the house.

"Where have you been? Are you mad?"

"Don't worry Rosa, I kept an eye on James the whole time and stayed out of his view. I made sure to leave long before him."

"You put us both at risk, if he finds out..."

"He won't, but in the chance that he was to know, it's my head, not yours. I promise," Marie assured her.

Rosa, still upset, started setting up for supper.

"Did you at least have fun?"

"It was amazing! The food was so good, and this old man even gave me this," Marie exclaimed as she held up the beaded necklace to show Rosa.

"It suits you well."

"That's what he said as well," Marie dazed as she smiled and looked about thoughtlessly, twirling herself down into a chair at the table.

"Who did?"

"What?" She realized she had gotten lost in her thoughts and wasn't sure of what she may have just accidentally slipped.

"Who told you that? I'd assume the old man, but you did this weird thing with your face when you said 'he', so I don't think it was him."

"What thing?"

"You were blushing, child. And you still are," Rosa teased.

"It doesn't matter. He disappeared in the smoke before I could find out more about him, and that's a good thing," she fibbed. She didn't want to admit she had become smitten with a wanted man, but she also knew she could never put Rosa at risk by leaving either.

"I'm sorry, dear, it's better this way. You have to promise you won't do that to me again. You really gave me quite the fright. If he had returned before you, or if anything had happened to you..."

"I know I broke your trust. I am so sorry, Rosa," she apologized as she helped her finish supper.

James returned late, and Rosa and Marie both sat uneasily in their seats, anxious to know for sure if she had gotten away with her adventure. They quietly ate their meal, but James was tense and had hardly touched his food. He pushed his plate aside and requested that Marie follow him to her room. He took his time as he entered the room and watched as she slowly changed into a more comfortable dress.

He stood behind her as she unlaced her gown and twirled her hair around his fingers to firmly pull her head back onto his shoulder. He kissed her exposed neck, grabbing at her waist tightly. He became engrossed in his passion and was desperate to have her for his pleasure. His body pressed hers into the bed, but he quickly shoved her onto her hands. He kissed her as he leaned over her and lifted the skirt of her gown over her back. The excitement of doing something risky and not being caught helped her to truly enjoy the position he'd put her in. His grip on her hair tightened as his other hand held her down, but she had other thoughts as he moved inside of her.

She felt excited and anxious. She had a secret: the first she'd ever felt was important to keep hidden. Nik's face began to contaminate her thoughts. His smile was cunning, and his dark eyes made her weak. She felt a flutter as her body seemed to recall the way it felt when he had merely kissed her cheek. She imagined him in James's place, and it made her tremble. She grabbed the bedding tightly with one hand and covered her mouth with the other to prevent herself from saying Nik's name aloud. And in that moment, she realized she had to extinguish the fantasy. It would never be real, and she had to forget him. The reality of the situation left a disappointing burn in her chest, and when James had finished, she rolled to her side of the bed without much thought. James finished undressing and then sat next to her as he tried to talk with her and held her hand as he made himself comfortable.

"Where is your bracelet?"

Marie had always worn it, and James always noticed when she wasn't. She felt around, knowing she had been wearing it that morning.

"Oh, it must have fallen off, and Graci took it to play with, she loves that thing."

"Well it was very expensive, stop letting her have it. It's not a toy," he scolded.

"I'm sorry, sir. I'll get it in the morning."

"It's alright. I must retire for the night; would you like me to stay in here?"

"Of course. Goodnight, sir."

He kissed her on the forehead and laid back. She pulled herself under the blanket and curled up close to him. He fell asleep quickly, but Marie struggled to rest her mind. She was filled with excitement and anxiety. She had to find that bracelet but couldn't stop thinking about the day she had. She decided to get her fill of the joy she felt from it that night, because come morning, she had to realize it could never happen again.

Only a few hours passed before Claude woke for the day. It was still dark outside, and everyone was sleeping soundly. He left for the courthouse without waking them and met Charles in his chambers. He was anxious to get started. There was a rage growing in the pit of his stomach; it felt like both anger and sickness at once. Claude had been so careful over the years to hide his family's indiscretions, and Julien's stunt could risk exposing the lie and leave a stain on his reputation.

"Charles, move Julien to the front of the schedule. I want the bastard dealt with today," he commanded.

"Yes, of course, sir," Charles maliciously agreed.

# Chapter Twenty

20 August 1778

When countries were at war, governing bodies often implemented a draft to recruit its best men to fight and defend their land and honor. This typically applied when men were needed on its borders or in foreign territory to fight opposing forces, however France had become at war with itself. The king drafted his men against the other French who stood against the crown. The opposition was small and weak, but the king wanted to ensure it stayed that way. He imposed a recruitment upon France's best to keep watch in the night, and amongst this group of elites was Claude and Charles.

Every night they led patrols to suppress attempts at building a stronger rebellion, but there seemed to be a growing problem. More and more issues arose, and the king was in desperate need of more affirmative actions and willing men. Despite Claude's hard work as a lawyer and sheriff, the king demanded more from him. He could pick up on sounds better than most people and had a strong sense of hearing that suited him well for night patrols. His father was a charming, yet cruel man who had begun a reign of terror in the prior years to anyone who stood against his crusade. Their similar features made Claude the perfect candidate to one day manage the city of Paris in his stead.

"He swore they would be coming in at the northern side of the forest," Charles whispered.

"And this informant can be trusted?"

"As much as any gypsy that doesn't want to hang can be," he laughed.

They headed towards a sound coming from the woods, and Charles jumped onto his horse. The men stalked the scene and waited in the dark until finally a small carriage drove to right outside the woods, barely able to be seen in the moonlight. It stopped, and three figures appeared to unload some bags and cages. The carriage disappeared back to the woods as fast as it had come. They appeared to be smuggling exotic creatures into the city. Claude and Charles charged to surround the group and his stomach turned at the things they uncovered. Weapons and emaciated creatures were crammed into small holdings, but despite the evidence, the offenders denied their crimes.

"Please, we have done nothing wrong! The driver left those things, but they don't belong to us. The animals are safe and legal. I have their certificates," one of the men pleaded.

"It is also illegal here to be out after dark. And what about your papers?"

"We are citizens of France. We weren't aware we needed any."

"You are clearly not French. Therefore, you need proof of citizenship," Charles snarled.

"Please! We will get the proper documentation immediately," the third man tried to negotiate, but his cry was useless. Claude refused to listen.

"It's too late, Charles, arrest them."

As they gathered the gypsies to the hold, a man on a horse raced towards Claude. He was hurried and nervous. Charles raised his sword in preparation for an attack, but as the man got closer, Claude recognized him. It was Joseph; he was alerting Claude to his father's grave condition and insisted he come with him. Claude jumped on his horse and quickly followed to Joseph's family's private hospital. He ran through the halls behind Joseph to Augustus's room and fell to the bedside.

"Father?"

"My son! Come! Take my hand," Augustus beckoned.

"How long have you been sick?"

"I have been ill for a while. Unable to be cured, and now, I am dying."

"Of what? How long have you known of this? I don't understand why have you not told me before now," Claude panicked. He was very close to his father and hurt at the thought of losing him so unexpectedly.

"Because, my son, it was my weakness that has led me here. I have felt true shame."

"For what? What has happened to you?"

"I have missed your mother deeply and felt the sting of loneliness. I gave into a gypsy's tempting powers and lusted," Augustus confessed. He was weak and low on energy to explain much, but he tried his best.

"She bewitched you! Your love is for my mother, and the demon took advantage of your grief."

"She did, but son, that's not my true transgression." Claude couldn't believe his father could be capable of anything more and held his breath as his father explained what happened after he discovered his illness.

"Months ago, I was beginning to decline in my health. When I was told, I had an idea of where I had gotten the disease, so I called on her. Instead of repenting her sins, she came to me with a baby, swearing it was mine. She wanted me to pay for it and claim it to the world. I was already angered from my health, so I struck her down hard. I lost all control in my hurt and despair. It was only a moment after that I realized she was dead," he gasped. His breathing turned heavy, and Claude cried for his father's soul.

"It was an accident, but nonetheless, I killed her. I'm so sorry I failed you, James."

"You have never called me that before."

"Your mother loved that name, she insisted on calling you that. It's what she would want me to do. I need to make one last request of you, my dear James."

"What can I do for you, father?"

"I left the baby to the monsignor. We were once great friends, but he can't keep it there. The baby must be taken care of. In anger I left it, but I realize now that it must be taken in by family."

"But you are in no condition to raise a child."

"I can't, but once many years ago, I denied Rosa the ability to ever have children of her own. I did care for her once too. After your mother died, her mother tried to hold on, but after her death, Rosa was all that was left. Before I die, I will give her this child."

Augustus continued to beg him, despite Claude's attempts to assure his father that he would find the baby a good home. He was desperate to convince his son this was the only way.

"Please this is my only dying request. I will not be allowed into the gates of heaven until the baby is safe with Rosa," he pleaded.

"Indulgences, father. We have plenty of money."

"I am afraid that won't do for this. The child is your brother, and this is the only way. Please, Claude, save my soul. He is an innocent child, and you can train him like I trained you to be a great man. You have great power, and I know you will be the firm hand this half-gypsy offspring needs to be just as good. It's all I need from you, my son."

His mind was spinning with the new information. He suddenly wiped his tears and went to the Monsignor. He would do anything for his father, even though he had no interest in this baby being a part of his life. Claude arrived late that night to the church. He explained his new discovery to the monsignor but was resistant in his words. Claude had a vision for his life and an order he intended to follow.

He worried of the scandal that would be rumored should he bring a child into his home. He was nineteen and unmarried with a single housemaid now. He considered sending her away with the baby, but she was like family to him. Abandoning her or the child was not an option, so he struck a deal. If he kept the boy in his home, the monsignor would take him in when he was of age to serve in the church. Servants were given a bed and meals, but Claude would be responsible for providing education and clothing. Hesitantly he shook on the deal.

Claude was reluctant to receive the child, but he brought him to Rosa as his father so desperately desired. He handed her the baby when he arrived home that night.

"What is this? Whose baby is this?"

"Father's. He lusted with some whore," he explained angrily.

"Oh, I see. And where is the master? Is he going to keep it here?"

"He left it for you to care for, to pay a debt he feels he owes you. It can stay until he's old enough to live in the church. As a penance, he will serve there for his mother's sins. You will help me keep this secret, and no one can ever see it. Father will be gone within a matter of weeks."

"What?"

"She diseased and cursed him," Claude scowled.

"Such an evil thing to do. I am sorry for him. So, the child is mine now?"

Claude nodded as he left her for the night. Rosa looked down at the baby sadly. She cared for the Master Augustus and was eager to care for his baby, but she knew he would not have an easy life. She named him Julien and wrapped him in a soft blanket as she brought him to her room.

"On this day, the seventh of March 1798, we the jury find Julien, no know family name, guilty of abandoning his church duties and attacking an officer of the law," Claude heard as he brought his attention back to the trial presently taking place. Over the years he began to pay less and less mind to any evidence or facts of the hearings; the jurors were always selected in Claude and the king's favor. For hours that day Claude struggled to pay any attention.

"Thank you. Let us recess while the jury deliberates sentences and when we return, they will announce as many as possible today."

"Yes, your honor."

"This court is now in recess," the judge announced.

As the crowd of people scattered out of the room, Claude stayed for a moment to write something on a piece of parchment, and Anthony walked with him as they met one of the jurors outside of their meeting room. He handed the man the paper, and they quickly parted ways.

"What was that sir?" Anthony inquired; he followed Claude's ways and was curious to all of his dealings.

"The jury often seeks my advice on how some prisoners should be dealt with. I give them any help I can."

"Is that not illegal?"

"Anthony, tell me, when you burned down that home, why did you do it?"

"To set an example?"

"Precisely. Arson isn't exactly legal either. I am simply advising this jury on how to best set an example for the people, much like you did when you burned down that home with the people and even a child inside. Sometimes our duty to this city calls for what may seem like questionable actions."

Anthony nodded in agreement. He was truly beginning to understand. Claude could sense he was troubled and offered to pay for their meal at the tavern. Charles joined them, and they discussed the trials and any questions Anthony had. Claude was careful to guide him in feeling just and confident in his position. They finished their meal and drinks and returned to the court room to wait for the jury to complete their deliberations.

The typical punishment for any attack on an officer of the law was severe time spent in prison. In the moments of that court session, Claude was reminded of why he had begun the mission to destroy the gypsies. It pained him to punish Julien, his own brother, but it was his brother whose life was to blame for his father's death. He played the images back in his mind as he waited for the courtroom to fill. The jurors walked out one by one and stood in their position. Claude stood tall as he approached his bench.

He took his seat and then gestured for the court to take theirs as well.

"Members of the jury, you have found these prisoners guilty according to the evidence shown in court. We appear in this courtroom to assign rightful and just sentences. Am I to believe you have sentenced these persons who appear here today accordingly?"

"We have your Honor. For the crimes deserving of a public chastise to include, but not be limited to, the mark of a criminal branded on their chest, a flogging in the public square, and their name listed in the public post of dangerous persons, goes as follows: John Ellis for partaking in illegal protest and rioting at Notre Dame past curfew, and Julien, no known family name for the first offense of attacking an officer of the law," the juror announced.

"For the crimes deserving of time served in the prison goes as follows: Jordan LeJeune for impersonating a physician and the theft of opiates from the hospital. Hera, no known family name, for the repeat offense of rioting in the streets causing injury to soldiers of the king, and Terrance Jones for aiding the escape of known fugitive Nikolais Quinn," a second juror read, "and each prisoner's individual time sentenced will be posted in the square at dawn."

"Your Honor, we the jury have taken a considerable amount of time to discuss and think upon these punishments. These are our official decisions."

"And so, it is official. Sentences will be drawn out in the morning," Claude concluded.

"But sir, tomorrow is only Thursday, and those are usually handled on Friday," Anthony whispered. He tried to speak low to prevent from embarrassing Claude in case he had forgotten what day it was.

Claude, however, had not forgotten the date or the regular order of his court. He knew that it would cause commotion to change the schedule, but he had prepared to set an example to the people. He spoke loudly as he announced, "and they still will be. I told you all, in this very room, that things were going to change and less mercy would be shown to any offenders. With the chaos of the previous days, I feel it is necessary to take care of more prisoners this week. Does anyone have a problem with that?"

"No, of course not," Anthony mumbled.

"Very well. Then tomorrow will be the first in our new order, and it will be a very dark day for those continuing on this treacherous path. Court is adjourned."

# Chapter Twenty-One

08 March 1798

The house was dark and quiet. James was asleep in his room, but Marie and Rosa had not been to bed. They spent the entire day tearing through the home to find the bracelet. They were cautious as they continued their hunt in every place they could imagine it could fit. They worked tirelessly into the night without success and had given up hope that it would be found in the home.

"Well we've cleaned through everything today, and I can't find it anywhere."

"I must have dropped it in the city when the crowd behaved so disorderly. If James finds it out of this house he will know I left. I will have to sneak into town again and find it."

"If you lost it out there then it is gone for good. Someone would have picked it up by now."

"The vendor, maybe he will know if someone did. He was one of the last to see me out there."

"This is a terrible idea, child. I should go, I won't be in trouble for leaving the house today."

"And how will you explain searching for a bracelet that was seen on another girl? Or how you know me? People know you keep the house for James, and they may figure it out and then he will know you conspired in this madness. I am the one who messed up. I'm the one who lost it, so I have to be the one to find it. This is my burden, not yours, Rosa."

"There won't be as many people as the other day in the street. Wear my hood, it will make you seem like a peasant, and you'll less likely be noticed," Rosa advised.

"Thank you. I will leave soon after James." Marie prepared herself for another secret adventure into the city.

"It's Thursday, he always stops in the tavern just before 8 o'clock and is usually in trials all day, so he shouldn't be out in the city once he goes in." Rosa was nervous about sending her out, but knew there was nothing she could say to change her mind. She woke James and prepared his breakfast before he left for the day, but he quickly got dressed and left without even eating.

Marie followed behind as soon as it was safe, but when she arrived at the square, there was a crowd. She had expected the town to be in the court or going about their lives, not gathered in the town square. Anxiously she tried to find the man who'd given her the necklace just two days before. The vendor didn't have it, and she felt discouraged before she had even begun her search. She wanted to just give up when suddenly, a familiar voice spoke behind her.

"Are you looking for this?"

Marie jumped back and quickly turned. It was Nik, and he was holding her bracelet.

"Yes, how did you know it was mine?"

"How can one not notice everything about you?"

Marie smiled shyly and then looked around at the crowd.

"What's going on? Why is everyone here today?"

The vendor stood behind them, "it's sentencing day. They are about to start the public chastises."

"But I thought Thursday was sentence deliberation and trials. I wasn't expecting the whole town outside," Marie anxiously spoke as she searched for James; she had to be even more careful now.

"The judge is a sadist, this is wrong!" Nik spoke with contempt and explained the judge was rushing the normal protocol.

"I don't understand."

"He's losing control. He feels himself starting to fail, so he's working faster to destroy any who are different than himself whether they have truly done wrong or not."

Marie watched as they tied a man to a post and began. Looking at it, seeing the man bleed and scream as the guard flogged him gave her a nauseating feeling, and she couldn't stand another moment of it. She looked around at the crowd gawking and observing, and it disgusted her.

"I'm sorry, I can't watch this." She tried to leave as she watched the second man on stage being tied to the flogging post. She heard him call out and recognized the man's voice. She turned and stepped closer.

"Help me, Please," the prisoner begged out toward the judge, but James looked angry and just watched.

"Who is that on stage?" It was the same man again. Her heart dropped for the poor soul; she had seen the damage James had just recently caused him. She knew he had been at the house, but she still didn't know who he was.

The vendor once again interjected, "they are the prisoners found guilty of causing trouble in the city! They are being punished. The ones on the stage now will be flogged and humiliated. The ones on the left will be hanged."

"Yes, but I mean that one on the post now. Do you know who he is?"

"I don't know for sure. He is a servant in the church. He helped my friend from one of the disgusting guards, and they are brutalizing him for it. They need to be stopped!"

It made sense. He may be a servant in the church, but Marie knew he had been in James's house before. She had so many questions in her head, but no one to ask them to. If she queried too much about him and his habits, someone may become suspicious, so she remained silent.

Marie's thoughts were disrupted when she watched as Natalya climbed onto the stage. The gypsy dancer tried to help him and stood as a shield between the guard and prisoner.

"He didn't do anything! He was trying to save me from YOUR guards," Natalya defended.

"Get down from there now, gypsy, or you will be arrested for disruption!" Claude called out to her.

"Disrupting? Is this a joke?! The war you've waged on innocent people is the disruption!" Natalya turned to the crowd to give her speech, "this judge mistreats you, and his men terrorize my people! We must stand up to him! He is the real problem here!"

The crowd began muttering amongst each other, shocked at her boldness. Some started to cheer, others were disgusted, but they remained tame until another appeared on the stage next to her. The people turned in an uproar as Nik climbed onto the stage and joined in her protest. He was recognized almost immediately.

"Guards! Arrest the man and the woman as well. Arrest anyone else who interferes," Claude ordered.

"Go to the church! Claim sanctuary! I know the place well and will find you when I get out of here. Then... I will tell you everything I know of my master." Julien whispered to Natalya as she tried to help him. Nik taunted the guards and then ran to escape with Natalya. The soldiers charged to her, but as they got close, she lifted a scarf and twirled it around her. It fell, and she had disappeared

"Witch! Find her!" Claude shouted as they seemed to reappear near the cathedral. Her and Nik had barely made it to the doors in time, where the monsignor prevented the soldiers from entering the sacred house.

"They can't stay in there forever!" Claude, enraged by their escape, ordered a guard to post at every entrance. He shut down the rest of the sentences for the day and sent everyone on their way. When Julien was released from his punishment, he snuck back to his workshop and went to find the two fugitives that were hiding.

The crowd had become even more chaotic with the scene, and Marie could see James growing angrier. She froze, never taking her eyes off of him; this was a side of him and life in Paris that she hadn't witnessed in a long time. She saw as he turned her way but couldn't move. He spotted her, and they locked eyes in the chaos. Tears began to fall as someone pushed into her and knocked her down.

She stayed on the ground until the crowd disbursed. She looked up, and he was still standing there staring down at her. Without a word, he turned and left her there. She was alone in the street. Slowly, she picked herself up and forced her feet to walk back. She stared straight ahead, too afraid to cry, as the road seemed to narrow in front of her. She was unsure of what to do next; running or staying could both be fatal choices.

Claude reported to the palace immediately. The shouting and insults began as soon as he stepped his foot into the meeting room where the king and his queen were waiting. He knew the king would be upset after the catastrophe at the festival, but he wasn't prepared for what was to come of it.

"I apologize your majesty, but we had every single guard we could manage on those streets. We did everything as you commanded," Claude mumbled as he hung his head in dismay.

"As I commanded? I told you all to cancel the damned festival, but you swore to me that you could handle it! Clearly, what you did wasn't enough! None of this would have happened had you listened to me! You're failing me, and I've lost my patience for it. We've spent far too many years on this hunt and absolutely nothing to show for it, because you are soft. You're in charge, so it's you that is falling short! This is on you! I'm sending the Captain of my guard to ensure that every possible measure is being taken to apprehend this culprit! You're a real disappointment, and your father would be ashamed of-"

"Husband," the queen abruptly interjected, "I believe our dear friend has a grasp of your point. There is no need to insult him more."

"Damnit, woman," the king shifted in his seat.

"You're sending your best man to aid him, and that is all that can be done for the time being. You must have faith in your loyal and dear friend."

"Fine, but I expect a change soon. Enjoy your new partner, Claude. I hope he improves your results," the king scowled as he left the room to calm his temper. The queen stayed behind and smiled. She always took advantage of any time they had alone and was sure to make Claude uneasy.

"His paranoia has grown. Some might say he's losing his mind," the queen suggested as she moved closer.

"Speaking ill of the king is…"

"Don't recite laws to me that don't exist. That is what he makes the people believe to merely frighten the public into silence. You will not speak to me as they are spoken to," the queen scolded.

"Pardon me, your highness."

She stood as close as she could to him, and it made Claude uncomfortable to be alone with her. She smiled up at him, touching his shoulder, and her hand swept down his chest.

"Our king is going mad, it's alright. Deep down he knows it as well," she whispered seductively.

"I do apologize your highness, but the patrols are beginning and I must see that the captain is set to lead the first shift, but I need to take care of something at home first," Claude muttered as he stormed from the palace.

# Chapter Twenty-Two

09 March 1798

Marie walked through the gate just after midnight. She had stood outside of it for hours and couldn't make herself go inside. She looked through the window at Rosa reading to Gracianna by the fire. She finally was able to pull herself together and join them.

"You're far past late! Did you find it? You're lucky you made it back before the master. If he finds out…"

"He already knows," Marie stared blankly. She could feel her heart pounding in her chest. Even saying the words was terrifying.

"Dear God, child. What happened?"

"It doesn't matter. Before he gets home I need you to take Graci into your room and keep her quiet. I don't want her to hear anything, and she doesn't need him angry at her too."

"Marie…" Rosa's voice dropped with worry.

"Don't be concerned, you're not in danger."

"That's not what I'm afraid of. I'm surprised you didn't think to run."

"I'm surprised you don't think that was what I desperately wanted to do the whole way here, but I couldn't force you or Graci to suffer for me."

Rosa hugged her tightly and then picked Graci up from the floor.

"Come here, Graci. Go give your mother those sweet goodnight kisses."

Gracianna ran and threw her arms around her. Marie began to cry and put the necklace from the festival around the little girl's neck.

"I love you, my baby," she whispered as she handed her daughter back to Rosa.

Marie sat nervously at the table until James returned home. When he walked through the door, she stood up. She could feel herself shaking in fear of what was to come. The light of the moon surrounded his silhouette. It made him even more intimidating, but she tried her best to speak as he stepped into the home. She could see his face clearly in the fire's light; there wasn't a single emotion upon it. His lips were tight, and his eyes were glaring, but no way of knowing for sure how he felt.

"Sir...I..."

"Go downstairs... now," he commanded. His voice was calm, which was more terrifying to her than if he had just shouted or hit her as he usually did.

"Please, just listen," Marie hoped he would give her a chance to explain, but he slapped her face as hard as he could. She couldn't hold her balance and fell into a post. He crouched beside her and spoke in a hauntingly low and firm tone.

"I refuse to shout at you. You will get up, now. I said to go downstairs." He grabbed her and pushed her into the doorway, but she tripped and rolled down the steps. She felt a cracking pain in her arm. She desperately tried to pull herself up as she heard him coming down the stairs, but he struck her as hard as he could with his cane. She attempted to defend herself, but he kicked her down. She could feel him putting all of his strength into every hit, showing more rage than he ever had before. Her voice began to slip from her, and she was no longer able to even scream as she endured his beating.

Rosa shut the door upstairs to keep her screams from waking Graci and sat against the door as she cried for her. She wanted to protect the child; she knew it was her fault for letting her leave the house, but James would surely send her away for her betrayal as he often threatened. She couldn't leave them alone with him, but when she stopped crying, she realized it had become very quiet. Her worst fears flashed before her, and she ran downstairs to find James standing over Marie who was covered in blood. She knelt to the ground and held the girl who was motionless, almost without a breath on the cold floor.

James had not moved, his face was flush, and Rosa demanded to send for Joseph. The bleeding was too much, and the girl needed a doctor. Without his response, she rode as fast as she could to Joseph's home and beat on the door. She was panicked as she explained to him what had happened and cried of her fear that she had come to him too late. Joseph gathered his equipment and hurried to do anything he could to save the girl. They arrived back shortly, and neither Marie nor James had moved. Joseph picked her up from the floor and gently laid her on the bed. He wanted to treat Marie privately and shoved James back to reality as he told them both to leave the room.

Joseph tried to keep her awake to know if she would make it. Marie nodded, but she was weak.

"This hurts the most right now; I can't really feel the rest," she whispered. She stretched out her arm to him; it had been broken during her fall.

He gave her something to make her sleep so he could see where all the bleeding was coming from without hurting her more. When she was finally asleep and her breathing was stable, he turned her to her stomach carefully. Her back was covered in blood, and he did everything he could for her. He cleaned her up and realized the true extent of what she had gone through. He stitched any major wounds and covered the rest. He put a light clean gown over her and laid her on her side to ease the discomfort.

He had expected her to sleep through the next days, but as he cleaned his equipment, he heard a light humming from her bed.

"Have I heard that before? It's lovely," Joseph whispered.

"It plays in my head whenever life feels unbearable. The writer was a very emotional man, and he used his daughter's talent to introduce his work."

"Victoria Vincent? I remember her playing in London when I was there. She was the youngest cellist I think the world had ever seen. You saw her play?" Joseph was surprised to see her awake and wanting to talk at all. He sat on the end of her bed to listen to anything she had to say.

"You could say that," Marie mumbled. "I also heard they told her to play the violin because it would be easier for a young girl. No one had faith in her to be exceptional on that great instrument."

"Well, I'm glad she chose that for herself despite all doubt. Young girls are far stronger than they are given credit for; much like yourself, Marie. I'm very sorry. You don't deserve this," he said as he kissed her forehead.

"I'm not really certain of what I deserve, sir. I make quite a few bad choices."

"Does this happen often?"

"The bad choices? I'd say quite often over my lifetime," she weakly giggled.

"That's not what-"

"I know what you meant..." Marie struggled to sit up and get her glass of water.

"You really should get some rest; your stitches could only stop most of the bleeding, but not all. Has he done this to you often?"

"Never this bad before, but I usually try to just lie still, stop screaming, and he stops, but this time I would say I really made him angry."

"In all this time, why haven't I known? By the looks of your body, there is a lot you've been through. The scarring on..."

"I'm a stupid girl, and I've done a lot of stupid things. This was, by far, the stupidest. I really don't know what I was thinking."

"But that's no reason for this!" Joseph was getting angry, and the conversation became tense and awkward.

"I think I need to rest now." She knew how bad things could be, and she didn't need to hear it, especially from Joseph.

"No wait, I'm not getting angry at you. Please don't take it that way."

Marie laid on her side and pulled the blanket over her head.

"I'm sorry child... you should never have to go through this." Joseph went back upstairs even though he didn't want to leave her.

"This is just the way things are now. He owns my life, and even if the world knew, who would really care what he did to me? I'm just a poor, dead man's daughter with no real family left. You shouldn't even waste your breath for my sake," she reminded him.

Joseph couldn't accept that. He wished he knew how to help her right then, but there was nothing he could do. She was right; the Beauchene and Fontaine families had worked side by side for generations; they were two of the most prominent families in France. Who really would care what any of them did? All he could do was try and keep the girl alive.

Rosa ran to Joseph when he arrived upstairs, but his sight was set on James.

"She almost didn't make it. She's weak and her arm is broken. I've stitched her up where I could and wrapped her arm, but she lost a lot of blood. She was conscious and able to converse, but that doesn't mean she is safe yet. Her breathing is shallow, there's no telling what kind of internal damage may have been caused. I've put her to sleep, and she'll stay that way for a few days to allow her body to heal."

"Thank you, Joseph. Please, eat some food I prepared before you leave," Rosa insisted before she went down to be with Marie. Joseph sat at the table next to James and grabbed a plate. He tried to remain calm.

"I don't know what she did, and it doesn't really matter. She is small and can't handle that much. You should know and understand that much better than you seem to," he warned James.

"She tried to-"

"I don't give a god damn what she did! Next time she'll more than likely be dead if you lose control like this," he shouted. His fist slammed onto the table, and James realized what he'd done. He shoved his plate aside and grabbed his coat to make his way to the church where the fugitives were last seen.

# Chapter Twenty-Three

10 March 1798

Before the sun rose over the horizon, Julien had been released from the prison in front of the courthouse. He managed to leave before his master had returned and snuck back to the church before he could get caught. He wanted to help Natalya and her friend, but knew it would be a betrayal to Claude. He crept and crawled around the halls and spaces until he finally found the two hiding near the servant's quarters. He showed them a way behind the walls to get to his workshop where he offered a place for them to stay safely without being found.

They were shocked by his knowledge of the church, and he admitted that he was not just another gypsy vendor in the city. The truth was an interesting surprise to them as he told of his relationship to Claude and the life he had lived. Julien was saddened as they expressed their shock and disgust by what he was led to believe about his own people.

"So, he obviously cares about you so little that he makes you live here and call him 'Master'. Why even bother with you at all? Madame DuPont takes many children in," Nik remarked.

"His father made him keep me, to pay his way into heaven for lusting with a gypsy."

"Why would his father care about you? Or is it your father? I'm not understanding."

"He is my father and my master's. We are half-brothers."

"And this is how he treats you?"

"He may seem harsh, but he does care about me. I have a good life here," Julien defended.

"He has a funny way of showing it," Nik sneered. Natalya noticed Julien's wounds and jumped to try and help him, "are you alright? Do you need medical aid? I can clean this up," she offered.

"I'm fine, I'll heal." Julien grabbed a cloak from his wardrobe and put it on. He didn't mind the pain, he was used to it, but he hated for Natalya to see him like that.

"He needs to be taken down; it's not right what he does to the people."

"He only means to maintain order; the gypsies are the ones-"

"Do you even know what you're talking about, or are you just your brother's little oaf? Our people-"

"Nikolais! That's enough!" Natalya was sympathetic to both sides. "I'm sorry Julien; his family has suffered the judge's wrath. It still hurts him."

Julien felt for Nik. He longed for a family as well. The gypsies were rising, and maybe they could stop his brother from hurting more people. If only he knew how to convince his master that some gypsies were good. He wanted peace amongst the city. He loved his master, but knew Nik was right. It was in that moment he thought back to the woman in the square. He began to piece it together, but he couldn't know for sure.

"I think I know something that can help you," Julien confessed.

"What is it?"

"I go to his house every week."

"He's brought you there? You've seen it?" Nik's tone seemed to change.

"I told you, he does care about me. I go there quite frequently to see Rosa."

"Who is Rosa?"

"She keeps his house, but she is like a mother to me."

"Do you think she would help us?"

"I don't want to put her in danger, you can't involve her. I just think someone should check the cellar. There is something there; I've been told it's dangerous for me to question of what may be hidden. I think it may be a person."

"What makes you believe that?"

"I'm not sure, but I used to always play down there, and then a few years ago, he put a lock on the door. I think there is something, maybe even someone he doesn't want anyone to know about down there. He says it's just some old relics and family heirlooms down there, but Rosa has gone down there in the night many times. And last week I think I may have met them, but I don't know for sure," Julien mumbled. He didn't want to speak too much of that encounter. It was shameful to admit he was still disciplined as a child and didn't want them to think he was more of a freak than he already felt he was.

"That doesn't seem likely it would be a person. That's a long time to keep a secret when you frequently have guests in your home," Nik assumed.

"What if maybe she is hiding someone down there, a friend or family member? The best hiding places can be right under one's nose. This could be her secret," Natalya added.

"Maybe so. That's why someone should just sneak in and see without her knowing. But I'm afraid if I'm wrong and someone got hurt because of me, I would never forgive myself."

"It doesn't help if were trapped in here," Nik grumbled as they looked down the building to the guards below. "There's a guard surrounding the place at every corner. They are just waiting for us to try something."

"I can get you out. I've been here my whole life, I know of other ways out of here, but we can't go tonight. It's not safe," Julien smiled. He wasn't worried about the soldiers. He was, however, very hesitant, but also hopeful as he gave Nik directions to the home of the only family he had ever known.

# Chapter Twenty-Four

14 March 1798

The room was dark except for a small light. It was the reflection of a flame that danced on the ceiling above her. She envied it. It moved with the air as it pleased. It was a free and happy element, and she stared at it, dreaming of the sun and people dancing without care. She pulled herself up to be closer to it, but the pain from her wounds forced her to realize where she was. She would never dance or be free; the pain reminded her of that.

"I'm glad to finally see you are awake," a voice muffled beside her. She could barely hear it, like she was still dreaming. She closed her eyes and hummed her favorite melody in hopes her nightmare would end.

Her mind told her to just give up, to lie back down, and there was no use in trying. But Marie never listened to her heart. She opened her eyes and looked around to find that James was sitting next to her.

"How long have I been asleep?"

"Three days."

"Oh."

"Why did you leave this place?"

"I don't know, I just thought-"

"Impossible. This kind of disobedience is not the result of someone who 'just thought'. Maybe if you had truly thought about anything, it would have occurred to you that nothing good would have possibly come from this kind of act."

"You don't understand; I wasn't trying to be seen by others or leave; I've just been locked in the dark for so long, and it was such a beautiful day. I had no idea what was going on before I left the house, and I was surprised by everything that had happened. I wish I could explain... I don't know what made me believe it wasn't a completely stupid idea."

"Someone could have seen you. Your appearance makes you alluring to the rebels. If they found out who you were, they would use you against me. I thought you were intelligent, but maybe I have thought wrong all this time," he scowled as he stood to leave.

"Please, I'm really sorry. I won't leave ever again."

"I trusted you, Marie! How could you betray me? I should lock you down here and never let you out again."

"No, please! I'm begging you," she cried. She tried to get up and run after him, but her arm jerked her back. She realized James had locked a new cuff around the wrist of her unbroken arm and wondered how she hadn't noticed it until that moment. It must have been there a while; she must have slept on it, because it was warm with her body. She looked up at him, quickly growing dizzy, and she sat back onto the bed.

"Yes, I was very disappointed to have to get another. I thought I would never need one again. I should be going, now. I'll leave you to your thoughts."

"Wait, James! Please don't leave me. I'll do anything. Please," she pleaded with him. The room was growing dark around her, and she was afraid to be alone.

"There's nothing you can do for me in your condition. Joseph has warned me of how weak you are for the time being."

"We have shared many times together without such things. Or should I forget the times you've been so kind to me?"

"As I look at you, I hate myself for the pain I've caused you. You are so beautiful," he whispered as his thumb rubbed across her bruised face. "I love you and want to be with you. Rosa has prepared some stew, are you hungry? I will stay with you for a while until I have to go for patrol tonight."

Marie nodded, and he ran up to tell Rosa. She returned behind him with a tray for Marie, but seemed to be avoiding eye contact with the girl. Marie placed her hand on top of Rosa's. She looked up at her while desperately trying to hold back tears, but a few managed to slip before she quickly looked away.

"I'm sorry dear. I must go, lots of things to take care of, and Graci can't be left alone long."

"Can I see her?" Marie wondered if Graci had heard anything or worse, seen her in such a condition. She longed to hold her baby.

"Later. Rosa, can you please leave us for a bit?"

"Of course," she promptly, and meekly responded without ever looking up, like she was afraid. Marie wondered if she was worried more about what James was capable of, or the fact that she didn't expect to live beyond that night. She tried to eat her food as quickly and quietly as possible. She knew she had to be careful with any future actions or inquiries, but something about the other day was still nagging at her.

"James, would you be upset if I asked you something?"

"What is it?"

"When I was in the square, a man was calling out to you on the stage. I saw him look to you and call you 'master'."

"I suppose you'd like to know who he is."

"Only if you wish to tell me. I don't want to impose."

"He's the man that has visited every week or so. He was imposed on me when he was an infant after my father died. His mother was a gypsy that cursed my father with him, and I have taken him in as payment for our parents' sins. He has been blessed with a gift I cannot give to you; freedom. He has the freedom to roam wherever he wants in the church as long as he stayed there. He was even rewarded with visits here to see Rosa. A few days before you saw him, he had asked me if he could attend the festival."

Marie hoped James didn't know about her venture to the festival, and she was careful to avoid talking much about it. She shifted silently as he continued.

"I granted him the freedom once again to do as he pleased. He was able to sell some of his art for the church, and all he had to do was stay at his booth. The day when you saw him, he was being punished for leaving and attacking a soldier of the king. His betrayal hurt me enough, but then to see you there as well..."

"I'm sorry, James. I never meant to betray you."

"I believe you are sincere, but for now, as long as I'm gone, this is where you'll remain. As for this moment though, you need to get some rest." He kissed her forehead and then helped her under the covers.

"Yes sir, I'm sorry."

"And I expect you to never speak of what you saw of the man in the square to Rosa. Is that understood?"

"Of course. Never." She was confused by his request, but she dared not ask more. She felt she had already pushed her luck and was afraid to go any farther. She laid in her bed on her side, trying to fall asleep before she turned in a way that would hurt.

James sat next to her until she fell asleep. She looked uncomfortable, and it hurt him to see her in such a way. He had to make it up to her and hoped his actions wouldn't forever erase the beautiful smile she had just days ago. He sat with her until Rosa came down. She alerted him to news from Charles regarding the fugitives hiding in the church. She told him that he didn't share any information, but the look upon his face told her it was urgent, and he needed to come quickly.

# Chapter Twenty-Five

17 March 1798

Claude arrived at the church every morning like clockwork. His guards were surrounding the street and had been gathered since the fugitives first claimed sanctuary. No one was allowed to leave a single entrance or wall unsupervised. They had done everything they could, but there was rumor that Nikolais had escaped.

"Charles, how many guards are at the church? The gypsy witches can't hide in there forever," Claude growled. He had taken every precaution to secure the area and keep Nik and Natalya captive, but since he couldn't be there every moment of every day, he needed to be sure.

"The girl has made her presence known, but we haven't seen Nikolais all morning. We have twelve guards on each wall, and this man-"

"Ah yes, Captain Lemieux," Claude interrupted. "I'm so glad you could make it, and thank you for coming at such a short notice."

"Please, call me Ivan," he greeted, attempting to be friendly.

Claude couldn't put his finger on why, but something about the captain's appearance irritated him. The man was tall with tanned skin and blue eyes. He had a ridiculous, goofy smile, and Claude could tell he spent far too much time on his physical training than was necessary to efficiently fulfill his duties. It was clear he wasn't chosen to lead the king's guard because of his intelligence or wit, but solely on the fact that he was mostly blonde-haired muscle.

"Captain, please take your armor off and leave your weapons. I need someone to go check and make sure they haven't escaped," Claude snidely replied.

"My armor?"

"The monsignor has forbidden any armed guards from entering."

"I've called the sisters to meet in the sanctuary for a meeting so all quarters are clear for search, but I expect you to respect this holy house of God," the monsignor commanded clearly and would not tolerate any misconduct.

"Of course, Father," Ivan agreed.

He went inside and quickly disappeared to the halls alongside the building. Claude waited impatiently with his men, but after a half hour, he insisted the captain needed assistance. The monsignor, however, did not trust Claude to abide by his rules and sent Anthony to go in after Ivan. Within a few moments, the two men returned with bad news.

"It seems as though the female gypsy had demised a plan to help the leader escape in the night. She has been taunting everyone, and causing mischief. We could not find him anywhere on the grounds."

Claude, infuriated with this news, set Anthony up to lead a search party. He demanded they turn over any suspicious home that may be hiding the gypsy fugitive. They sent out their best search parties, and within minutes, a man had been caught in the woods near a place the hounds had last caught Nik's scent. It was past curfew, and he had promised less mercy to anyone who seemed to get in his way to finding Nikolais. Charles bound the man, and Claude led Ivan to their favorite place under the courthouse where Joseph had also met them for the evening.

"Captain, maybe you would like to perform the interrogation," Claude suggested. The king seemed to think the captain was more capable, so he allowed him to take over for the night. Claude was tired and growing weary of the hunt anyhow.

"Certainly, your honor," Ivan said to Claude as he approached the prisoner and immediately began punching and beating him.

"Now, I expect you to tell us what we want to know, or we could do this all night. The choice is yours," Ivan threatened.

"What do you want from me? I don't even know why I am here," the man cried as he was pleading for his life.

"You're lying! You were brought in because you were found in the area where Nikolais had last been spotted, and I don't believe in coincidences."

"I don't know this man you're speaking of, I swear!"
It was clear why the king had chosen Ivan; he was a brute during interrogations, but Claude, Joseph and Charles were getting bored. They went outside for a break and allowed Ivan to stay behind to continue his questioning. He continued to abuse and torture the man without clemency for over an hour, when finally, he gave up. After many fruitless attempts, he began losing patience and realized he needed to take things a step further.

"Since you seem incapable of speaking when it is required of you, I will ensure you never speak again," Ivan laughed as he pulled out a knife from his belt.

"Please! I don't know anything! I just came in from London, and I have my papers. What more do you want?"

"I need to know the location of the gypsy harbor and Nikolais." He pointed the knife to the man's face and was determined to get information from this man at any cost. He pressed the knife to his cheek.

"What are you going to do with that?" The man was afraid but he stood firm.

"I heard the doctor likes to cut out prisoners' tongues. Usually it's just to keep them quiet, but since you don't know anything, I think I'll just do it for the fun of it," Ivan smiled at the man as he pried open his mouth.

"You can't do this! Not all gypsies are alike and know each other. If I could help you, I would," the man screamed, but it was too late. Ivan didn't even care anymore. He snuck his knife in the man's mouth, but he jerked his head, and the knife sliced his tongue.

The prisoner began to bleed heavily, and despite his best efforts, the man bled out. Ivan called for help, and the others returned in a hurry to see what had happened.

"Why would you perform a procedure you know nothing about?" Joseph was angry. He didn't appreciate the newcomer using his tools to do things he was not capable of successfully carrying out.

"I know you hate my presence here, so I am trying to do things as I've heard you do them. I'm under the king's orders to do whatever is needed of me."

"I'm a doctor and this is my specialty. I can do it without killing the person we need to get information from." Joseph became defensive.

"He was useless anyway. I know what I'm doing," Captain Ivan shouted arrogantly.

"The hell you do," Joseph blurted.

The captain was offended and began to react aggressively. He raised his fist in an attempt to retaliate before Charles separated the two men. Claude pulled Joseph out of the room. Joseph didn't want to continue the night with the captain alongside.

"Claude this is ludicrous. He can't be here butchering our witnesses and prisoners."

"I mean, we were going to end up killing the man anyways. Why are you so upset by this?"

"Because he is using MY tools and invading MY space."

"And you think this is not an invasion upon my territory as well? What would you have me do? He was sent by the king personally, so he's in charge of things now," Claude shouted.

"Everything we've worked for so far will be destroyed in a single evening if things progress this way."

"Ultimately, he has the same goals we do; we'll just have to adapt, Joseph. You should get back to the hospital anyways, and I'll take care of things here," he sighed. He wanted to calm the situation before it escalated any further.

"Fine, do whatever you want," Joseph scoffed, and Claude went back to the room with Charles and Ivan and agreed to deal with the deceased prisoner if everyone just went home in peace.

From the shadows of the alley ways, Nik had escaped to the last place any of them would have expected. He stood outside of Claude's gate, but it was locked. He tried to break into the lock when Rosa came out and snuck behind him. She put her knife to his throat, and backed him into the wall.

"If you're going to break onto a property, you should try to be a little less conspicuous. I've been watching you scope this place out for nearly an hour. Tell me, what are you doing here," Rosa questioned as she pressed the blade into Nik's skin.

# Chapter Twenty- Six

18 March 1798

Julien often kept watch over the church at night. He would sit along the ledge just outside his workshop and watch the people below. He was finishing a very special doll for Natalya. He was proud of this one and wanted to show her. He searched the quarters and the church and heard a noise near the room of baths. Natalya was speaking with a rather drunk man. He was the captain of the king's guard, and Julien moved closer to hear their conversation.

"The way you touched me before, men have touched me in such ways, but it never felt like that," she giggled.

"So, you liked it," the man smirked.

She nodded and led him into the room, and the man kissed her. Julien could feel a pulling in his gut telling him to leave, but he wasn't sure if Natalya was truly wanting the man to do such a thing to her. He waited for her to push him away as she did with the other offensive guard, but she never did.

"You serve the king, you should be trying to arrest me," she whispered.

"Is that what you like? Because I can do just that if it makes you wet," he howled as he spun Natalya around and pushed her down to her hands and knees. He knelt behind her, spread her legs, and began vigorously rubbing her. It made Julien sick to see her in such a position.

"I've never fucked a gypsy cunt before," he told her.

Julien was confused; he was speaking such vulgar language to a beautiful lady like Natalya, but she didn't seem to be fighting this guard off. He was doing the same thing the last guard had tried to do to her, but she was letting him violate her. As the Captain began thrusting into her, Julien felt something break inside of him. He charged at them and threw the guard into the water and held his head under. Natalya grabbed Julien, begging him to stop. Julien was shocked and confused. He stared at her, and she looked afraid. He followed the guard as he crawled out of the bath. He kicked the man and straddled him. He looked at the mouth of the man who had spoken such filthy words to a beautiful woman and he punched him as hard as he could. He punched him over and over, there was blood everywhere. Julien looked up and Natalya was crying. Julien left them and threw the doll on the floor, shattering his artistic creation.

"There's a tunnel under the church, down in the cellar, and past the wine shelf. It leads to some woods outside of the city. I want you gone!"

"Please Julien, let me explain," Natalya pleaded.

"No, I don't want to hear anything you have to say."

"Please, just come to the hidden city with me, you'll be safe there from the judge, and I can explain this."

"The judge is my master, and you are nothing but gypsy trash. Get out," Julien shouted as he turned to hide the emotions he was feeling.

"I know you don't mean that. Keep this should you ever want to find me or Nik for safety. Please, Julien. I do care about you, I simply wanted to use his stance to gain information."

"So, you use men for your own gain? I'm not as stupid and naïve as you see me. You should go," he demanded.

His heart was breaking, but he took the small paper with a picture that she had left for him. At first glance, the picture was nonsense, but to anyone needing to find refuge, it would be understandable. She expressed that she wanted to stay and speak, but Julien felt it was time for her and the captain to leave. He returned to his room with a rage in his heart. He threw another doll he'd made for her into the glass cabinet and watched as its door shattered. He tried to clean it up before his master arrived for his lesson, but a shard cut his foot. Every emotion he had suppressed in the recent weeks flowed from the wound with all the blood. His anger surfaced, and he trashed the workshop in his fit. The tantrum felt justified until he threw a doll at the door and nearly hit Claude as he entered the room.

# Chapter Twenty-Seven

02 April 1798

Claude spent every night patrolling the city and the woods outward of the town. He had little patience and was willing to do anything to bring the people back for justice. They needed Nikolais to find the leader and how they were getting people and weapons in and out of the city. Claude brought many gypsies in for interrogations but his tolerance was wearing thin. Unaware of the Captain Ivan's affair, he promoted him to lead out many patrols and interrogations. Some prisoners were helpful, others were not, but few made it out alive.

He arrived at the church and met up with Charles and Anthony. He sent Captain Lemieux and all the best guards to find her. He overthrew the Monsignor's request to keep out with force and weapons. It was late in the night and the town's people were in their homes due to the strict curfew. There was no help for the Monsignor or his church, and the soldier's raided the quarters and every crevasse of the building, but she was nowhere to be found.

"Sir, the girl has escaped the church. I've sent my best men to search for her," Anthony assured Claude.

"Impossible, there are guards surrounding every entrance and opening of the place. My men would never fail during a watch, I refuse to have my team being called into question," Charles exclaimed!

"I have an idea as to what's happened. I will get to the bottom of this," Claude assured him. He had a suspicion that he was certain to be true and immediately went to Julien's workshop.

When he got to the loft, though, he found quite the mess of dolls and glass smashed all over the floor.

"What has happened in here?"

"Nothing, master, don't come in. I don't want you to get hurt on the glass."

"My boots are thick, now, tell me what has happened."

"Nothing, sir. I just didn't get much sleep and knocked a shelf over. I'll clean the mess. I promise."

"Very well. I have word that the gypsy girl has escaped. The only one who knows this structure better than anyone is you..."

"I didn't help her escape," Julien fibbed. He tried to be short; he didn't like lying, especially to his master.

"Then how did she get out?" Claude was losing patience. This girl had caused enough grief in his life, and he was ready for it to end.

"I don't know..."

"I think you're lying, Julien, you defended her in the square before, are you defending her now?"
Julien's eyes darted around the room. He was nervous. He didn't want to get her killed even if she had hurt him.

"You have inappropriate thoughts of her, don't you?"

"No," Julien screamed!

"Don't lie to me! I know you helped her! She's a temptress, and you fell for it. You have lusted, haven't you?"
As he continued in his accusation, he could see Julien's emotions rising. Claude knew he was on the brink of confessing and pushed a bit more, but the anger surpassed his expectations as Julien grabbed dolls from the floor and began throwing them. His eyes seemed to widen as he picked up a small figurine, and in his passion, Julien threw the doll and hit him with it. Claude was shocked by his behavior and grabbed a cane from the wall. Julien began to fold before him, but the damage was done, and Claude felt he needed to remind him of his place once more.

"I didn't mean for that to hit you, I swear! I was just angry. Please, don't," he begged, but Claude was not forgiving.

"Put your hands on the desk," he commanded.

"My back hasn't healed at all from the punishment I endured in the square, please don't do this. I am so sorry, master."

"I believe my order was clear. I will be sure to not interfere with your back's healing process. Now, elbows down on the desk. Or do you want to test my aim when I'm especially frustrated?"

Julien took his punishment once more and felt defeated. The mere twitches and spasms of the muscles in his back were enough to throw his pain into an intensity like no other. He threw himself to the floor but remembered what the mysterious girl had told him before. He stayed on the ground and forced himself to quit screaming as he silently prayed for mercy. Claude stopped as she had predicted, and he threw a towel to Julien to clean himself.

"That woman is a whore! She will do anything to get what she wants, and you gave into her. That makes you worthless gypsy trash like her."

"Brother, please! I am not the one who-" Julien had never called him that before, but he thought if he did, maybe Claude would take back the harsh words he had just spoken and forgive his transgressions.

"We shared a father, but you are no brother of mine," Claude snapped. He put the cane back in its place and walked away, leaving Julien there without care or remorse.

James returned home late that night. Rosa was bathing Graci, but Marie was already asleep; her body was still frail and weak, so she slept often. He sat on the bed, and she woke up briefly to spend a moment with him. They talked a bit about his work and how she was doing, but James seemed distracted. His thoughts drifted, and she fell back to sleep. He laid next to her but couldn't rest his mind. He thought about the gypsies who had escaped and the pressure from the king to find them.

He thought about the woman who had sexually shown her leg to him in public. The skin was dark and appeared to be very soft. She was a curvier woman, more mature and not of the girlish qualities Marie possessed. She was sensual, experienced in her movements, and her hair was thick with a curl towards the ends. It flowed beautifully over her corset, which was smaller than appropriate for a woman with breasts the size of hers. He found himself more intrigued by her than he ever thought he would be. His thoughts disturbed him, and he was unable to sleep.

Marie woke again to find her chain was still unlocked. She knew James was close, and called out to him, but there was no answer. She was thirsty and went upstairs to get some water, but he wasn't in the kitchen either. She searched for him in his room when she noticed an opening behind the tall mirror along the back wall. She had never known about it or even suspected it to be there, so she looked inside. There was a hallway with a light at the end, and she quietly followed it to a room where she had finally found him.

He was sitting in front of a fireplace with his back towards her. He was moving violently in the seat and making grunting and moaning sounds. She moved close enough to see what he was doing and saw he was holding a scarf. It was the one the dancing gypsy at the festival had wrapped around him. With one hand he was rubbing the silk cloth, and with the other hand he was stroking himself. She was confused and upset as she tried to back up, but tears blinded her, and she ran into a small table. He anxiously turned to fix himself and then faced her. He stared at her for a moment, and she stood frozen. He had sinned, and she had witnessed it. He could feel her judgement upon him and became angry; this was his private room, and she wasn't supposed to be there. He charged at her and grabbed her arms. He started to shake her violently, but she slipped from his grasp and hit her head on the wall.

When he saw blood, he knelt beside her. She wasn't moving or responding, and he remembered Joseph's warning. He had lost control and was certain this time he had killed her. Tears rushed down his face, but he quickly composed himself. His despair turned to anger, and he knew of only one way to make it right; the gypsy had to die. She had caused him to sin, which led to the death of the girl he loved, and the mother of his daughter. He threw the scarf into the fire and left toward the church. Rosa saw him leave in a hurry and tried to stop him, but he was incoherent.

She rushed to find Marie and tried everything she could to get her to wake or respond but failed. She quickly rode to find Joseph, and in her hysteria and anxiety, she pounded on the front door until he answered. She was unable to stop crying, making it difficult for her to speak. It was hard for Joseph to understand what had happened, so he left without another word, hoping it wasn't too late.

# Chapter Twenty-Eight

23 December 1791

The theater was bright and busy throughout the entire day, and everything was almost ready. The Christmas Concerto in London was an affair like no other, and everyone was preparing for it. Workers had filled the house early that morning to dust and clean the seating for the event and ensure the lighting worked well. Dancers had spent the afternoon rehearsing on the stage while the orchestra practiced below. The day was coming to an end, but there was one that had not yet been allowed to leave. A young cellist was rehearsing with more intensity than the entire orchestra combined. She was small; much smaller than the instrument she played, but she performed better than anyone had ever heard. She was headlining the concerto, and her instructor expected nothing less than perfection.

She practiced her solo repeatedly and was forced to start from the beginning every time she made a mistake. The day had been long, and her performance was worsening as the afternoon progressed into the late evening. The frustration between the girl and her teacher began to fill the room, and it made for a miserable practice for them both.

"It's as if you're not even trying, Victoria. You miss the same notes every time."

"That's not my name... and I am trying! It's hard to twist my back and reach the stupid note at the same time. I'm too small to do both!"

"I don't care who you are outside of these walls, in here you are Victoria, and you will keep playing until you get it right. The concerto is tomorrow night, and everyone will be there. All I am hearing from you is excuses!"

"I want to go home," the little girl cried.

"When you play the entire piece without mistake, then, and only then, may you leave."

"No! I'm done!"

"Your father finished with the orchestra hours ago, because they had a very good rehearsal. You are not even paying attention. He has hired me to make sure you play perfectly, but I can't do that when you keep joking around."

"I heard this theater is haunted. They say a ghost spooks people at night, so we should go," the girl giggled, but the woman was not sharing in her humour.

"Play again, Victoria. From the beginning."

"This is the worst life ever! I am not playing tomorrow!"

"Then you will not only let everyone around you down, but you will let yourself down. There are people who have been playing for twenty and thirty years that would kill to be featured in front of the king and Pope Pius. This is the highest honor for any musician, and you should appreciate such an opportunity."

As she continued in her tantrum, a man walked into the room. He smiled as he watched the child in her fit and stepped in to try and cheer the exhausted girl. He picked her up and wrapped her tightly in his arms as he sat down with her to talk.

"I don't want to do this anymore. Please, let's go home," she cried.

"I understand you're tired and not connecting. Why don't we take a short break, and you can tell me of your partner?"

"He's not my partner, he's a stupid cello! I hate it, and I hate you!"

"He? Look, I know this is hard, but a nine-year-old has never once been considered to receive an invitation to play for the Christmas concerto. I have heard you hit that note flawlessly along with all the rest, many times. Now, my daughter, tell me about your partner."

The girl looked down at the cello on the stand. It stood tall, and its build was strong with dark stain. Her small fingers grazed the gold lettering of her name across the side; it had been custom built for her, as she was the youngest and smallest cellist that had ever played. She couldn't recall when she first began, but she always remembered a calling for the strings. Her father was a great violinist, and she had always dreamed of following in his footsteps. The first concerto she ever performed was standing on a chair next to her instrument. It was a simple tune, and she didn't play well, but her passion and skill for a six-year-old turned many heads that night. She had become the star of her father's show, and it changed their lives. From that moment on, her life became all about the cello. There were times she was exhausted and couldn't stand it, but she knew deep down it was what she loved.

"His name is Mirecourt," she finally told him.

"Like where we got him from? Do you remember when we went there?"

"Yes. Monsieur Didier told me he was the most special voice anyone would ever hear, because he is one of a kind and only for me. He is my partner, and only I have the magic to make him sing."

"My darling, you are more than the prodigy Victoria, you are my brilliant and fierce Marie. You ignored us all when we told you to find a more suitable instrument and defied the odds. You were much smaller when you stood next to that cello that was far bigger than your whole being and still played all those notes. We have nine months left of our tour. How about when we finish, we move to Paris where no one knows us. We can hang the hat on Vince and Victoria Vincent, and we will just be Vincent Adams and his mischievous daughter, Marie. You can play on your own time, but I will never make you perform after you retire, unless it's what you want. Would you like that?"

"You would really let me do that?"

"If you finish the tour we agreed to, then yes. I want you to always practice, but we can be done with this," he promised.

"I love you," she smiled.

"I love you too, now, we need you to be Victoria Vincent. Go, introduce the world to the melody we wrote together."

She kissed her father's cheek and positioned herself to finally play with every drop of energy she had left. She straightened her posture and inhaled the cool air deep into her lungs. She closed her eyes, her fingers lightly stroked over each string, and her nose pressed against the neck. There was an art to her routine, and Mirecourt became her partner once more. She opened her eyes slowly to the theater filled with strangers and looked out amongst the people. She could see her family and instructor, but she noticed a man and woman dressed in lavish jewels; it was the king and queen. She smiled at them, and they seemed to notice her, because they smiled back. She tapped her nose three times for luck, and they seemed to find it funny as they giggled to each other. She turned to the conductor, and the room fell completely silent as he stood. She took another deep breath and raised her bow to begin.

The theater darkened over the auditorium, and her vision narrowed on Mirecourt. Her magic brought him to life, and they were in perfect harmony. She gave her heart to the music, and it rewarded her with a melody like no other. It was her best performance yet, and she gave it her all as she captivated the souls of everyone who heard. There was an eerie silence as she struck her final chord. She looked above her and could see a ghost-like figure watching from the catwalk and smiled; she knew the theater was haunted.

And Marie, the great Victoria Vincent, took a final bow before her audience. She ran to her father in excitement as the crowd stood to cheer and applaud her. She hugged him tightly, crying as she told him how much she had missed him. He didn't speak, but he knelt in front of her and kissed her forehead. He smiled as he turned her around and pushed her back to the stage. Confusion overwhelmed her as the spotlight hit her face and nearly blinded her. She tried to go back to him, but he was gone, and her body began to shake from an unbearable pain.

# Chapter Twenty-Nine

03 April 1798

Claude raced through the city as he woke every able-bodied man he knew. His soul was slipping from him, and his demons were taking over as he gathered the soldiers to the edge of the city. He commanded them to search deep into the woods for any traces of where the gypsies may be hiding. He was on a witch hunt, and no one would get in his way. The king was right; he was soft and would continue to fail if he didn't change. He thought of his motherless daughter as he headed the largest patrol Paris had ever seen. Despite the men's lack of knowledge on why this hunt was necessary, they trusted Claude and could sense his urgency. His passion spread amongst the people, and they all began to feel as angry as he was. As he encouraged them, his emotions passed through every single man; they began to feel what he felt and hate what he hated.

The search excited them all. They flew to deep in the woods, and Captain Lemieux was the first to find a small camp of gypsies. He alerted the others to interrogate, and Claude and Anthony quickly responded. After scouting the area, Claude found it to just be a small, unimportant camp, and left the sheriff and captain to deal with it. He pulled most of the men as he led them on the hunt for something much bigger.

Anthony dismounted his horse, and the captain helped him gather the family. They tied them together inside their home.

Anthony attempted to interrogate them but realized they only spoke a foreign language.

"I assume these just came in from the Romanian lands... Usually they try to learn the language before pretending they're one of us," he complained.

"The Romani are from India, not Romania. Those are two completely different countries."

"I don't give a damn, Ivan... These people are useless, let's go," he growled in disappointment. He wanted to impress Claude and prove himself in his position once again, and as they left, Anthony locked the door behind him with the family still inside.

"Useless squalor!" Anthony was angry and grabbed his torch to burn the home, but the captain was uncomfortable with his solution and tried to help the family escape.

"If you go in there, you will be a traitor, and I will kill you like one, Captain," Anthony threatened.

"This is wrong, and you know it. These people didn't do anything criminal as of yet, and you didn't give them a fair chance to talk!"

"A fair chance? This is our duty, given by the king. You're not here to decide what's fair or not!" Anthony raised his weapon to intimidate Captain Lemieux but was unsuccessful. The captain punched the sheriff and knocked him down to the ground. He put out the fire before it spread and took the family in as suspects to be questioned.

"They deserve a fair trial," he huffed to the sheriff as he pulled them past.

Anthony trudged through the city to get a bandage for his eye when a messenger found him. The man helped him to the church infirmary as he relayed an important message to be delivered to Claude. Anthony tore a piece of his sleeve to stop the gash from bleeding and immediately found a horse to search for the judge.

"Judge Fontaine! Sir!? Has anyone seen the Judge Fontaine? I have an urgent message for him," Anthony called out as he rode throughout the woods. Finally, someone was able to lead him to Claude.

"Judge Fontaine," Anthony called out one last time before he finally found him.

"What is it Anthony? Claude is busy interrogating some gypsies we found," Charles snapped.

"I have a message from the monsignor for him," Anthony told him, who then promptly retrieved Claude.

"Sir, the monsignor wanted me to inform you that a servant is missing from the church and may have gone to join allegiance with the rebels."

"And why would I care about that right now?"

"It's the one that's been helping the fugitives we're searching for, the one that gave them sanctuary and then lead them to escape."

"Damnit!" Claude was even more furious. He was losing everything and slowly failing his entire mission.

"And another thing," Anthony added.

"What more could there possibly be?"

"The Captain Lemieux... I believe he doesn't support our cause."

"That is quite an accusation. And what leads you to this belief?"

"The gypsies we uncovered were uncooperative, and so I set to make an example that he did not agree with. He attacked me and brought the gypsies in for a trial."

"I see. Thank you, Anthony. I will take care of this personally," Claude nodded as he made his way back to the palace. Anthony returned the gesture and continued on to the search with a lot of ground to cover and no time to waste.

Moments felt like hours, and Rosa was becoming more worried. She didn't know Marie's condition, and Joseph refused to let her down to check. She tried to entertain Graci to keep her own mind occupied, but little was working to calm her. When he finally returned, he was very quiet with a grim look upon his face, and Rosa feared the worst.

"I very much almost lost her. She's weak, but she is alive," he assured her.

"Oh, thank you," she sighed as he fell into his arms in gratitude.

"The girl may be small, but she's surely a fighter. The head tends to bleed a lot, but it's surprisingly not a very big gash. It's most likely that the other pain in her weakened condition was too much for her, and she fell unconscious. I've stitched her up, but I can't imagine she'd be strong enough to endure anymore.

At this point, I truly believe she's living on borrowed time and growing even weaker," he explained.

"I swear I thought they were both asleep. They had been in bed when I last checked them. I just don't understand what happened," she sobbed.

"It's not your fault, Rosa. This is Claude; he has a problem, and only he is responsible for the torment she endures. I've done my best to get her through, but it's no longer enough to keep her alive."

"Thank you, Joseph. I will do everything in my power to protect her. I swear it."

"If anything were to happen to Marie, I fear for the fate of that precious child," Joseph advised Rosa as he kissed her forehead.

Joseph packed his equipment and left to join Claude's search for the escaped gypsies, and Rosa just stared down at Marie and Graci. She pulled out a piece of paper from her coat that Nik had left her; she knew exactly where he was hiding. She had managed to discourage his interests in what was hidden in her master's home, despite her pain at learning what had happened to Julien from the rebel. She had kept his family a secret, but Claude had betrayed her last confidence, and she found herself in search of his enemy, Nikolais Quinn.

# Chapter Thirty

04 April 1798

    Rosa rode out just after midnight in search of the place Nik had left for her to find. She knocked on the door of the marked home when she finally found it and Nik opened the door. He expressed that he was glad to see her have a change of heart and welcomed her in. He opened the door to her, but she stayed outside. She took a deep breath, trying desperately not to lose her emotions as she begged for him to come rescue another that was in much more need. Claude could return at any moment and find them, but she had to shove aside her fears and take the chance to save Marie. She promised him that it was safe, but knew that too many people might be overwhelming, and he agreed to come alone.

    They moved quickly and quietly in the darkness. When they got to the house, she checked to make sure Claude had not returned. His horse was gone, and it was safe for her to lead him inside the house to the stairs that led down to Marie's room.

    "What's down there?" Nik asked. She could see that he was nervous and understood the fear of being in his enemy's home alone. His fears of walking into a trap was obvious, and she finally broke herself down to tell him the truth she had been hiding for so long.

    "Three years ago, the judge Fontaine brought someone down there; a young girl. He's hidden her here, and she's been forced to endure him ever since." Rosa showed him Marie, who was still asleep from the medicine Joseph had given her.

"The judge has been hiding a gypsy sex slave?" Nik was surprised, but was even more taken back as Rosa pulled the hair from the girl's face. "Wait, I know this girl. I've seen her before, at the festival. We spent time together there. I had hoped to see her again but not like this..."

"So, you're the handsome man that disappeared in smoke."

Flattered, Nik smiled back, "she called me handsome?"

"No."

"Oh..."

"But I could tell she wanted to," Rosa smiled.

"Wait, why didn't she say anything to me then? I thought you said he was forcing her to stay here for the last three years? If she wanted to leave, why didn't she ask for help?"

"She's a child. She got out for an adventure after being locked away for so long. That's how her arm got broken when he hurt her the first time. She is afraid, but truly believes that he loves her and would never go against him.

"But if he does these things to her then why wouldn't she go against him? Someone could have helped her before it came to this."

"To protect her baby, she loves that child far more than anything and would risk her own life for her," she told him as she pointed to a small cradle that held the sleeping Gracianna.

"So, tell me what happened? Why now? I came here, and you sent me away. Why didn't you say anything?"

"I was afraid for her. I never imagined things would get this bad. I still don't know what happened this time, but he clearly lost control of himself and has hurt her for the last time. She'll die for sure if he hurts her again. I thought I was protecting her before. When you told me about Julien, I knew I had to do everything I could to keep her safe," she cried.

"She looks so young."

"Yes, she will be seventeen next week," Rosa told him as she rubbed her face with the palms of her hands. Nik became angry; he knew the judge was a corrupt man, but he never imagined him to be this evil.

"Help me get her wrapped up, and I'll carry her out. You bring the baby and whatever you can carry by hand; we have to go now," he instructed.

"Thank you."

Rosa woke Graci and dressed her warmly to keep her content. She grabbed what she could and followed him back to the place where the other gypsies hid. Marie slept the entire journey, and they found an empty tent. Nik laid her down inside on a small cot and left Rosa to get the baby cleaned up and to bed. It had been a very long day for everyone, and the group of refugees extinguished their lights early to get some rest. Rosa was sure to stay close by the next morning, and as soon as Marie realized she wasn't at home, she began to panic.

"Why did you bring me here? We belong at home. If we hurry maybe we can make it back before he becomes too angry." Marie started to gather the few things she knew to be hers.

"Joseph said you'd die if the master ever hurt you again. This was the right thing to do, I had to protect you and Graci," Rosa tried to explain.

"No, that's not true! I know he didn't mean to, I just walked in... I was stupid to go into that room. He won't do it again; I know he loves me." Marie was frantically pacing the tent and collecting her things. Nik had been eavesdropping and finally came inside.

"You're stupid if you think there's anything you can do to stop him from doing this again. It's just a matter of time before he gets worse to you or your baby," he interjected.

Marie was startled by the intruder, but she seemed to almost instantly recognize him. Rosa held her hand and convinced her to settle for a moment as they sat on her cot. She smiled to Nik, and he smiled back and knelt down next to her. They worked together to comfort Marie and assure her that they were right; she couldn't survive with James any longer.

"I came to make my family safe, I can't leave him now. He'll find me," she mumbled.

"We can make you safe. Our people are growing in numbers and were getting stronger. He can't hurt you with us here," Nik assured her.

"Graci means the world to me..."

"She's a beautiful little girl, she looks like you."

"I never want her to be like me. I've made so many mistakes, and the thought of her hurting kills me inside. Do you promise to take us far away from him?"

"Yes, you are safe now, and we'll take you far away." Rosa wrapped her arms around Marie as tears welled up in her eyes. She was overwhelmed by a sudden flood of relief and worry at the same time. She spent her recent years in fear and unease. That wasn't going to go away instantly, but it was comforting to think of the future without all that.

"Come with me, I'm sure you're hungry, the others have gathered to eat," Nik told them. He held her hand and led them to a much larger area with tables and old stumps as chairs. As they walked through the cavern, Rosa saw Julien and ran to him. Marie recognized him and expressed that she was glad to see he had found safety as well, but he did not seem to recognize her.

"Have we met before?" he asked.

"Julien, remember when you told me there was something or maybe someone to find in Claude's home? Well..." Nik told him as he pulled Marie closer to him. Julien thought for a moment.

"You're the girl that helped me in his home when I was hurt. I just knew I wasn't dreaming that night!"

"What day?" Rosa asked. She had never known Marie to be unlocked from her room nor Julien able to unlock the door for them to have met.

"The day I had asked Master to leave the church, he was very angry, and she helped clean me when he punished me."

"Impossible, I always made sure she was locked downstairs when you were at the house," Rosa said with certainty.

"Not this one night, it was an accident. You had an emergency with Joseph, and James didn't lock my door. I heard him fighting with someone and snuck upstairs. There was a stranger bleeding on our floor, so I tried to help him. When I saw him in the square, I didn't want James to know I had ever left the room, so I didn't say anything. I'm sorry," Marie explained.

"Who is James?" both Nik and Julien queried.

"Oh... That's the master's real name; he said very few knew it, I suppose I wasn't thinking. I'm sorry I never helped you more and ran from you at the festival. I was afraid of you trying to figure out who I may be," she continued.

"No, it's alright. Is that your sister? She's so beautiful," Julien asked as he tickled Graci's foot.

"Who, her? Thank you, but she's mine. Her name is Gracianna, or Graci for short."

"Who is her father?" Julien asked. He was confused at why his master would have been hiding a girl with a baby in his home.

"She is his, isn't she? She has some pretty little curls," Natalya intruded. She had been listening and was able to connect the dots much easier than Julien could.

"Who's baby?" Julien still didn't comprehend the situation.

"She is the judge's," Natalya informed him.

"I don't understand, the Master has said that gypsies are such evilness. Why would he lay with and have a baby with one? This makes no sense."

"Julien! That's enough," Rosa scolded him. Marie began to feel ashamed. She began to draw back, but then she recognized Natalya from the festival. All of her memories of what had happened came reeling back.

"You... you are what he's looking for. He wants you! He got so angry at me for seeing…" Marie's breathing became heavy, and she started to panic once again.

"What?" Natalya stepped back, and Nik grabbed Marie before she could run away.

"What did he tell you about Natalya? Why was he angry at you about her?"

"No, don't! I saw you dancing at the festival; you gave him your scarf... I don't want to be here, Rosa!"

"Ignore everyone else. Just breath, dear. Tell me what happened."

"Rosa, please just kill me. I don't want to be here. When I found him that night…he was doing a vile thing with it. He was angry at me because of whatever she did, or made him do. I don't understand why, but he was just so angry," she cried and threw her hands over her ears.

Everyone gathered to help her, but she knelt to the ground and continued to cry for silence. Rosa knew her upset often made her feel dizzy and ordered for space. She held her, trying to calm her down, but it was clear that Marie was done talking with anyone any longer.

"I see. I'm sorry to upset you-" Natalya was sympathetic.

"She'll be alright, she just needs some to be left alone." Rosa helped Marie to an open area so she could get a bit of fresher air and calm herself.

"Come with me," Nik told her. He brought them to a remote area where a few gathered in front of a fire. He never let go of her hand as they sat. They watched as the flames of the fire danced, and Rosa finally got up to get Graci to bed. The others began to leave one by one until the two were left alone.

"I'm sorry for calling you stupid earlier; I guess it was just hard for me to understand. A beautiful girl like you should never have to endure so much from anyone like that man."

"It wasn't always like that. I know what you think but I know he cared about me more times than he didn't. He wasn't so hurtful that often, I just deserved it sometimes." Marie could never explain to anyone what she knew James and herself had between them. Despite everything, she still cared about him.

"No one deserves to nearly die," Nik told her. As it grew later in the evening, Marie noticed many of the torches in front of the tents being extinguished one by one. Marie wiped the tear that had fallen from her eye and stood to find Rosa. As she walked away, Nik pulled her back to him. He reached both of his arms around her and held her tight. He simply kissed the top of her forehead, and for the first time in years she felt safe.

In the city, Claude finally returned to his home. He immediately went to the spot he had left Marie, but her body was gone. He touched the wall she had fallen into and the blood where her head had hit. He kneeled down to where she had laid so still. There was blood on the floor; much more than what was on the wall, and he went down to her room. He realized she was gone, and Rosa must have taken her and the baby away. He wondered if Marie could be found at the hospital or the mortician. Either way, his mistake had cost him his family. He thought of what he had done and became infuriated. As he stormed through the house, he began throwing everything in sight, kicking furniture and shelves. He saw a bottle of wine that had been left on the table threw it into the fireplace, but some had spilled out.

The fire contained in it began to spread out of its place and rushed along the rug. It quickly crept along towards the window and lit the drapes. He tried to extinguish the flames but couldn't get to it in time. He gave up and ran outside as his home, the place his parents had raised him in, and he had his first child in, burned. His neighbors hurried outside to put out the fire, but it was too late. He stood back and observed the madness as everyone worked to stop the spreading, but when they finally killed the flames, his home was completely destroyed. He sent for his men, and Joseph was the first to arrive.

"What happened here?" Joseph looked around for anyone that may be listening. When the area was clear, he continued. "Where are the girls? What happened?"

"They are gone. I don't know where they went to, but they are not here."

"Don't worry we will find them," Joseph assured him as he looked upon his distress-filled eyes.

When Anthony, Charles and Ivan arrived, Claude ordered a more intense hunt for Nikolais and Natalya. He encouraged their fears that the gypsies had begun a war, and they needed to prepare immediately for a fight.

"Do whatever it takes; take down anyone who refuses to cooperate. If we don't find these heathens then the whole city may burn at their hands!" he shouted. The men lead the searches. Other family men of the city began volunteering to aid the judge and the king's soldiers. The city wouldn't rest until the fugitives were found.

# Chapter Thirty - One

12 April 1798

Marie decided she needed to give the camp a real chance. She knew she would always be on guard, but she was beginning to feel as if she didn't have to keep watching over her shoulder for James to find her. The camp was set up to look like a small city, and there were tents for people to sleep in and bigger tents to store food and water. There was an area full of tables and chairs where people gathered to eat and congregate. There were torches along the walls and each tent had a light outside the entrances. The evening meal was being served. The gypsies all gathered together, and the young helped serve food to the older. It was a community full of love and hope. Marie had missed this feeling and was grateful to have found it again.

"Niko we're clear, everyone needs to get ready to go," Lee informed Nik as he began rounding up the people and their things.

"Yes, we must move quickly, I want to get some rest tonight. Everyone! I know this place is amazing, but this is only the first step. We have a much larger home that is safer, and we believe you all are finally ready to make the journey. We must move now," he announced. Marie was nervous, but he was reassuring as he held her hand.

"It's the first step to freedom," he whispered as a few people gathered at the entrance.

Nik led them through the city; it was a tedious journey, and they had to be very stealth. The camp had been separated into groups, and the first three groups seemed to make it through the obstacles with ease. Nik realized there were more and more patrolmen out as they wandered further from the safe house and into the deeper parts of the city, but it was too late to turn back. He continued to lead his small group towards the wooded area near the city border, but as they crept through the alley ways, Marie noticed a light heading towards them. She showed Nik, who then signaled the others to halt. They waited, too afraid to move and be even more conspicuous, but the light only got closer. Suddenly, a peasant walked past and saw them. The man was clearly not friendly, and Nik tried to stop him, but he got away.

"We have to hurry; he's most likely one of them." Nik was afraid, but just as they approached the edge of the town borders, the group was surrounded by guards. They had caught the others before them and were waiting. James expressed his disinterest in the rest, he was only after a handful of gypsies. The guards began executing the ones he deemed useless, and it turned into a bloodbath in the street. Marie and Nik held each other's hands tightly as they witnessed the slaughter; there was no use in fighting.

She looked up to James as he led the massacre and kissed Nik goodbye. She could see his rage and began to scream as the guards took Nik and held him. Charles grabbed his sword and held it to his throat as James confronted Marie.

"James, please don't!"

"Marie, you betrayed me. I made a mistake, but I would never commit such a sin against you. Your betrayal will end his life," James snarled.

"Please, don't!"

"This is your fault, Marie," someone called out. The voice was not one she recognized. It was muffled but kept calling her name.

"Marie!" The voice was now crystal clear, and she jumped up and looked around in a panic. It was a dream. She realized that she had fallen asleep by the fire, and two girls were trying to wake her up.

"It's just us," they chimed together. It was her younger sisters. They were much smaller when she last saw them, and the years had changed their girlish looks into features of young women. She almost didn't recognize them.

"Valerie? Cordelia? My goodness, what are you doing here?"

"We've been here for over a year now. Is it true you have been a slave to the judge?"

"That's bold and inappropriate. Why would you ask me that when you've hardly even greeted me?" Marie was bothered by what people may think they knew about her and James, and felt embarrassed. It wasn't something she was comfortable talking to anyone about, much less her younger sisters.

"It's the word around here today, we just came to welcome the newcomer, but we had no idea it was you until we saw you."

"It's still impolite to ask a stranger such a personal thing. Where is Giselle and the children? Is she here as well?"

"She was pregnant with another baby but died during the labor. Alexander saved their child."

"He always was a good father to them," Marie sighed. She felt a twinge of anger and disappointment at never knowing what had happened to her family, but she knew it would do no good for her. She wanted to be happy for her sisters and do whatever she could for them.

"We tried to stay with him, but he could barely provide for the children. His light hair and complexion helped him blend with the French well enough. We came here when the gypsy hunts became more severe, and even established residents of the city weren't safe. We didn't want to risk the children losing their father as well."

"I'm so sorry I wasn't there for you." Marie could relate to what they may have felt. They lost their family and were forced into hiding with no one to protect or care for them.

"No, we're just glad to have you back alive now. We stuck together and quickly found safety here. Marie, there's so many people here from the old camp we used to visit with mother. It was like finding home again," Valerie told her. The girls seemed happy, and Marie started to feel much better.

From a short distance, Gracianna could see that her mother was awake and ran to her, throwing her arms around Marie's neck. She clung tightly having never encountered so many people before. The crowds were a bit overwhelming for her.

"Gracianna, meet your aunts. Girls, this is your niece."

"Oh, she is lovely, we would love to play with her. There aren't many young children around here," the girls squealed. They were gleaming with excitement over the newest member of the family. They played with Graci for a moment while Marie assured her child that the strangers were safe to go with. They offered to take her to get something to eat. Graci began to follow, but when she saw Rosa at the tables, she led her aunts to where she felt most comfortable. Marie watched as they all seemed to giggle and have fun when she wandered to the fire nearby and sat next to Nik. He had been listening to a group of men play their instruments together, and she was sure to remain quiet as they enjoyed the music together. It was a familiar melody, and Marie began to recognize the tune.

"I've heard that before," she whispered.

"My grandfather used to play it for my family. He always played at gatherings when we were younger."

"I remember an old man with the purple coat played it." Marie tried to remember the man's face but she had lost so many memories of her childhood over the years. Things were getting harder for her to recollect.

"That was my grandfather. I believe we played together many times as young children. I thought you looked familiar when we first met."

"I think I do remember you. I used to love dancing to that song; it's one of the few melodies that's played in my mind since I left home."

"You mean since you were taken from home?"

"Yes, I suppose you're right," she admitted as she stared at the ground.

"I'm sorry, that wasn't appropriate."

The moment felt awkward and strange. She could tell that Nik was sincere in his kindness, even when his words didn't quite come out that way. She could see that he was simply trying to know her, but a strange feeling overcame her, and she felt unsure of herself. She could find a thousand words and put them together to form the perfect conversation, but none of them ever seemed good enough to escape her mind through her mouth. She sat silently and was relieved when he finally started asking questions. She was good at answering questions, but she struggled with finding anything else to say.

"Tell me, Marie, do you still dance?"

"I haven't in years. After father took me on his tour, I never had time. Besides, I was barely seven or eight the last time he let my mother bring me to a gathering," Marie laughed.

"Well, I vaguely remember hearing you play, but your sisters often talked about their father's little starlight. I would rather see you struggle on the tips of your toes again," he teased.

He grabbed a fiddle from the band and began to play. She closed her eyes to absorb the melody, and after a moment, she reluctantly stood up and danced as well as she could remember. Nik watched as her silhouette twirled and moved in front of the fire. He put the instrument down and danced with her to the music of the trees surrounding them. He put his hands on her waist and moved with her, pulling her close. His eyes never strayed from hers as their bodies pulled to each other until the movements stopped. She felt frozen as she stared up at him. Everything in her head and heart told her that she wanted him to kiss her, but when he finally did, she found herself pulling away. She didn't feel afraid, but it must have looked like she was by the way Nik repeated his apologies.

"I'm so sorry, Marie. I thought... never mind. I'm sorry if you were not ready for me to touch you, it wasn't ill-intended, I promise."

"Stop. Please don't apologize. It's me... James is the only man who... No, you did nothing wrong," Marie paused, realizing she didn't want talk about James to Nik anymore.
Something was different, and she didn't want to force him to listen to her speak of that life anymore. Instead, she wanted to just be with him, knowing there was nothing to be afraid of with Nik. She enjoyed his company, and he could always make her smile with his silly faces when they would be with the others at meals. He never cared how others saw him and always found the opportunity to be fun and playful. It made her feel like she could be herself for once.

She found her fingers drawing up his chest and around his neck. She pulled him into her to kiss him back, and her body didn't shudder. The way she had always expected her first time would feel is exactly how she felt when Nik touched her. His lips, his skin, and warmth he shared was everything she imagined it to be. Her skin felt a small chill, like her body knew he was the one meant to be there. He pulled her in close and held her but then did a strange thing; his hand wisped and waved as it did when they first met. He smiled and a small, yellow flower appeared once more.

"I was told a special girl turned seventeen today," he grinned.

"You never cease to make me blush. I know it's silly, but that's such a fun talent. I think you should show me."

"Marie, I want you to know that if you become uncomfortable in any way, I will stop. I don't want you to think you need to return my affections because of anything I enjoy doing for you. I do it because your smile is cute, and I'll admit, making you blush can be entertaining."

"Thank you. I want to lay here with you. I feel good about that, and I have never once felt uncomfortable with anything that has happened between us."

"I'm glad to hear it," he whispered as he kissed her once more. His face was soft, and his facial hair well kept. He was beautiful, and she wanted more of him. But as Nik had suggested, they took their time. He taught her some of his little street tricks. When Nik wasn't busy organizing his men, he would stay with her and Graci to just relax and play. She enjoyed just listening to his stories and talking for hours. They had many common interests that she had forgotten she liked over the years, and he reminded her of the good things that life had to offer. The days passed, and she began staying with him more. They grew closer, building a more intense physical and emotional connection than she had ever felt before.

The camp was quiet, and most everyone was sleeping at the late hour. Nik and Marie had just gone to sleep when Lee snuck in to wake Nik. Lee seemed nervous, and he could tell it was serious. His urgency pulled Nik from his drowsiness, and he was quick to focus on the matter at hand. Lee had done his own patrolling and alerted Nik to a smaller camp that had been discovered by Claude and his men. There was only one survivor, and they knew he had been left as a message to the rebels and gypsies. It was a brutal scene, and it terrified them to see the messenger in his condition. The plan they'd been so desperate to stick to was now escalating. Nik wished to deny it, but Lee made his point quite clear as they whispered to each other privately.

"Nik, we have to do this soon, Fontaine is burning the city searching for you, but we both know what he's truly after."

"It's not like he can tell anyone without exposing himself."

"He's telling people he's looking for you and Nat, but we both know he wasn't this destructive until you took that girl. I imagine he is assuming she came here. He's not going to stop until we act or he finds what he's looking for, and we both know what it means if he finds them. You should have known he was going to get worse when you decided to steal what he thinks belongs to him. He doesn't have to tell anyone what he's really after, you are a good enough reason to burn this city to ash. Her being here has changed everything. It's getting far too dangerous, and we can't let this go on any longer," Lee warned.

"You're right, but we can't say anything to anyone right now except the strong few who can help."

"And the girl?"

"Let me deal with that; you just worry about the others."

"Alright. I know you care about her, but we have to do this. There are too many lives on the line to pull back or wait any longer."

"I still don't feel right about this without, you know..."

"It's too late for that kind of doubt, Nik. If he isn't returning then the decision is on us, and I say we strike now," Lee decided.

# Chapter Thirty-Two

03 May 1798

There was a quiet intensity amongst the camp before dawn. Marie had spent the past few days watching the others train in different skills to benefit the community. Some volunteered to protect and fight for the cause, others cooked or taught the children. They each contributed to the greater good of the people, but Nik and Lee seemed to be planning something more. The morning was busy, and Lee had been waking a few people since before the sun showed itself.

"Niko, it's time buddy, we've got to head out now."
Nik was slow to wake but quickly realized how much there was to get done. He lightly touched Marie, but she jumped up and screamed. Nightmares continued to afflict her. Living in terror forced her to find the most pleasant memories to hold on to before she slept, but now, the fear of going back overwhelmed her dreams at night.

"I'm sorry. It will get easier as time passes," she sighed. She didn't want him to see that she didn't hold on to much hope of being released of the fear. She felt safe with Nik in the camp, but there was always that small unease. Whether it was physically, mentally or even emotionally, she knew James would haunt her for the rest of her life.

"It's alright. We need to hurry and get washed up. It's a big day," he kissed her on the forehead and smiled. His eyes made her weak. He wanted her to go with him somewhere, but her mind was distracted. There was an odd feeling in her gut, but she couldn't quite figure out the words to describe it. She tried her best to listen despite her aberration. She heard him promise her they would change the world, and that all she needed to do was share her story with some people. She lost track of the rest of his words as she focused on the fear of reliving that horror enough to speak of it. Her mind began to race, but she remained calm. She watched his lips move as he spoke, but she struggled to hold on to his words long enough to understand them.

"Marie, do you trust me?"

His question forced her back to reality. She knew that she didn't know him as well as she would like, but he had given her no reason to not trust him. He was so kind and patient as she had been learning to live again like she had once before. He was helping her reclaim her life, and there was no cause for doubt.

"Alright, I trust you. Now, I must get dressed," she told him as she grabbed his shirt. She pulled him in to kiss him but then pushed him out. She quickly made herself up for the day and met the others in the dining area. Rosa was feeding Graci before leaving her with Marie's sisters to play.

She sat next to Nik, who was convincing Julien to also tell his story to a few people. Julien seemed even more anxious than she was, but Nik was very reassuring. He always made sure that everyone felt as if they belonged. He believed the gypsies were a family made up of many unique parts and did everything to bring lost souls together. When a few of the gypsies with similar stories had gathered, Nik and Lee packed everyone into a covered wagon. It was daylight, and they couldn't risk being seen before they arrived where they needed to be. It was a bumpy journey, but the wagon stopped after just a short time. Lee opened the back and rushed everyone out. Nik grabbed Marie's hand and helped her out. She looked around and realized they were in the town square and became nervous.

"Why are we here? I don't understand."

"It's a sentencing day, all the people are here, they can hear your and Julien's story along with the others, and that will make the town's people realize who their leaders really are. Taking him down is the first step to taking the king down."

"No! You said you'd take me away from him and here. You promised."

"But I need you to do this Marie! It's the only way."

"You don't understand, Nik. We really shouldn't do this," Marie pulled back.

"She trusted you. We trusted you! Why would you bring her here? She has nothing to do with this," Rosa scorned.

"She has everything to do with this! You may not realize it, but everything changed the moment you brought her to us, so don't tell me she's not a part of this," Nik argued.

Lee ran up on stage where James was standing. He was less than half the height of the average person, which made him more noticeable to the crowd. Everyone turned their attention from the sentences to him.

"People of Paris! This mutiny and genocide committed by the king and his men has got to stop! Your judge claims to be a just man, pure in the law, but he's a truly vile and dangerous criminal. I have testimony of the evil things he's done! He is a hypocrite and liar, far worse than most of the people he's arrested and even tortured in the name of the king," Lee shouted.

The people stared at him and muttered amongst each other in confusion. It was going to prove near impossible to persuade an entire town who felt saved by the judge to believe that he could ever be considered an evil person. Marie knew him to be charismatic and charming with a flawless reputation to his public. James didn't seem amused and tried to brush it off as nothing, but Lee continued to challenge his character as he had planned to. He was threatened with arrest for causing a disturbance but refused to be intimidated by the judge as he turned back to the people.

"This is what your judge does, anytime a person calls him on his transgressions, he shuts them down with threats!"

"That's not true!" James argued.

"Then let us speak!" Lee shouted. The town's people grew in their curiosity, and he would have to prove himself to an unwitting crowd.

"Very well, have your slanderous words. It will get you nowhere," James grumbled and stepped back, entertaining the idea that they had a chance against him.

Nik pulled Marie onto the stage. She begged him once more to reconsider using her story to sway an entire city, but it was no use. As she desperately pulled back, she tripped and fell in front of James. She didn't even need to look at him to see his anger and refused to stand before him. She feared what he may do to her, but Nik stood in between them to speak out.

"Your judge is a truly evil man. Three years ago, he kidnapped a child, raped her, and has forced her to live in his cellar as a slave to him," he shouted. The people looked at the girl with dismay and confusion at the accusation. They appeared unsure of what to believe as they listened to Nik tell her story with biased ears.

"This is absurd!" James tried to blow off the accusation, but Nik had raised the peoples' curiosities. He grabbed Marie off the ground and shoved her to face the people.

"Fine. Speak for yourself, girl," James commanded. She couldn't seem to force the words out of her mouth and stood frozen. She didn't want to let Nik down, but she was even more terrified of James. She looked back at them both and began to cry.

"This is pointless, they're all liars!"

"It's you! You've made her afraid with the things you have done to her, and the years you have spent torturing her," Nik recoiled.

"I have done no such thing. There have been no crimes committed in my home!"

"You're the liar! The vile things you've done to a girl who was barely fourteen. You killed her family to hide her existence! You should burn in the fires of hell for your crimes."

"If the girl is legally bound in wedlock, then no acts, be it sexual or physical, are considered a crime. Her father was sick and dying, you all remember Vincent Adams; he was ill. Her mother went missing years ago, and I had no part in that. She has yet to be found, but there have been many rumors of her lechery and evasion."

"You're lying!" Nik screamed.

"You see, when the girl went missing, I assumed a stunt like this would be committed. I have my proof, although the chain around her neck should be sufficient evidence as to who she really is."

Nik pulled the necklace that was tucked under her corset. There was a ring around the chain, and Nik looked confused and almost angry as if he'd been betrayed.

"It's engraved J. Claude Fontaine. That's my name, Nik. And see here…" James pointed to a spot on a piece of parchment, "her name is signed right there."

"She was fourteen, and that means she cannot make that decision on her own. You forced her."

"I also have a signed document from her father. He granted her to me before he died," he announced. Marie grabbed the paper in disbelief. She swore he would never do such a thing but James had convinced the people that she was being manipulated into lying. He was charming in his speech, and the people only saw her as Nik's victim. There was nothing she could say to persuade them of the truth; they had decided.

"You should have told me. This ruins everything," Nik scowled.

"I had to, I'm sorry. I just wanted you to take me away."

"So, as all of you can see, this girl belongs to me, and these men's credibility is lost," he snapped as he turned back to them, "Nikolais, I do believe you are under arrest for, now, kidnapping along with crimes of treason and leading the gypsies in their rebellion. Guards, set him to hang immediately and arrest the others!"

"No!" Marie felt responsible for Nik's plan failing and stood tall beside him in his defense.

"Excuse me?" James glared at her as he moved closer. He was an intimidating length taller than her, and she became skittish. James looked at her as she stood closer to Nik and grabbed his hand.

"Fine, Charles tie him in the square, it seems as though my wife has grown sentiment for her captor. She needs to see what his crimes cause for him and others, should they defend him."

Marie tried desperately to stop them. She didn't want Nik taking the punishment for her mistakes but was shoved aside. Charles tied him up and began to beat him. James stood behind Marie and grabbed her broken arm, twisting it behind her back.

"How dare you think you could come here and embarrass me like this? You know better," he whispered in her ear.

"I don't know what the plan was, James. Please, stop. Don't break it again, that really hurts."

He kissed her neck as Nik was finally able to pull his head up enough to look to Marie. Her body tensed at his touch, and she looked to everyone in the crowd. They could all see but allowed it to continue; no one would dare make him stop. She could hear Nik; his suffering was unbearable to her. She wanted to look away, but James pulled her hair and forced her to watch as blood began to cover him.

"Every strike he endures, every painful shriek and cry, is because a selfish girl refused to obey her master and stay in her place," he continued. It had become too much, and Marie couldn't take anymore. She screamed out for them to stop. James let her go, and she turned and knelt down, pleading with him.

"Please, James! Just stop! I'll do anything," she cried.

"Why is that, Marie?" he queried.

She hung her head and began to sob, "because he did not force me to go with him. I went willingly."

"You, adulterous whore..." James walked to the front of the stage and looked up at the crowd. "I take back what I said. This girl has sinned against me, lusting with a wanted criminal! She is not mine! Hang him and punish her in the square for their crimes."

"Please, James. Don't do this!"

"Confess your sin, or he will suffer more before he dies, Marie!"

"Yes, alright, I did. I'm sorry! Now, please stop!" she begged, but James didn't seem satisfied in the least.

"Admit it louder! Tell the people of your transgressions!" he shouted as he grabbed her arm and threw her in front of the crowd.

She could feel shame stripping her of every bit of dignity that had once covered her. She was left to stand before everyone, vulnerable and exposed as they stared at her. She knew society expected her to feel shame for what she had done with Nik, but her true regrets were in letting him down. The sun's warmth grew hotter as she choked up the words she thought may save the man she had grown to care for. She ignored Nik's pleas for her to stop and choke back her tears.

"Nik, I'm sorry. I don't want anyone going through that, especially for me. I did it, I lusted and ran away by my own free will. It's all my fault."

"She's lying! Marie, stop!"

"You all heard her admit it. The punishment for adultery is public chastise by means of flogging. Guards, get him down, and let her take his place."

"Marie! No! Damnit, you can't do this! She didn't do anything wrong! You'll kill her if you do this, and you know that!

"You will always have a look about you that makes it impossible to kill you," James growled as he grabbed her face and held it close to his. She held back her tears and pulled away.

"For what it's worth, Nik, I'd rather die at his hand than live without you here," she called to him as James shoved her past his hold. She could feel James grow angrier and he pushed her along. The glare in his eyes, and the heat coming from him intensified. She knew he would never allow her to get away with such boldness. In his rage, he grabbed her by the back of her neck and threw her down in front of Captain Ivan. Her arm was still weak, and she was pretty sure the break had gotten worse as she fell on it once more and heard another snap.

"Tie her up. Five strikes."

"Your honor, the felon was one thing, but you're asking me to punish this young girl without a fair trial first, and not to mention your wife. You can't use the system for personal vendettas."

"Your constant need to undermine me at every turn and to attack the sheriff in defense of these gypsies forces me to call your loyalties into question."

"How dare you question my loyalty to our king? I will not be involved in your personal affairs," Ivan shouted. They began to fight, but Anthony broke the two up, and Ivan angrily left.

"Anthony! Take his place! Five strikes, do you understand?" James commanded.

"Yes, your Honor," he replied, securing her tightly. She could hear Nik screaming and shaking the bars of his cage. James bent down close to Marie. She looked up at him, staring into his eyes daringly, but he e smiled at her.

"Today will not go as you wish. You are mine, and I will make sure that you will live to remember this day for many years to come."

As Anthony prepared to strike, an arrow darted into his arm, and he fell to the ground. Marie could hear the confusion and chaos break out amongst the people in the crowd, and her heart began to race. She couldn't comprehend everything going on around her, but she listened as guards frantically searched for the culprit. A soldier ran to help Anthony and get him to Joseph at a nearby clinic before he could bleed out.

A masked man was running with a bow in his hand. She watched as the soldiers chased after him, but he disappeared. There was a look in James's eyes; he was losing control of the situation and getting angrier. She knew he was panicking to regain control of himself and everything going on. She recalled her boldness and what she had told Nik just moments ago. It was out of order, and James would do anything for order to be maintained. She gripped the post tightly as she saw him grab the whip and strike her. She swallowed her scream; she didn't want to give James the satisfaction. Her breaths were staggered as she realized it would never be good enough for him, He felt betrayed by her, and she flinched as he lifted his arm to strike her again.

She waited anxiously for the torture he would inflict, but it seemed to never come. She took a breath and looked back at him. The masked man had returned and was now holding a sword to his throat. A wave of relief poured over her as she watched Nik run past the men to untie her. She fell into his arms, but he was covered in his own blood.

"How did you get out?" James shouted, "unmask yourself, coward! You help these vile creatures commit treason against your king! Show yourself!" James could feel everything he had worked for slipping from his grasp as the masked man made a small cut on his neck. Charles charged at them, but the man shoved James into them, and knocked them all to the ground. He grabbed Marie and Nik, and they managed to escape to a hidden tunnel system under the city.

As the mysterious man helped them to escape, Nik collapsed. Marie reached around him and felt something from his back. There was more blood than she'd ever seen before.

"He's bleeding out and running short of time. His breathing is shallow, and there's no telling how bad it is. They had every intention of killing him. He's too weak to continue on foot, help me hold him up, girl," the man asked of her. He lifted Nik over one shoulder, and Marie did her best to help get Nik to safety.

"There's so much blood," she cried.

"I'm afraid it could be too late. We have to get him back to the camp now. You must hurry," he spat the words as she followed closely through the tunnel.

The square filled with screams of Claude shouting commands, panicked civilians, and his men apologizing to him profusely. The city was under attack, and they had fallen short of their duties to apprehend all the rebels and protect Claude from the masked villain. The people fled in such disarray which made for an easy escape, but not for many. His soldiers assured him they would properly question the gypsies who had been captured and find the whereabouts of their camp and leader.

"That's not enough! Where is Ivan? This is no longer a personal matter, and the king will agree with me. He should be leading these interrogations."

"But sir, no one has been able to find him."

"That is suspicious. Find him, but keep this to yourself. We will find out where the captain's loyalties truly lie."

"Yes sir. Oh, and I almost forgot to mention that we found the servant you used to care for. We caught him as the commotion had begun. He's been to their hiding place, so we could call Joseph for a special interrogation."

Claude forced himself to calm down and think rationally about what to do next. He instructed Charles to bring Julien to the church tower where his workshop was and secure him there by any means necessary. Charles agreed with a smile and immediately left to retrieve their next victim.

# *Chapter Thirty-Three*

04 May 1798

      The streets echoed with silence, and there was a tension in the air that cut through the city like a knife. Everyone kept quiet in their homes over the next night. The king called for a meeting, the previous day's events had caused quite the stir, and none of them could know what to expect for the future. Claude stood alongside Joseph, Charles, and Ivan, who all hung their heads as the king paced angrily about the room. They all waited tensely in a row, rigid in their stance and nervous as the king scolded them like misbehaved children.

      "Again, I will ask, 'what in the damned hell was that today?' Are you trying to send me to an early grave? The town's people are tired of these insects causing chaos in our streets. Why is this still a problem?" the king asked.

      "We have the gypsies that were caught locked away. Very few escaped," Claude explained.

      "Don't forget to mention that the most important ones got away, Claude. The only one we have been after for years managed to slip through your grasp yet again!"

      "We had everything under control!" Claude shouted. He was beginning to snap and lose control of his temper and emotions as he spewed out his next words, "we were doing just fine. We had captured every single one that rebelled against us, until someone attacked us by surprise. I believe it to be someone else who also works against us."

"And who do you think this mystery culprit to be, Claude?" Claude hesitated. What he was about to say could go one of two ways, and he was unsure of which it would go, but given the circumstances, he had to say something.

"During the sentencing, the Captain Lemieux disappeared after a quarrel, just before the attack. The guards didn't find him again until much later. He had opposed my rulings and refused to carry out a sentence. He even tried to fight me in front of our civilians."

"I had nothing to do with that attack if that's your accusation. I disagreed with your ridiculous form of whatever you call justice and went to the pub. The owner was in the square, so I did take a few drinks, but that's where I was all afternoon," Ivan defended.

"So, he claims to have been stealing drinks from the pub at the time of the masked villain attack, but since the pub owner was not present, we cannot verify this claim," Claude retaliated. He had a gut feeling that the captain was up to something and refused to back down.

"What are you saying? That my best guard, my number one soldier is a traitor?"

"I'm just inquiring to his suspicious behavior your Majesty; he had the most open opposition to the sentences that were to be dealt."

"Is no one going to question why you've been hiding a wife for what appears to be a few years now? I don't know how legitimate those papers that you shoved in front of the ignorant street people are, but if you really had nothing to hide, then why has no one heard of it until you were accused of rape? That girl was at least half gypsy, so maybe we should be questioning where your loyalties lie, Claude. You are nothing more than a judge, a glorified lawyer really. Your majesty, he really has no business running things like he has. He's resented me since you told him I was due to aid him. He abuses his power to take care of personal business, and when I refused to get involved in his home affairs, he found it his business to come to you with accusations of treason! This is absurd!" Ivan debated.

"Absurd?! You've-" Claude recoiled.

"Enough!" the king scowled, "I refuse to hear that either of my best men would commit treason. I will listen no longer! Claude, this is the final chance I will grant you. Take care of these gypsies and drop all personal matters. Your father was my friend, and I have trusted you, but should you fail again, you are done!"

"Your majesty!" he called as the king left with the captain. As much as Claude hated it, he was forced to keep Ivan on guard.

That evening, Claude, Joseph, and Charles brought Lee, who had been captured, in for interrogation. Captain Ivan was brought back and given a chance to prove himself. They had spent hours questioning all the other rebels without success, and Lee was all they had left. After burning, cutting and beating him relentlessly, Joseph realized they would not get anywhere with him. The ones that had been caught were all trained and prepared for such interrogations. They pondered on what to do next.

"We can't kill him; he's the leader's right-hand man. We need him alive."

"Then set him upon the stocks. Maybe his friend will save him from the sun's brutal glare. Set two guards in hiding and gag him. He must not speak to anyone," Claude instructed.

"Are you sure? I think the Captain would fancy another tongue in his collection of royal failures," Charles taunted Ivan, who did not find the humour in his jokes.

"Very well. I'll get on it right now. Let's get this done with so that we can all go back to our respective jobs and not see each other again, shall we?" Ivan huffed as he pulled their prisoner down to set him in the square.

They stripped him of his clothes and laid out a table of rotting food to humiliate and torment him with. As the night grew to morning, the people of Paris would see the criminal. It would only be a matter of time before word got back to Nik of his dear friend, but hopefully before the dehydration and heat took his life.

# Chapter Thirty-Four

07 May 1798

The masked stranger carried Nik and led Marie a strange way to the camp. It detoured from the normal route and led to a small building. She didn't recognize where they were, but she helped the man get Nik inside. It was quiet outside, they couldn't even hear the chaos from the square, so she knew they had to have gone quite a distance away. The room had a few food and water supplies, but there was also an odd bed with various hinged sections that moved to suit whoever needed it. There was also a small glass cabinet full of medical equipment and tools. The man picked Nik up and laid him on a table to clean him up. He told Marie to simply be there for him through his suffering. Her mind was rushed with emotions, but she did her best for him.

Marie held Nik's hand tightly through his screams. His body shook as the man poured a cleansing liquid on the wounds and cleaned him to prevent infection. He commanded her to hold him still while he worked. She took his orders, but also demanded to know who the man was. She tried to coax his identity from him, but he was busy wrapping Nik's injuries and refused to answer her.

The man continued to work without response. He focused on the task at hand until it appeared as though the bleeding had stopped. He assured her that Nik would be alright when he finally looked up at her. He promised her that they would meet when the time was right, but he needed her to keep a look out for anyone else as he transported Nik back to his own tent. Marie didn't like trusting someone whose face she'd never even seen, but she was left with little option.

"I gave him an elixir to help him sleep. There's more by the bed," the man whispered. He laid Nik down on his cot but disappeared before Marie could thank him.

She felt angrier at herself than she ever had before and knelt down beside him. She cleaned the blood that was left and put him in a clean shirt. She gave him the medicine to keep him asleep as he healed and ensured that no one bothered his rest. When Nik finally woke up, he was in immense agony, and she came to help him before he hurt himself any worse. She grabbed the bottle from his table and carefully poured it into a spoon.

"Here, drink this. It's been helping you with the pain," she soothed.

"For how long?"

"About two days."

Nik jumped to sit up, but the burning sensation took over, and he nearly collapsed. He vaguely remembered what had happened and was afraid for the rest of his people.

"Stop, you'll open the wounds that are starting to heal. Lie down."

He looked around, realizing where he was and tried his best to recall the events. Marie had hoped he would remember the important things so she wouldn't have to relive it to tell him.

"I really don't remember much, and by the feel of my back, that's probably a good thing. I can see us in the square confronting Fontaine, but it's all a bit blurry from then on."

"Lucky you, then… You missed all the fun," she quipped as she helped him change his shirt. His muscles twitched from the throbbing of his injuries, and he shifted to ease some of the discomfort.

"Oh my, Marie it feels like you gave me quite the beating. I must have been a really bad boy," he smiled painfully. She choked back her tears and playfully shoved him sideways.

"Stop it," she giggled with heartbroken tears in her eyes. She loved that he could find the humour in every situation, but she truly felt terrible for everything that had happened.

"Goddamn, this is hell," he moaned.

"I'm so sorry. This is all my fault."

"Whatever you did, I'm sure I deserved it," he teased.

"I should have told you," she cried. She handed him the necklace, and he read the engraving on the ring. "Ah yes, I remember that now," he mumbled as he rested his head on his hand and got comfortable.

"I never wanted you to suffer for me, but being forced in front of him felt shattering. That man terrifies me, and I didn't know what else to do."

"Marie, stop! I'm just glad you're alive. I thought for sure we were dead."

"I just feel terrible for ruining your plan."

Nik sighed as he held her hand and rubbed it with his thumb. She expected him to be angry or even upset, but he wasn't. There was a sadness in his eyes that was sincere, and while she blamed herself, he wasn't pointing a single finger at her for how everything turned out.

"It's not your fault, Marie. I was too eager and just hoped that would be a good place to start. I thought if his true self was seen to the people, they would realize his evil ways are a result of work for the king and dethrone him. I shouldn't have listened to Lee and just waited for orders."

"We will find a way- wait, what orders? You aren't the one who gives-"

"No, and that's all you need to know for now. Could you please give me another spoon of that medicine?"

"Is it the masked man who brought us here? Is he the one who..." Marie was even more confused and didn't know the exact words to ask.

"The pain is getting worse." Nik looked at her; and she knew she wouldn't get an answer from him. It was now just one of many questions that she had to keep inside.

As Marie poured the elixir, Rosa came into the tent. They hadn't seen each other since that day, and she hugged her tightly. They expressed their gratitude in escaping and finding each other again. Rosa seemed much better at concealing her emotions, but even she couldn't stand up to the fear that overwhelmed her at the thought of losing Marie. They spent a moment talking, but Rosa seemed in a bit of a hurry to shift the conversation.

"Marie, Graci is fussy and needs her mother."

"Of course," she smiled as she looked to Nik, "you need to get some rest anyhow. Now, take this, and get some sleep. I will see about the others as soon as I can. Will you be alright for a while?"

"Yes, I'll be fine. Thank you, love."

Marie kissed Nik on the forehead and followed her from the tent. The air outside was refreshing, but it brought with it a wave of emotions. There was a clarity that hadn't been there in the last weeks since they had left James and much more that had been left unsaid. Rosa held her face and brushed over her shoulders as they both tried to hold in tears. Marie knew there was something she needed to say but was caught off guard when Rosa discreetly handed her a small bag.

"What is this?"

"It's just a little silver I took from the house before we left James."

"A little? This is heavy... Rosa, we shouldn't have this. Why would you give it to me?"

"Because I want you to listen very carefully, Marie. This is important."

"You're worrying me. What is it?"

"James thinks your family is dead. He assumed your younger sisters were abandoned and died after they were orphaned. He doesn't even know of your older sister or her husband's existence."

"Are you sure? I don't understand-"

"I'm absolutely positive. I had asked him years ago; he thought all of your sisters were much younger, he's mistaken you for the oldest."

"Yes, but what does this have to do with the silver?"

"Marie, as long as James is looking for you, and I know he is, he will not be forgiving."

"I'm as good as dead if he does. After what I've done, he will never grant me mercy, even if he doesn't execute me the minute he lays eyes on me again."

"I know James loved Graci, but she deserves safety and trust. Not to be a prisoner in her home."

"What are you saying, Rosa?"

"All of this: the gypsies, James, the king, it's all bigger... so much bigger than you or I. There is a war waging, and it could get very messy. I imagine the casualties will be great."

"So, you think I should bring her to Alexander's home?"

"I imagine this isn't what you want to hear, but I also know that you want her to be safe-"

"I get it... I've made such a mess of thing, and you think I should hide her from this. From James..." Marie paused; she could barely spit out her next words, "and from me," she cried. She didn't want to think more on it, but she knew Rosa was right.

"I know you don't believe me, but you are the strongest woman out of anyone here and the least selfish person. You have been denied so much and given up everything. I shouldn't ask this of you, but we both know that she can't stay here."

"I know. Graci deserves the best, and I'll do anything I need to make sure that happens. When Nik is awake, he can bring me."

"Marie, are you sure about that? He's-"

"I trust him, Rosa," she interrupted. "I understand how messed up things got at the square, but I do think he can be trusted with this."

"Just because he saved you, and has charmed himself into your heart, it doesn't mean that a thing so delicate like a baby should be-"

"Stop it, Rosa. You think he is the one who rescued me? Or that I look to him as some type of hero? Rosa, I may find myself attracted to him in many ways, but you are the one who saved my life. I would have never survived the first week at James's home if you hadn't been there for me. I could have never made it through my pregnancy or giving birth to my only child if you hadn't held my hand through it all. You cleaned me up when I was sick or hurt, you made me feel safe in my darkest days, and always brought me to light. Nik only 'saved me' because you risked your life and safety to bring him to me. I owe... everything to you. You are truly a lionheart, and I look up to you whenever I have doubts."

"You just might make me cry," Rosa laughed as she sobbed. "I love you with all my heart, child. Your words will never leave me, thank you. I'm scared for you as well, but I trust you to decide what's right for our precious girl," she mumbled through her tears. They held each other tightly, squeezing every last emotion from them. Rosa finally let her go and sent her on her way to get everything ready.

Marie tried to sneak back to the tent and pack Graci's things, but Nik was regaining his strength and sat up. She could see his curiosity and caught him before he could say a word. His lips drew her close, and she wanted nothing more than to touch them with her own, but her finger came between them to hush his concerns. She knew that if he began to talk, she may change her mind. She quietly told him of her discussion with Rosa and asked him to help her when it was dark out. She needed his guidance through the city. She whispered of where she needed him to lead her to, but he refused to put Graci in danger.

"Don't treat me like a child, Nik. I wasn't asking for your permission, just your assistance. I know where this road leads, and it's the only way to keep her safe," she could feel her breathe slipping from her as she spoke. She tried to be strong and set her fears aside, but it proved harder than she imagined.

"What road? What are you talking about?"

"The road that leads to you not being able to defeat James or the king without anyone getting hurt; the other day in the square proves that. That was a very close call, and if anything were to happen to Graci... I'm begging you to help me, Nik. I'm not willing to bet her life on the next time. It has to be tonight."

"Where do you need me to take you?"

"James thinks I am my eldest sister, which is actually Giselle. He thinks all of my younger sisters are dead, but even if he were to figure out the truth of my younger sisters, Giselle's marriage was never made official. They didn't have the money to officiate, so her children were deemed illegitimate at birth. There is nothing tying my brother-in-law, Alexander, to my family. I know Graci will be safe with him. I have enough silver to get their family out of France if he takes her. It is for the best," she said with maybe too much confidence. She pondered her last words as if she were convincing herself that this plan was truly the best choice. This could be temporary or a forever goodbye; was she really capable of that? She knew deep down that there was no other option. It had to be now, or she could be risking her daughter's life.

Just after sunset, Nik led Marie through the city. As they walked through the city they stayed close to the shadows and alley ways. Nik noticed a light as they approached the street and looked around the corner. It was a patrol crew. Marie picked

Graci up, and they leaned into the wall to keep from being seen. As the group passed, Marie noticed a tall man on a horse; it was James. Her body froze.

"Daa-" Graci tried to call out to him. She must have recognized him as well. Marie threw her hand over Graci's mouth and turned into her to muffle any more noise she could make. Nik leaned into them, preparing for the worst. Running now would only make them more conspicuous, so they remained as still as possible.

"Did you hear that? It sounded like..." she heard James call out. "I don't know for sure, but I could swear it was..." James continued, his voice lowered as he turned back to follow the sound.

# Chapter Thirty-Five

10 May 1798

The small voice pulled at Claude, and he immediately halted. His men stopped ahead of him, but no one else seemed to have heard it. They waited for his orders, but Claude knew he wasn't imagining things. He paced back slowly and silently in search of where it came from.

"What was it?" Charles queried.

"It sounded like a child called out… like my child," Claude told Charles as he backed his horse up. The shined his light back toward the street.

"Nonsense, this is a family area, there's many children here."

He looked into the window of a home and there sat a family with a few small children. He missed suppers with his daughter beside him, playing and laughing together.

Claude loved his daughter; he would recognize her voice anywhere. He steered the horse closer towards the alley way, but stopped as he heard another child laughing. He looked in the window of a house and saw five small children sitting at a table with their parents. He missed Graci sitting across from him at supper; but maybe his longing was causing him to imagine things. He knew the odds of Marie keeping Graci in the city was extremely small and ordered the others to continue forward.

His men rode on, but Claude began to feel sentimental as he glanced at the smallest child once more. Her smile reminded him of the family he once had, and he decided to pay a visit to the only person he had left. It was dark, and he lit a couple of lamps around Julien's workshop. He looked around and complimented him on how well he had cleaned and reorganized his space. Julien was quiet as he got up from the new cot that had been brought into the room. It was felt that Julien was no longer worthy of boarding with the other servants, and Claude had him chained up to keep him from leaving his workshop. He set out a basket he had bought from the tavern and offered it to Julien.

"Thank you, master."

"You're welcome. Have you made any more dolls with your new clay wheel lately?"

"No, sir. I have not had the desire to create anything yet."

"Shame. What's the matter with you?"

"I miss Rosa," Julien muttered.

"Yes, well she made her choice."

"Like the girl? Your wife?"

"Just like my wife."

"Master, do you mind my asking why you never told me about her? I came to your home many times."

"I was afraid. She looks like a gypsy; I didn't want anyone thinking inappropriate things about my work, so I kept her a secret."

"You said 'she looks like a gypsy'. Is that not what she is, sir? Her being a gypsy could have helped people see you are not just against gypsies but against law breakers."

"But she's not a gypsy. Her father was a well-liked Englishman."

"So, that may not have helped against the gypsies, but the French would have certainly accepted you marrying an English woman."

"It doesn't matter what I thought at the time. Just leave it alone."

"I'm sorry, sir. I don't mean to push my boundaries, I'm merely curious. Who did you tell her had visited all those times I was there? Did she know about me?"

"She knew nothing of you until she saw you at your sentencing."

"You mean at the festival?"

"What about the festival?"

"Oh, I'm sorry, I must be mistaken."

"Did she tell you she was at the festival?"

"Only that she saw Natalya dancing and give you her scarf."

"Really? What else did she say, Julien?"

"She was very upset, but I don't know anything else, I promise."

"Brother, I want you to know, despite any accusations, I did care for her. I did everything I could to make her happy. I've made mistakes with her and you, and I want to make it all right."

"But they said you-"

"I didn't mean to hurt her so badly. I was so angry with you for getting into trouble and the gypsies protesting. It was overwhelming for me. The king is persistent. His paranoia of the gypsy uprising, it's a lot to handle." Claude became emotional. "I never wanted to hurt her. I just want her back. Her and my child. Now that I know the people may accept her, if she only chooses me, we can be a real family." Claude had a hard tone. He wanted someone, anyone, to know how he felt about his family. He had very strong feelings for Marie, and he wanted his family back with him.

"I'm sorry, master. I didn't know."

"Well, she's lost now," Claude huffed. His tone changed and became cold.

"Maybe if she felt like you wouldn't hurt her again, she would-"

"Like you, she would have to work hard to earn my trust. She committed a serious crime; to sin against your marriage is a crime against God. It's the gypsy in her blood. She craves disobedience at times, much like yourself. Now do you believe me when I tell you that gypsies are dangerous?"

"Can't some be good?"

"If you are referring to Natalya then again I say 'no'. She has seduced you to her ways much like Nikolais has seduced my dear Marie. Even Rosa has abandoned her French upbringing to this gypsy folly."

"But..."

"She is a witch! She has broken you down to such naive and immature thinking. They are nothing more than criminals, Julien! When they hang, you will be free of their mind games."

"Yes, I'm sorry. I understand."

"I must leave now, but I will be back soon. Take care of yourself," Claude pat his back and then left to meet Charles. They needed to devise a plan to find the escaped and hiding gypsies; he was getting more and more desperate.

"Of course, master." Julien moved slowly. The chain around his ankle dragged, making a lot of noise. It was heavy and Julien didn't feel like picking it up so he just allowed it to rub across the floor. His ankle had blood, dried from the cuff rubbing his skin. He felt like all hope was lost to him. He cringed at the thought of what would happen to those he considered friends for a short time.

As Julien cleaned his workshop, a loud screech blared through the city. He ran to the window and saw it had come from the square. The short man from the camp had been posted on the stocks for days, and a figure seemed to be coming to his rescue. He could see they were running short on time; the sound had to have alerted everyone for miles. It was still night, but the morning would soon come. He waited and prayed as the soldiers marched toward them, hoping they could escape in time.

# Chapter Thirty-Six

10 May 1798

Marie could feel every fear and life moment flash before her as she caught her daughter's gleeful shriek. She didn't have a single thought as she threw her arms around Graci and quickly covered her mouth before she could make another sound. She held the child snugly against her, and her heart stopped at the sound of the patrol halting in their steps.

"What is it?" Charles asked James.

"It sounded like a child called out, like my child..." she heard James mutter as he backed his horse up. The lantern he held moved closer to them, but she felt stuck and unable to even move or run.

Marie knew that James loved his daughter and would recognize her voice anywhere. She held her breath as he steered his horse closer towards the alley way. She covered Graci's eyes to prevent her from seeing the steed she had spent so much time riding with her father. Marie watched as he looked in the window of a home with children playing together at a table. She could see his expression, but it didn't change the facts. She had every confidence in her choice to do what was best for her daughter and pushed aside her doubts.

As James shouted for the other patrolmen to continue on, Nik quietly signaled for Marie to be ready to move. She massaged Graci's scalp in an attempt to relax her and tried to direct the child's eyes into her shoulder to get her to nap. They continued on their journey when it was clear and followed the map her sister had drawn to get them to the right house. When they finally found it, Marie approached the door, but her body and will froze at the door. She realized the burden she would be asking Alexander to bear and was afraid he wouldn't help her.

"Are you going to knock, or should I?" Nik asked her. Marie finally got up the courage to force her hand to the door, and Alexander answered nervously. He didn't seem to recognize her at first, but upon closer look, he appeared quite surprised and anxious.

"Marie?"

"You look like you've seen a ghost," Nik smirked.

"Come, come before the patrols pass by again," Alexander muttered as he looked around and pulled Marie inside. He lit a candle and offered them a seat at the table. "I can't believe it's you. We thought you were dead. Have you seen your sisters? Are they alright? It killed me to not take care of them any longer. The times have been tough on everyone."

"They're fine and completely understand. Look, I do regret everything you had to deal with, but that's not why I'm here, Alexander."

"I'm sorry. It's just, seeing you here. Giselle looked for you for months. She never believed the rumors of your mother taking you and running away."

"I know, and I'm sorry for her passing. I've missed her most in these last years, and it hurts that she's no longer here," she whispered as she grabbed his hand from across the table, "but that's why I've come to you. I really need your help. This is Gracianna, my daughter."

"Who's her father? Is this why you've been missing? I don't understand why you came here," he seemed anxious and full of questions; none of which Marie had time for.

"Alexander, please! I need your help!" Her voice was stern, but she tried to be quiet and carefully placed the bag of silver on the table in front of him.

"What is this? Where have you been all this time? Where did you get this, Marie?" His anxiety seemed to be growing, and he was losing focus on the problem at hand.

"Stop! Just listen for a moment," Marie barked.

Alexander sat back down, but was very shifty in his seat. He found it hard to be comfortable with anything Marie could ask of him.

"The judge Fontaine. He-" Nik interjected.

"Excuse me?" Alexander jumped from his seat.

"He took me years ago. He killed mother, and he's hunting for me now."

"And you came here? I've got children, Marie!" Alexander began to pace the room in panic.

"I know, just listen. Please. He doesn't know who you are and would never look for Graci here. I need you to keep her safe until he is no longer looking for me."

"I don't know, it's not just me at risk here. Fontaine has been harsher than ever, and they have no mercy, even with families, anymore."

"Please. There's plenty of currency to get you all safely out of Paris."

"Isabelle is old enough now, she can watch her here when I'm gone and keep her inside. They have a hiding place in the woods with a secret escape route in case of... well they know what to do."

"If anything happens to me, you and the children need to find a new home out of this horrid place. I don't want him ever finding her."

"I promise, Marie. We won't look back if that does happen. I will care for her as my own, you have my word," Alexander assured her. He hugged her tightly, and Marie knew her daughter would be in safe hands. She simply thanked him; it was all she could find left to say.

Marie brought Graci into one of the rooms and cradled her in her arms. She wrapped the child in a blanket and held her tight against her chest. The soft lullaby that had always lingered close to Marie's heart began to play in her mind as she rocked her daughter back and forth. As she whispered the lyrics into Graci's ear, a giant knot grew in her throat. Her face burned, but she refused to cry. Sadness would not be her daughter's last memory of her. She twirled her baby's curls around her finger and caressed her forehead until the baby fell asleep in her arms.

As she watched Graci fall deeper into her dreams she tried to hold back her emotions. Every smile, every tiny 'I love you', and every sweet snuggle came to Marie's mind. She squeezed her gently, but couldn't let go. This was it, this could be the last time she ever saw her daughter again. She tried to stop the tears but they forced their way out. She cradled the baby soundly and laid her head into her. She heard a horse drawn buggy race by; she knew if she were to be the best mother to Graci then she would have to let her go. She deserved a safe and happy life, and Marie would do anything to give it to her. She quietly laid Graci in the bed and covered her up. She did her best to quietly sneak out the room, but as she got to the door, she heard Graci's voice.

"Mamma? Mamma!" Graci cried. Marie hid behind the door, the tears streamed down her face but she did her best not to let her be heard. That was it; Graci didn't make another sound and must have fallen back asleep. Marie grabbed Nik's hand before she could wake again and pulled him out the door. She couldn't stay a moment longer.

Nik did his best to comfort her as he whispered promises of seeing her child again. She fell into his arms and wept. Nik nestled her face into his shoulder to give her the ability to cry as much as she needed safely. His hand rubbed her back, and he held the hair from her face and just let her be free with her emotions without speaking. There wasn't a single word he could say to ease her hurt, so he kept silent. He couldn't imagine her pain, but he knew this was more traumatic for her than anything James had done to her before. When she could finally stop long enough to take a breath, she looked around. The area was clear but the patrols were getting more intense, and Marie knew she didn't have much longer to safely get back to the camp. She took a deep breath and forced herself to focus on what she needed to do in that moment. She kissed Nik, and they began their journey to the camp without the child.

As they made their way back, Marie noticed a small man tied to a post in the square; she pulled Nik in for a closer look. It was Lee, but there were two guards discreetly posted out of sight from the stocks. It was an unusual situation, and Marie wanted to approach with caution.

"It's bait, they want me."

"So, then we need to really stop and think about-" but before Marie could finish, Nik was gone. She tried to stop him, but he cut the guards' throats in a rush. As one of them fell, Nik noticed something strange hanging from the man's waist, and when it hit the ground, a loud sound emerged from it. A high-pitched screech filled the city, and Nik and Marie fell to their knees, covering their ears. When the sound finally stopped, they were able to shake off the shock of what had happened.

"You shouldn't have killed them. Half the town had to have heard that. The patrol wasn't that far away; they could return at any moment." Marie was growing more and more worried, but Nik was determined to save his friend, who was barely conscious from heat exhaustion and dehydration.

# Chapter Thirty-Seven

21 November 1798

The months passed slowly with Graci gone, and Marie knew she had to protect herself from exposing her daughter's whereabouts. There was a quiet tension from the failure they endured trying to save Lee, so she didn't want to press too hard, but she asked Nik to help her train to fight. There was rumor that Lee was still alive and locked separately from the other prisoners, and she was determined to help Nik rescue him. He was reluctant to teach her, but she was persuasive. She insisted on being outside every chance she could be to practice privately, especially since the warmer months had passed. The season had grown cold quickly, and the autumn was brisk and short.

After much convincing, Nik finally gave in. He grabbed two rods from the weapon tent and brought her into the woods where they could be alone. He worked with her every day that week. They went into the woods daily to work on her movement and the best ways for her to defend herself. As they practiced one evening Nik's rod swung around, hitting Marie on the back of her shoulder. She cried out and nearly fell, almost.

"See, I hate doing this. You've broken that arm twice in the last six months, because you're not giving it the proper time to heal. I can tell it bothers you."

"But it does help me get better. I can feel myself getting stronger, so you have to keep going."

"I don't want to, Marie! You're not very good, and you keep getting hurt."

"Stop it! I need you to do this. If I don't, what do you think James and especially Charles will do if they find me, and I don't fight?" she argued. She ran towards him, swinging her baton as hard as she could, but he blocked it and knocked her to the ground.

"I know but-" he hesitated.

"But nothing! We keep going!" she snapped as she stood to continue. She was relentless in pressuring him to really give her the chance to work harder. She refused to give up until he really trained her. Finally, Nik gave her what she wanted and kicked his foot behind her as he slapped his weapon against her stomach. She fell on her back, and the air nearly escaped her lungs.

"You should protect your face, but knowing these men, that's not what they're aiming for. They'll do anything to get you on your back. Keep your strong foot behind you and lean forward," he advised.

"Got it." She stayed there for a moment, staring above her. The sky was filled with grey clouds. She knew it was a sign of harsh weather, and was glad to be getting the practice in, because she could tell there would be freezing rains and possibly snow to come. She sat up to catch her breath but noticed something in the distance.

"I think someone is coming."

"Where?" Nik searched around.

"There," she pointed in the distance, "don't you see?"

"I do now. Stay hidden, and I will go take care of it," Nik told her.

Marie hid behind a tree and waited. She feared it could be someone spying for their whereabouts. After a moment she looked to see what was going on. She saw Nik with a man. When they made their way closer, Marie realized who it was, and she ran to hug him.

"I'm so glad to see you! You must tell us how you escaped," she exclaimed as they made their way back into the camp. He was weak and looked almost starved, but he had pushed with everything he had left to get to them. They helped him to a quiet tent, and he sat to catch his breath and try his best to explain.

# Chapter Thirty-Eight

23 November 1798

     Life in his workshop had grown much easier over the months for Julien. His master would visit three times a week just like they used to. Aside of the chain on his foot, his routine had returned to the way it had been his entire life. They continued in their lessons, but his rewards had been changed to suit their new life. Claude no longer had a home for him to visit, so he would take him to the tavern at night or sometimes a sweet shop in the evening when he did well in his work.

     Julien began to excel, and dedicated all of his focus and concentration into his lessons. He would occasionally work on new dolls, but not as his once did. He was all Claude had left, and he wanted to keep him happy. It was a little before noon one day, and Julien eagerly awaited as his master checked his work. He had passed all of his exams. Claude presented him with a new suit and treated him to a lunch in the royal court. It was a lavish event, and the guests were well dressed and handsomely groomed. Julien couldn't take his eyes off the feast that had been set, but Claude insisted on keeping him close by. Musicians played in the far side, and there were tables of different foods, sweets and treats for everyone to enjoy. A small group of both men and women gathered around Claude, eager to gossip and speak of the current events.

"Do tell us Claude, how is the hunt for those filthy gypsy animals progressing?" one man scoffed.

"Personally, I can't wait until you've eradicated them all," another woman chimed.

"Awful creatures," someone else added.

They barely gave Claude the opportunity to respond, but when he did, they would eat his words like cake. They admired his charm and looked to him as a hero amongst men. Their distaste of the gypsies was abundantly clear. They spent the afternoon complaining about them and the conditions of the city because of them. Julien was forced to silently endure their ridicule and taunts and teases. He knew his master's patience was short, so he didn't want to seem rude and excuse himself. He sat quietly until the party died down and everyone went home. He was tired, and happy when Claude led him back to his workshop. He immediately went to his bed to set up for the night, but Claude seemed to want to sit and converse for a moment. Julien was nervous, but he didn't have a great time and decided to talk about it.

"Why did you bring me to that? Those people were terribly mean," Julien whined.

"Have you not always wanted to attend a banquet?"

"Yes, but-"

"I just thought you may be old enough to come out and enjoy a nice afternoon with what I consider to be my friends. I'm rather offended you would insult them in such a way. Did you not enjoy the food and wine? And the games they played?"

"I beg your forgiveness. I do appreciate that. It was a very pleasant day."

"I'm glad, and I hope you can forgive me for my past mistakes against you, Julien. I never meant to hurt you before. From now on, I will treat you more as a brother. You can join me in my social life and will no longer be required to wear your chain. I know now it is not right," his master confessed to him, and Julien could see that he wanted to gain their relationship back.

"Thank you, Master."

"You can call me James; we are family."

"James... I've always respected you. You should know I never touched the gypsy woman."

"Then why did you help her escape?"

"I will not lie to you, I did feel affection towards her, but she betrayed that. I just wanted her away from me."

"And how did she do that?"

"She did sinful things with a soldier in the church, vile things really."

"What soldier? Who would abandon their oath and commit treason against the king in such a way?"

"I don't know his name, but I did hit him. He was left with a bruised and cut face."

James thought for a moment. He recalled Captain Ivan had a similar injury just recently.

"Thank you for trusting me with this, but I must go, Julien. Charles is meeting me before we report to the king. I think we may have found where the gypsies are hiding."

Julien did his best to trust him, but hearing the fates of his friends made him feel sick. He wanted to know if James had truly found their camp and quietly followed down until James ran into Charles. He hid behind the stairwell to listen to what they may know and have planned.

"So, do you believe Julien will be able to help us?" he heard Charles mumble to James.

"No. He's just as useless as the gypsy trash he was spawned from. He's lucky I'm not hanging him with the rest of the degenerates when they are gathered. Tomorrow night is the night, we have finally found the vermin's hiding place."

Heartbroken would hardly be a suitable word to describe how Julien felt in that moment. He thought things had truly changed, but he was wrong. He would have done anything to help his master had he asked, but he revealed his true feelings in that moment. It was obvious that he never loved or even cared about Julien, and he couldn't hear another word of it. That was all he needed as he trudged back up the stairs and contemplated his life the entire way to his bed. He couldn't stay, but he wasn't sure if he wanted to go back to the camp either.

The church had always been his home, but as he stared at the chain lying on the floor, he made his decision. James had ruined everything he loved about his safe place, and he snuck out of the church just after dark to find shelter once again with the gypsies. He felt wanted in the camp despite any tense feelings between him and Natalya. He didn't want her nor anyone else to die, so he had to warn them immediately. He walked until he couldn't take another step and could barely recall Nik finding him. He tried to hold himself up enough to speak, but his throat was dry and the words wouldn't come out.

"How did you escape?" Julien heard Marie exclaim as he tried to catch his breath. She hugged him and helped Nik support him as they walked back to the camp together.

"I will tell you everything just as soon as I can get some water or eat. I'm glad you all made it out, I was so worried. The camp was much easier to find the second time," he told them.

"Did you see Lee? How was he?" Nik interjected.

"I never saw him, I was locked in the church away from the others," he confessed.

"Oh." Nik worried of his friend's condition. His regret for having to leave him was apparent in his eyes.

As they walked inside, Natalya noticed Julien. She ran up and stopped him; placing both hands on his shoulders. They had never truly had a chance to talk the last time they were together, and she expressed that she was thankful for him to be safe at the camp once again. They stared for a moment; Julien could feel the pain in his chest intensify, but she pulled him close and wrapped her arms around him. She hugged him tightly, and after a moment, he gave in and reached his arms around her as well. All the pain and hurt she had caused him was vanishing, and he was just glad she was alive and safe.

"Julien, I feel I owe it to you to make things right, I never wanted to hurt you, and I'm so sorry," she cried into his shoulder.

"Please, I don't want to think about those things anymore. I just want to forget everything that happened."

"Can we start again? I want to show you who I really am."

"I would like that very much," he smiled at her. Just then she bounced back in cheer.

"Oh, Julien you must come see. While you were gone a man arrived, a glass blower from Romania was passing through," she told him, knowing it would peak his interest.

"I'm surprised he would stop here."

"He wasn't aware of the city's condition when he first arrived. He was lucky that Nik found him first. With everything that's been happening though, it hasn't been safe for him to travel any farther, so he set up his equipment here for the time being. You should see it, Julien. I know you would just love it."

Her words were soft, she spoke to his heart, finding a new art for him to love. He had forgotten his mission for returning.

They sat on a bench nearby as the man worked and watched in amazement as he spun the molten glass. He made it seem so easy as he shaped it into something beautiful. Julien was most impressed.

"I would love for you to show me how you do this, sir. Is it difficult to learn?" He was shy to approach the man. Someone with his skill deserved much respect, and Julien didn't want to bother him.

"I wouldn't say it's hard, sometimes challenging, but it's what I love doing."

"And that shows in your work; it is something to be admired. I've worked with clay before but nothing quite this spectacular."

"He's being modest, Julien makes beautiful dolls with his clay," Marie chimed in.

"Is that so? And you say you'd like to learn to work with glass?"

"Yes, I really would."

"There are many opportunities for me in London and even Spain, but I don't like staying in any one place for very long. I travel frequently and set up shop wherever life takes me."

"That sounds fantastic sir, a life's dream.

"I'm glad you think so. I'm getting older and my equipment is nothing less than a chore to pack around. If you were to help me I would gladly teach you everything I know," the man offered. Julien's heart jumped with excitement, it was his fantasy to travel with his art. The man's wagon had room for his wheel, he could sneak in the night and get it from the church, they could travel together trading art forms and selling their work to the high class and wealthy.

"That would be a great honor to me, sir!" Julien exclaimed.

"I'm running out of the supplies I need, and I can feel the weight of the French government. This place is not safe, and I would like to leave as soon as I can. I am giving my mule one more day of rest, but I plan to leave by this time tomorrow. I would very much appreciate your company."

"And I've always longed to leave this place." Julien took almost no time to consider the proposal; there was really nothing in France for him anymore.

He immediately ran to tell Natalya, who had gone to eat with the others. At first, she hugged him in excitement, but then the reason for him telling her sank in. He wanted her to join him in his adventures. She too had thought of leaving France but was afraid to leave everyone she knew at such a trying time. They laid a blanket near a small fire, and he asked her to at least take the night to think on it. He kissed her forehead, and she leaned into him. They sat together and watched the musicians play their instruments, calming the camp as the sun set for the evening.

Suddenly, the torch near the gathering table was extinguished. It was the fire that had always remained lit, and the gypsies began to worry. The smaller lights in front of the tents went out one by one from the outside of the camp, and the darkness quickly worked its way to the center. Everyone was forced together in the middle. A scream came from one side of the camp and then two and three, but before anyone could react, the valley was filled with screams and terrified cries. The soldiers had found the camp and invaded quickly. As they watched the camp crumble before them, Nik pulled Marie back into their tent and kissed her.

"You have to go, I can't let them catch you."

"No, I'm not leaving you," she insisted. She was becoming panicked, and Nik needed to calm her down. He grabbed her face and looked her in the eyes as he instructed her on what to do next.

"Marie, you don't understand, I need you to get out. You need to send for help from the brothers and sisters of the east."

"What? Who are they, and how will I know them?"

"You just will. Please trust me, Marie and leave now. Go past the wall of the outer city limit. We have allies on the other side, and the leader will be there. He needs to know of this right away, and he'll keep you safe."

She wanted to refuse and stay with him, but there was a pleading look in his eyes that wouldn't allow her to let him down. She listened carefully to his instructions, and did exactly as he instructed.

# Chapter Thirty-Nine

25 November

The camp was completely surrounded. Nik held her tightly as chaos took over the home outside of their tent. Marie didn't have faith in herself to escape the siege and get to help, but Nik assured her that he could distract the guards long enough for her to get out. She knew it wouldn't take long for the soldiers to get past Nik, so she would have to give it her all and be quick. She kissed him and followed him out. She knew the pace at which her feet could carry her would mean life or death for so many. She used this motivation to escape and run as fast as she could into the trees.

There was only a short distance before the wall; she just needed to get past it. She ran so quickly that she didn't see how deep the snow was getting. Charles was catching up; his hands nearly touching her. He was after her and her alone while James and his guards were chaotically rounding up the others. She could feel the cold air filling her lungs in her panicked pace, but she pushed herself all the harder to make it out of the city. She could see the wall. It wasn't much further, and she was determined to make it.

Marie was focused on it so intently that she missed the small drop. She lost her footing and tumbled down the side of a hill, rolling through the snow. She looked up as he was standing near the top trying to figure a way down. She was so close and knew she could make it. Charles was fat and wouldn't get over the wall anyhow. She picked herself up and brushed the snow from her dress. That's when she saw him; James had come to find her as well. She continued on, finally reaching the wall but soon realized she wasn't tall enough to climb it. She searched for a crack, an opening, anything, but when she finally found one, it was too late. Charles shoved his hands into her back, throwing them both to the ground. She struggled to get away, but he pinned her down.

"My, my sweet girl," he snarled as he ran his finger down her chest. "It's just like the first time we met," his voice whispered in her ear. She kicked his stomach and almost escaped, but didn't make it very far. James had gotten there as well and caught her. He wrapped his arms around her tightly, and his hand pulled the hair behind her ear to ensure she heard his next words clearly.

"Marie, you need to stop fighting this. It's over, and you will watch as they all die."

She kicked and thrashed her body around, but he was stronger. James brought her back to the valley where Anthony held Nik captive, and the guards had captured the others.

"Keep her away from the rest of the swine. She is mine to deal with."

"James, please stop!" Marie cried.

"You betrayed me. Now come along and stop making this harder on yourself. You won't win, do you understand me?" He commanded the guards to escort the rest of the prisoners to the jail as Anthony and Charles led Nik and Marie to the interrogation room under the courthouse. There were many things James was concerned with, but his main focus was on Gracianna.

"The guards have searched every tent and element of the camp. Damnit, tell me where she is, Marie!"

"Whether I'm dead or alive, you'll never find her," Marie threatened. Her stare was daring and taunted James. He didn't even try to control his anger as he slapped her as hard as he could. Nik tried to charge after him, but the guards held him back tightly.

"Maybe if I had my way with the girl, one of them would be inclined to tell us where your child is," Charles suggested.

"Don't you dare touch her!" Nik screamed.

"Nik doesn't know anything; the answer only lies with me, and I'm not afraid of you," Marie challenged. Even when she felt safest at the camp, she was always prepared for this moment.

"Do whatever you want to me, but please don't let him do this to her. I'm begging you!" Nik pleaded.

"Nik is useless to you, James; leave him out of it. This is between you and I."

Charles twisted Marie's arm behind her back. She let out a cry but stood firm in her refusal to tell them anything. Charles began kissing her neck, touching her back. Marie held strong, if she were afraid, it was hidden deep and she refused to let it show.

"You can let him do whatever you want to me, I don't care. Our daughter is safer without you." James stared at her for a moment; the look in her eyes was enough of an answer to him.

"That's enough, Charles. She won't tell us anything. Yet."

"Shame. Next time, the judge won't interrupt, and I will have you one day," he grumbled in her ear.

"Gag her, Anthony. This is the time where Marie will watch silently and witness what these gypsies and revolutionaries will all be facing soon enough. Charles, make sure Nikolais is comfortable; we have a long night ahead of us."

As Anthony and Charles prepared their tools and equipment, Joseph came rushing in. He told them that news had just arrived at his hospital of what had happened, and he was surprised. For years they had searched for the camp, and he was curious as to how it finally came together. Marie's heart broke for Julien as she listened to Charles explain how James had manipulated him into leading them to the gypsies, his friends, unknowingly. She listened as Joseph congratulated him on the win, but wondered why he had not been called to be a part of it. The king had given orders to not disrupt important work he had been doing with his father for the palace. Joseph expressed his appreciation but was glad to finally be informed. He wanted to continue in his work with James. Together, they interrogated Nik for hours about who the masked man was, but Nik refused any information. If Marie could be strong, then he would give it everything he could to be as well.

"Even if I did know, I'll die before I help you."

"And what about the girl, you care about her, don't you? Would you speak if it would save her?" Joseph was curious to see if Marie would be Nik's weakness. Maybe they could bargain with her.

"I can only pray for her soul. She knows that. She would rather die than see you rise even higher. For her child..."

"She's MY fucking child!" James snapped. He stabbed Nik in the leg with his knife. He grunted but quickly worked past the pain.

"For HER child, she'd endure anything to bring you down, she already showed you that. She's the strongest woman I've ever known, and I would follow in her every step. You can torture me, or try to kill me, but I've prepared for this! You get nothing, and the gypsies will rise and tear you down like the lonely pathetic horse pile you are!"

James pulled the knife from Nik's leg to stab him in the chest, but Joseph stopped him.

"Not like this. Anthony, I think now would be a good time to escort Marie to a cell in the courthouse." He looked at Nik when she was gone from the room, "maybe harsher than instant death would be to tie him to his lover and burn them both in the square." Joseph advised.

"But Marie..." James hesitated.

"You know as well as I that she is no longer yours. She's taken your daughter and lusted with a traitor of the king. I didn't want her to hear, because maybe you can try again to persuade her, but if not, they should suffer death together."

"You have a clever way of thinking, Joseph. I would like to do that much better. Go, lock him up."

"Consider it done," Joseph said as he took Nik away.

As Marie sat alone in her cell, she worried of all her friends' fates. She waited in the cold darkness until she finally heard the sound of someone in the doorway. An overwhelming sensation filled the room, and a darkness began creeping in. She was terrified but couldn't let her strength falter. She looked into the shadow at the entrance and took a deep breath to toughen her voice.

"What are you doing here, James? There are no more questions you could possibly ask that I would answer for you."

"This is not what I want for you, my darling. They wish to kill you off with the others, but I can save you from all of this if you just chose to be with me again." James was seductive, and Marie thought on his offer. Could she bargain herself for others?

At what price could she sell her soul to the devil and save all the innocent? There were many questions, but only one that would make her sacrifice worth anything.

"Would you end this war on these people? You know that you don't have to do any of this. I believe there has to be a better way."

"This is not just my war, Marie. The king has demanded this. It's what he wants, and I must abide."

"Nik and his people should be free to live peacefully. They're not hurting anyone."

"Their kind has hurt everyone! That man you think you know, he's the worst kind of deceiver. "

"Nik isn't bad. You don't know-"

"You love him, don't you?"

"What?" She hadn't thought on it. She trusted Nik, and he made her feel something she could never truly describe, but to love him?

"Don't deny it, stupid girl. You sure are willing to risk your life for him."

"I don't."

"You've let him seduce your thoughts. I know you. I love you, I just-"

"You never once told me you loved me before. Why now?"

"I took you for granted. I thought you would still be with me at home. I miss you with me, and it's made me realize what I've known to be true all along."

"I never had a home with you. I was too young to understand. The things you did to me, what you used me for; that's not what a loving husband does."

"You're still too young to really understand why I had to do it."

"I'm not a child anymore! You didn't love me, you loved controlling me. I see that now. If you really loved me, you would have trusted me. I had proved years ago that I would stay with you. I proved myself to you when I came back to you after seeing you in the square. I saw how you looked at me, but I came back home. Even after seeing how angry you were, I still went to you and stayed. You could have killed me, but I continued to devote my heart to you. I can't ever say that you loved me, but I did love you."

James seemed insulted by her accusation. She almost felt annoyed by having to explain to him as simply as she could that the pain and anxiety he had caused her for so long was a life that no one should have to live. He had broken her heart and body for the last time, and she had no desire to return to a life of sadness and hurt. Her heart was not with him, but that only seemed to anger his ego. She did her best to stay strong as he shoved her down, demanding to know where she had hidden Graci. She held on to the knowledge that her daughter would always be safer, and that death would only seal her daughter's whereabouts in her grave. He grabbed her throat in his rage, but his face changed as she stared into his eyes. A look of sadness overcame him, and he let her go.

"Please, Marie, don't do this. Come be with me, and I will keep you safe. I will love you and promise to never hurt you again. If you come back to me, I will forgive all your sins against me and disregard your last words. Please," he whispered as he pressed his forehead into hers.

"I want believe you," she whispered as she laid back on the blanket on the floor. He got down in between her legs and kissed her neck. She put her arms around him. He rubbed against her and touched and kissed her. As he untied the corset string, she reached around his back. James jumped up, and Marie suddenly felt a cold chill on her chest; He had a small knife pointed at her, and the blade was cold on her skin.

"Are you looking for this? You made up lies about me when I did nothing but give you my love, and now, you want to kill me?"

"You're a cunning prick. You nearly killed me before, so why would I ever go back to you?"

"I disciplined you because you acted like a selfish brat, disobeying me and doing as you pleased."

"I couldn't stand the dark, no one can! It's not a way to live!"

"You're right. It's no way for you to live. Then, it is decided; you will burn at the stake with your lover."

"What?"

"Oh, didn't I tell you? You will be tied to him in the square and burned for your sins," James smiled as he spoke of her fate.

"We aren't witches, you can't do this!"

"Please, don't be so naïve, Marie. Natalya used witchcraft at the festival, the whole town saw. Nik's association with her and the fact that he leads gypsy witches in rebellion, the city is begging to burn him! And you, my little harlot... you confessed your lustful ways with him in front of all of Paris. You made it too easy, my dear! What other outcome could you possibly have expected?"

She stood, frozen in the fear and reality of what was happening. He shoved her back into her cell and locked the door. He touched her face as tears fell from her eyes.

"Just as beautiful as the day I found you, Marie. As I've said before, it's such a waste to harm that pretty face," he said as he left her. She stood there, unable move. She's prepared herself for this moment, yet felt the most unprepared when it finally happened. She tried to pull up every bad memory she had to figure out if knowing she was living her last moments alone in a cell could be considered her worst. She determined she had lived through worse, when she heard a terrifying voice come from another door into the room. It was Charles.

"You made the right decision, choosing to be alone is much better. I told you I would have you one day, and you just threw out the only person who has ever kept us apart," he smirked as he unlocked the door to her cell and let himself in.

She was wrong; there were far worse things than being alone. She felt even more afraid than she ever had with James and tried to fight him off. He shoved her into the wall, and she fell to her hands and knees. He had always wanted this, and no one was there to stop it. He came behind her and wrapped one hand around her throat, but she didn't even fight. She knew it would be a useless struggle; he had won. The tears fell from her face as he violated her, and she prayed for a quick death to come.

# Chapter Forty

14 December 1798

James gathered his men early that morning. He charged Anthony with supervising the other guards in retrieving every convicted rebel. He wanted them all to be locked together in a new arrangement of cages that had just been built around the square. He wanted every single one to be present for the day's events, and instructed him to have them packed in as tightly as possible. If there weren't enough cages, they had more that were ready for a quick build. He announced to all of his men that the madness would end that day, and they would be doing away with every single gypsy they found and caught. He felt a sense of relief. The day had finally come when all of his years of work were paying off.

They brought Nik, Marie and Natalya out first. In the middle of the stage, two poles had been erected for the burnings. James made Ivan and Charles handle his wife and her lover while he prided himself of taking care of the witch.

Ivan tied Marie to the pole first, binding her tightly. He looked down at her. She was so young and had a beauty that was of destroyed innocence. Nothing felt right about her there, but he had to do as the king ordered him.

"You don't deserve this; I know you are not evil," he whispered to Marie as he bound her arms. She looked away, silently staring off at the city.

As Charles led Nik to the pole, Nik punched his elbow back and broke Charles's nose, knocking him to the ground. He ran to Marie and kissed her.

"I had to kiss you one last time. I need you to know that I love you, and I'm sorry we're here. I never-" Nik tried to profess to her, but two more guards came and grabbed him. They kicked and beat him to the ground. Marie cried for them to stop, but Ivan had already broken up the issue.

"Get him up, and tie his hands," Charles demanded as he wiped the blood from his face.

Natalya watched Nik struggle as James pulled her up and tied her on the adjacent pole. He never broke focus as he twisted and hooped the rope around her. It was an art that he quite enjoyed, and he made sure to tie her there with care for the tool he placed around her body.

"Are you too coward to tie your own wife? You abuse her, lead her to her death but can't even tie her there yourself?"

"Dear, my wife is already dead, and that girl has chosen her fate with him," he whispered in her ear. His hand slid down from her neck and touched her chest as he tied her tighter.

"Yes, I heard about what you did with the thought of me. I could bring the fantasy to life, you need not imagine any longer. Just let us go, and I'll be yours."

"Please, don't try to flatter me."

"You were less cruel with a wife, and you can be that way again. Let me show you," she persuaded. Natalya's voice was seductive, tempting even. James pushed her hair from her eyes.

"You are very beautiful," he paused for a very brief moment as he brushed his hand over her cheek, "a beautiful kind of demon. Even if I wasn't repulsed by your kind, the desire to kill you all is not mine alone. And I will very much enjoy the sight of you burning, witch." She spit in his face. Frustrated, James slapped her. Ivan came back to James, he had more than enough.

"I have done my part and proven my loyalty. Everything is exactly as the king wants it."

"And we appreciate-"

"But I won't stay and watch you, Charles, and your other men abuse these people needlessly until you kill them."

"What are you talking about?"

"Charles and his men are boasting together of the prisoners they raped and tortured in the night. It's vile and wrong. And what I just saw you do... I'll be at the pub, I refuse to stay here and be a part of this," Ivan scowled, but before James could stop him, he was gone.

"Should we tell the king?" Anthony came up behind James. He was concerned of the captain's loyalty as well.

"No, let the coward hide behind his drink. Come, Anthony, there is much to be done."

Marie twisted and wriggled in the ropes until she was able to free her hand. She reached back and grabbed Nik's hand, locking her fingers with his.

"Nik?" she called to him.

"I'm so sorry! I never wanted this for you. I love you. You should know before-"

"It's alright, Nik. I told you before I would rather die here with you than live another day without you."

Charles came to Nik and Marie and pulled their rope as hard as he could, tightening it to painfully secure around them. He then stood in front of Nik, facing him while also caressing Marie's face as he spoke.

"Sweet Marie, the judge wasn't lying when he told me of your beauty; I just never realized that beauty was deep inside you as well," he smirked, staring into Nik's eyes as he taunted her.

"What did you do to her?" Nik demanded an answer, but he was afraid of the truth.

"I am so glad to have been the last to be inside of you before they burn you, dear girl."

Marie began to cry, squeezing Nik's hand tightly.

"You disgusting shit eater!" Nik screamed, but Charles quickly gagged him.

"Sir, consider yourself to die a blessed man, she is such a sweet little treat... Anyone who has felt that soft, lovely skin... such a blessing." He touched her chest and quivered as his eyes closed. He let out a giant evil grin. "Just the thought of what we did, Nik... and I know she loved it," Charles laughed as he enjoyed their pain. He watched as Nik angrily struggled under his ropes and left the stage to help James.

Marie took a deep breath when she heard Nik's cries. Suddenly, the knot in her chest went away, as if the end may not be as terrible as she feared. She felt a calm come over her even as she listened to Nik struggle to hold his emotions back behind her. She squeezed his hand tighter, letting him know she would be strong for him too.

"Nik, even through the pain, don't let go of my hand. I love you as well," she told him.

"That's very touching Marie." James had been listening. He stood close to her as he spoke. "I handed you every opportunity to save yourself, but you betrayed me yet again. I can see that wouldn't change if I gave you one last chance. If that is so, let us proceed, shall we?"

As James spoke to the crowd, Marie began to sing to Nik the same soft lullaby that had always comforted her through the toughest times life could hand out. She watched as everyone waited in fear, and felt her heart break once more as Charles brought Julien out and chained him to a seat in front on the stage. There were many people she pitied, but she really felt that Julien had endured so much more than the reset, and even worried of the life he would be forced to endure when there was no one to protect him.

"I first want to celebrate our guest of honor," he jeered as he faced the gypsies locked in their cages. "My friend and brother, Julien, is the one who led us straight to you. He followed in my plan precisely. Despite his association with you in the past, he has been granted amnesty for aiding us in your capture," James announced proudly.

"You're a liar! I had nothing to do with it, I swear!" Julien cried out, "I was tricked!"
James was the master manipulator, but Julien still felt foolish for falling for anything he had said. He was made to look like a traitor to those he cared about more than anything.

"Of course." Charles shoved a rag into his mouth and gagged him. James stepped to the front of the stage.

"People of Paris, today is a very big day! For years our city has been plagued with these gypsies. They've attacked our wives, terrorized our children, and stolen the goods and resources we've worked so hard for. They've torn down our community. Today that all ends! This man, Nikolais Quinn, leader of these gypsy witches and rebels, has been caught!"

Shouts of victory and cheers filled the city as James spoke of their success. He had built up their energies and worded his speeches to give them the same feeling of being a big part in the win.

"But it is with deep regret that he is not alone on his post. We unfortunately did not catch him before he stole my wife in the night, seducing her to his way, convincing her she was one of them. She has chosen to be with this man in his criminal ways and will burn alongside him," he shared with sadness. The people booed and hissed at her. They pitied the judge and the heartbreak he must have been feeling to lose his wife to the gypsies.

"And on the post next to them, Natalya is to burn for witchcraft. Gypsies are witches and use the black arts to seduce you. They try to win you over with their deception and cunning ways. After the burnings, the rest of them will hang. We will be rid of this disease in our city!"

The crowd cheered once again in excitement. Many were hurt by the curfews and restrictions on the city while the gypsies were at bay. They were convinced that ridding the city of them would solve all of their problems. James lit a torch, and the monsignor approached the stage to pray for their souls.

"Now! We watch them burn!" he shouted as the people applauded.

"No!" Julien screamed. He was forced to watch as the three struggled in fear and hopelessness. James knew it hurt him to see them like that. He felt a deep guilt, if he had just stayed in his workshop and not been so selfish then his friends wouldn't be here.

As the hay was readied for lighting, an arrow shot to the stage and almost hit James. The masked man had returned. He stood on a pillar across from the square, and the people looked around hoping the guards would catch him.

"Citizens of Paris! We are not your enemy! The king and his cabinet, as well as the judge and his men are paranoid and corrupt. They've tricked you into mass genocide for their own vendetta!" The masked man announced, but as he was trying to speak the people began to throw anything at hand at him. At that moment, all of the gypsies opened their cages while the crowd of spectators grew stunned and afraid.

"I have unlocked all their prisons in the square, and all the gypsies have been freed! They will fight for their freedom but they mean no harm to the people of Paris," he preached, but the crowd was not convinced and began to attack.

The masked culprit fled to the courthouse as the gypsies ran against the soldiers. James had an opportunity to catch him; no one knew the courthouse like he did. This was his chance, but he couldn't risk the three escaping their fates. He threw his torch onto the hay under them and watched as it went up in flames.

"Damn all of you! You will die, none the less!" he snapped as he ensured a good fire had progressed and then ran to the courtroom to find his enemy. He diligently searched each and every room using hidden entrances and blind corners. He opened the secret door to a large court when a peculiar smell filled the hallway. A few of his clerks and other judges and lawyers that had been working late ran to flee the building, but James refused to give up. As he searched the remaining courts, he ran into Joseph who was trying to escape the building as well.

"The building is on fire. Claude, we must go. They've won, the rebels' attacks are more than we can bear at the moment, you can't stay in here!" Joseph shouted over the sound of flames taking control of its victim, the courthouse.

"No! We must find the masked man. Everything is falling apart, and the gypsy trash is going crazy!"

"James, this is madness, what has gotten into you? Why are you so obsessed with this? You would kill yourself over these people?" Joseph realized that James had completely changed. The old James, full of virtue, morals and self-respect was gone. There was nothing left of him but delusion and paranoia.

"What do you mean? I'm trying to do what needs to be done," James replied.

"This is not the man you once were; the man I became friends with."

"And this is not the time for that. Are you going to help me?"

"Look at yourself, James! Years ago, you couldn't care less about these people, and you were repulsed by child brides, but now you've gone mad with anger and hatred for a race of people, and you're burning what was your own child bride out there."

James noticed the courtroom was burning around them, but humoured Joseph.

"I received my orders from the king, no different than you did, Joseph. We have been following the same plan for years together."

"The gypsies had nothing to do with your father's death Claude. The king made up some bullshit to preserve his reputation and motivate you with anger, but your father couldn't keep his prick in his pants and contracted syphilis. He refused to take care of himself, and it killed him, and I was bound by an oath of confidentiality. None of that, however has to do with you kidnapping a child. Everything you did to that poor girl... I couldn't let you kill her."

"I don't believe you. Why would you bring this up now? Why-" he stuttered, but it was in that very moment James noticed Joseph's clothes and the mask he was holding. "it's you... you're the..."

"This isn't how I wanted you to find out. It's disgusting what the king wants for these people. I know the things Charles did to turn the city against them. I thought you were better than that, but you have lost every bit of soul you had left. This wasn't my plan, but I had to save that girl. She couldn't die under my watch."

"But you were with me all that night."

"It didn't take but a few minutes. A few minutes to convince Rosa of whom you really were now. She would have done anything for you before... before all this."

"What are you talking about? All those interrogations and torture on rebels that you yourself performed... how are you better than me?"

"None of them generally knew anything important. They all knew the risk when they joined the cause. We had a plan, the tortures and manipulations, all for this. This day wasn't meant to come for a while, but I couldn't let you kill them."

"But Nikolais... even Ivan was suspicious, but you?" James felt the room getting hotter, and his heart began to race.

"Yes, Ivan has a good heart, but he's a drunk. It's merely coincidence he was never around when I had to interrupt your madness. And I made it so Nik would seem the likely suspect, always leading a protest or helping with whatever was needed. He agreed to act as the leader, as the distraction."

"Distraction for what?"

"For the events leading up to this! I needed you to follow him, so I could get the important things taken care of. I know you never believed a kid to be the master mind behind everything, James. You're smarter than that."

"You're a traitor!"

Joseph blocked James as he charged at him with his sword, and they began to fight. The building was quickly burning down around them. Joseph covered his face with a cloth knowing that James would choose to fight through. He was confident as they continued in their duel. He could see that James was giving it his all, but a dark fog began pouring through the hallways, capturing James's breath. He'd been distracted by the flames but caught off guard from the smoke and began to choke. James fought until the flames began entering their space, and that's when Joseph took his shot. James had grown weary from smoke inhalation, and he pushed him into the next room and locked the door. He could hear James try to scream and bang on the door, but the damage was done and the ceiling had collapsed. He took it as a sign to leave and quickly fled the building.

He found Charles, who was panicked and looking to him for what to do. No one, except James, knew who he really was. He continued in his façade as he advised him to gather the soldiers and wait for an order. Charles did as he said, and Joseph made his way into the crowd.

"Joseph!" Nik called out, but before anyone could spot them, Joseph pulled him into a dark alley.

"I'm so relieved you were able to escape the fire, Nik. James is dead."

"That's great news!"

"Yes, and my identity is still unknown, so we can carry out our plan as originally intended."

"We can go on like we should have."

"But we can only do that if I remain the physician for the king. With the current state things are in, we are more at risk than ever. We may have won this battle, but the war is far from over. I have been hearing rumor that the Bonaparte brothers are also working against the royalists. If that's true, we have a lot more to do to ensure we are on the same side," Joseph confessed.

"What can I do?"

"Be the leader, the real leader. You have to do this on your own for now. If I'm caught helping you in any way then the entire mission could be exposed."

"But I don't know how to lead. This entire mess is my fault. You left me in charge, and I destroyed everything twice. I can't do this."

"You can and you will have to. But for now, with the city in such disarray; it could be days before they find James. You have to be the one to announce his death; the guards will flee at his demise. That should give you some time to regroup and figure out your next step. The longer I stay here with you though, the more we risk."

Nik nervously stood to leave but Joseph stopped him.

"Wait, first tell me, how is Marie? Was she badly hurt? And you? Rosa?"

"We got burned, but there's nothing too damaging. We will be fine."

"Maybe physically, but this will take its toll on you. I will see to both of you in a few days when things have died down. My father will need me at the hospital to tend to the soldiers that have been hurt today, and it's probably best that I lay low there for a bit until things aren't as chaotic here. Now you must go."

Nik ran out to the stage and stood above the fading fire. He yelled out as loud as he could, capturing the city's attention. He announced the judge's death and where to find his body. The soldiers fled when they heard his speech, and the gypsies rejoiced in their victory. The citizens of Paris gave up and hid in their homes. The soldiers retreated in fear, and Anthony did his best to take charge, but he was alone. The gypsies fought hard, and now that the king's army was gone, he felt hopeless. Realizing that James was dead and Charles and Ivan were missing, he gave up. In a panic he fled to the king.

# Chapter Forty-One

15 February 1799

Life in Paris seemed to settle much quicker than people had anticipated. The fighting stopped within days, and the king withdrew his men. James's funeral proved to be a divider amongst the people, but it was a quiet tension. The gypsies found homes amongst the French, and the economy began to balance. The city had calmed, but the healing process had only begun.

One morning while Nik was helping Marie, he noticed her burns were still in bad condition. Joseph had given word that he could help safely and Nik felt it was important that she was treated immediately. She hesitated, knowing that he was already risking so much by continuing in work for the king while also leading the revolutionaries and gypsies. She didn't think going was a good idea, but Rosa promised she would ride to get Graci from Alexander in England if she agreed to go. She knew Graci would need a mother that was healthy, so she finally gave in. Her hand was still swollen, and the burn hadn't even begun to heal yet. Whether she felt good about it or not, she had to go.

The next morning, they traveled quickly through the outskirts of the city and when they arrived Joseph was almost finished seeing to Natalya. Nik went to speak with her and Julien as Joseph examined the burn on Marie's hand. He checked her body for any other injuries that may need attention, and gave her a few things to help in her recovery.

"This should work." He rubbed a cream on it and tightly bound her arm. "That should protect it so it can heal properly, but I'm really not worried about it. Some wounds just take longer than others do. Not to mention, this arm has really been through some trauma. Nik informed me you had broken it twice after I had set it the first time. You're really lucky it didn't shift the bone and cause more problems."

"That's good to hear. I'm so glad you could see us. I really wouldn't trust anyone else," she admitted. He gave her a small smile and looked back at Nik, who came over and put his hand on Joseph's shoulder. The two men exchanged a curious glance before Nik brought the others inside to give him some privacy.

"Have you seen my property, Marie? There's a boardwalk, and the trees are lovely this time of year," Joseph inquired.

"I would love to see it," she smiled as he led her to the walkway.

They enjoyed a simple conversation as they walked together, making their way off of the boardwalk. As they ventured through the brush, Joseph spotted an old tree that had fallen. It made for the perfect bench. He sat down and gestured for Marie to sit next to him. "Marie, there's something I should really tell you."

"I suspected that when you asked me away from everyone else." She smiled for a brief moment until she noticed he wasn't sharing in her same lightness. "What is it though? You look troubled."

"Do you remember in the valley when Nik was losing blood, and you asked to know the identity of the man helping you?"

"It was you," she answered before he could tell her. She didn't look up when she spoke, just simply smiled. "There was no one else in that place but the three of us, I know because I looked and never told Nik what I asked that man."

"Yes, that's right."

Marie looked into the forest of trees. Faint pastel shades and light greens seemed to surround them. Everything was just beginning to rebuild its life from the harsh winter, nature including, and the colors brought a promise of an early spring to come. Marie smiled and knew that if anyone was a leader and protector of people, Joseph made the most sense. She replayed events of the past over and over in her mind. It was like a giant puzzle in which the picture was clear now that she had all the pieces. But she could sense that wasn't everything he needed to get off his chest.

"What is it, Joseph? What else do you need to tell me?"

"Why do you think there's more?"

"Because no one else knows of your secret. I'm not someone of importance to this cause, so I don't believe you would be telling me if you didn't have more troubling news to share."

"First of all, you are of great importance to this cause. Something about you inspired me to push everything ahead. I treated you all of those months desperately wanting to save you, but I couldn't without compromising everything. I had to plan carefully, and even then, we almost failed. You are very important, Marie," he promised. He kissed her forehead then stared at the ground, preparing his next words. She held his hand, assuring him that she would hear whatever he had to say.

"I know you loved James. I can see you still mourning his death in secret."

"No, I'm glad he's gone. He wasn't a good man."

"Your first love never quite goes away completely, though. You don't have to say it; the feelings in your heart belong to only you, but I have seen you. I know some part of you still hurts for what you had with him during those times that he seemed to not be such a bad man."

Marie thought on his words. James had once been a loving husband and father of her daughter. There were many times she remembered having with him that she wished she could still enjoy, but those times were over. She had to put it out of her mind. It hurt too much, and she had Nik now.

"Why are you saying these things to me, Joseph?"

"Because I think you should know from me. You need to know why it happened the way it did. He had found out who I was. He had already been going mad with stress and anger, and it turned him into something that you wouldn't be able to love if you had chosen him. I didn't think, I just acted. We were in the courthouse that final day."

"You're the one who killed him..." Marie stared blankly. His shoulders dropped; the events had spun in his head for weeks, but it hurt more when she said it aloud. She put on a strong face but he knew the truth behind her mask. She turned back to the woods, stood and walked towards it. She didn't say a word; Joseph grabbed her hand, he didn't want to lose her.

"Marie, please speak to me," he begged. She looked at the ground, and couldn't make herself speak; she didn't know what to say. She didn't even know what to feel. He pulled her back and wrapped his arms around her, holding her close. A tear fell, but she couldn't cry. She didn't know what emotion would take over; so many ran through her mind and heart.

"Marie, I'm so sorry. I hate watching your pain and hurt. I know you may not trust me right now, but I love you so much. From the minute I saw you, I have cared for you. I've loved you for a long time, Marie." The words had slipped before he could stop them. He paused but she didn't look up at him. "Please, forgive me for any hurt I've caused you."

She pulled back and looked at him, staring for a brief moment. Maybe it was the rush and anxiety of everything he was and had done that would cause him to profess such an idea as to love her, but she couldn't hear any more of it. Men did many stupid things because of love, and she didn't see Joseph as a stupid man. She tried to comprehend her feelings, but it All she could do was walk away. It was more to take in than she could handle at the time. There were no words for what she felt. She left him there as he sat down and cried for her. She quickly disappeared into the distance without so much as a glance back.

# Epilogue

19 February 1799

It was a hard fight for the gypsies, but they gave it their all until the king finally pulled his men. They retreated in fear, realizing they had been outnumbered. Many people took their loss like a medicine and swallowed it with a shot, but Anthony seemed to take it harder than anyone. His realization that Claude was dead sent him into a deep depression. He'd found the judge to be a hero to him, and his world crashed down at the loss of his mentor and friend.

It had affected his marriage and family as he processed the events when a messenger sent for him to immediately report to the king. Anthony forced himself from the tavern bench he had slept on and followed the man. He began apologizing as soon as he stepped in the king's chamber, but the king was calm and smiled at him.

"Your highness, I am at a loss for what to do. The gypsies have taken over and the city is being turned upside down!"

"I know Anthony, it's quite disappointing."

"Why aren't you in hiding? They could attack at any moment with the guards having fled." Anthony was overwhelmed with confusion and worry.

"It is nothing for you to fret on. I pulled the soldiers back, because I need them at their best for what's to come."

"What is to come, your majesty?"

"A war. We have a plan," the king explained.

"When will this plan take effect, sir?" Anthony didn't feel any relief from the king's words, in fact, he felt even more unsettled. He wondered what could be soon to come of the city.

"Let me show you something."

"Of course, my king," Anthony said as he followed him to a far side of the palace. He opened a door to a room where Charles stood quietly next to a bed.

"When he is at his best, we will proceed with the plan," the king assured him.

Anthony moved closer, as the nurse began removing the man's bandages. Anthony soon began to recognize the man lying on the bed.

"But how can that be?" he muttered in shock; it was as if he'd seen a ghost.

"It's still too early, but if he survives, we will have everything we need to find our rightful criminal," Charles muttered. The nurse bandaged the patient back up, and the men felt confident that they had not yet been defeated.

38086434R00155

Made in the USA
Columbia, SC
08 December 2018